An American Politician by F. Marion Crawford

Francis Marion Crawford was born on August 2nd, 1854 at Bagni di Lucca, Italy. An only son and a nephew to Julia Ward Howe, the American poet and writer of 'The Battle Hymn of the Republic'.

His education began at St Paul's School, Concord, New Hampshire, then to Cambridge University; University of Heidelberg; and the University of Rome.

In 1879 Crawford went to India, to study Sanskrit and then edited The Indian Herald. In 1881 he returned to America to continue his Sanskrit studies at Harvard University.

At this time in Boston he lived at his Aunt Julia house and in the company of his Uncle, Sam Ward. His family was concerned about his employment prospects. After a singing career as a baritone was ruled out, he was encouraged to write.

In December 1882 his first novel, 'Mr Isaacs', was an immediate hit which was amplified by 'Dr Claudius' in 1883.

In October 1884 he married Elizabeth Berdan. They went on to have two sons and two daughters.

Encouraged by his excellent start to a literary career he returned to Italy with Elizabeth to make a permanent home, principally in Sant' Agnello, where he bought the Villa Renzi that then became Villa Crawford.

In the late 1890s, he began to write his historical works: 'Ave Roma Immortalis' (1898), 'Rulers of the South' (1900) and 'Gleanings from Venetian History' (1905). The Saracinesca series is perhaps his best work. 'Saracinesca' was followed by 'Sant' Ilario' in 1889, 'Don Orsino' in 1892 and 'Corleone' in 1897, that being the first major treatment of the Mafia in literature.

Francis Marion Crawford died at Sorrento on Good Friday 1909 at Villa Crawford of a heart attack.

Index of Contents

Dedication

To My Dear Friend, Elizabeth Christophers Hobson,
In Gratitude and Affection, I Dedicate This Story.

Constantinople,
October 7, 1884.

Chapter I

Mrs. Sam Wyndham was generally at home after five o'clock. The established custom whereby the ladies who live in Beacon Street all receive their friends on Monday afternoon did not seem to her satisfactory. She was willing to conform to the practice, but she reserved the right of seeing people on other days as well.

Mrs. Sam Wyndham was never very popular. That is to say, she was not one of those women who are seemingly never spoken ill of, and are invited as a matter of course, or rather as an element of success, to every dinner, musical party, and dance in the season.

Women did not all regard her with envy, all young men did not think she was capital fun, nor did all old men come and confide to her the weaknesses of their approaching second childhood. She was not invariably quoted as the standard authority on dress, classical music, and Boston literature, and it was not an unpardonable heresy to say that some other women might be, had been, or could be, more amusing in ordinary conversation. Nevertheless, Mrs. Sam Wyndham held a position in Boston which Boston acknowledged, and which Boston insisted that foreigners such as New Yorkers, Philadelphians and the like, should acknowledge also in that spirit of reverence which is justly due to a descent on both sides from several signers of the Declaration of Independence, and to the wife of one of the ruling financial spirits of the aristocratic part of Boston business.

As a matter of fact, Mrs. Wyndham was about forty years of age, as all her friends of course knew; for it is as easy for a Bostonian to conceal a question of age as for a crowned head. In a place where one half of society calls the other half cousin, and went to school with it, every one knows and accurately remembers just how old everybody else is. But Mrs. Wyndham might have passed for younger than she was among the world at large, for she was fresh to look at, and of good figure and complexion. Her black hair showed no signs of turning gray, and her dark eyes were bright and penetrating still. There were lines in her face, those microscopic lines that come so abundantly to American women in middle age, speaking of a certain restless nervousness that belongs to them especially; but on the whole Mrs. Sam Wyndham was fair to see, having a dignity of carriage and a grace of ease about her that at once gave the impression of a woman thoroughly equal to the part she had to play in the world, and not by any means incapable of enjoying it.

For the rest, Mrs. Sam led a life very much like the lives of many rich Americans. She went abroad frequently, wandered about the continent with her husband, went to Egypt and Algiers, stayed in England, where she had a good many friends, avoided her countrymen and countrywomen when away from home, and did her duty in the social state to which she was called in Boston.

She read the books of the period, and generally pronounced them ridiculous; she believed in her husband's politics, and aristocratically approved the way in which he abstained from putting theory into practice, from voting, and in a general way from dirtying his fingers with anything so corrupt as government, or so despicable as elections; she understood Boston business to some extent, and called it finance, but she despised the New York Stock Market and denounced its doings as gambling. She made fine distinctions, but she was a woman of sense, and was generally more likely to be right than wrong when she had a definite opinion, or expressed a definite dislike. Her religious views were simple and unobtrusive, and never changed.

Her custom of being at home after five o'clock was perhaps the only deviation she allowed herself from the established manners of her native city, and since two or three other ladies had followed her example, it had come to be regarded as a perfectly harmless idiosyncrasy for which she could not properly be blamed. The people who came to see her were chiefly men, except, of course, on the inevitable Monday.

A day or two before Christmas, then, Mrs. Sam Wyndham was at home in the afternoon. The snow lay thick and hard outside, and the sleigh bells tinkled unceasingly as the sleighs slipped by the window, gleaming and glittering in the deep red glow of the sunset. The track was well beaten for miles away, down Beacon Street and across the Milldam to the country, and the pavements were strewn with ashes to give a foothold for pedestrians.

For the frost was sharp and lasting. But within, Mrs. Wyndham sat by the fire with a small table before her, and one companion by her side, for whom she was pouring tea.

"Tell me all about your summer, Mr. Vancouver," said she, teasing the flame of the spirit-lamp into better shape with a small silver instrument.

Mr. Pocock Vancouver leaned back in his corner of the sofa and looked at the fire, then at the window, and finally at his hostess, before he answered. He was a pale man and slight of figure, with dark eyes, and his carefully brushed hair, turning gray at the temples and over his forehead, threw his delicate, intelligent face into relief.

"I have not done much," he answered, rather absently, as though trying to find something interesting in his reminiscences; and he watched Mrs. Wyndham as she filled a cup. He was not the least anxious to talk, it seemed, and he had an air of being thoroughly at home.

"You were in England most of the time, were you not?"

"Yes—I believe I was. Oh, by the bye, I met Harrington in Paris; I thought he meant to stay at home."

"He often goes abroad," said Mrs. Wyndham indifferently. "One lump of sugar?"

"Two, if you please—no cream—thanks. Does he go to Paris to convert the French, or to glean materials for converting other people?" inquired Mr. Vancouver languidly.

"I am sure I cannot tell you," answered the lady, still indifferently. "What do you go to Paris for?"

"Principally to renew my acquaintance with civilized institutions and humanizing influences. What does anybody go abroad for?"

"You always talk like that when you come home, Mr. Vancouver," said Mrs. Wyndham. "But nevertheless you come back and seem to find Boston bearable. It is not such a bad place after all, is it?"

"If it were not for half a dozen people here, I would never come back at all," said Mr. Vancouver. "But then, I am not originally one of you, and I suppose that makes a difference."

"And pray, who are the half dozen people who procure us the honor of your presence?"

"You are one of them, Mrs. Wyndham," he answered, looking at her.

"I am much obliged," she replied, demurely. "Any one else?"

"Oh—John Harrington," said Vancouver with a little laugh.

"Really?" said Mrs. Wyndham, innocently; "I did not know you were such good friends."

Mr. Vancouver sipped his tea in silence for a moment and stared at the fire.

"I have a great respect for Harrington," he said at last. "He interests me very much, and I like to meet him." He spoke seriously, as though thoroughly in earnest. The faintest look of amusement came to Mrs. Wyndham's face for a moment.

"I am glad of that," she said; "Mr. Harrington is a very good friend of mine. Do you mind lighting those candles? The days are dreadfully short."

Pocock Vancouver rose with alacrity and performed the service required.

"By the way," said Mrs. Wyndham, watching him, "I have a surprise for you."

"Indeed?"

"Yes, an immense surprise. Do you remember Sybil Brandon?"

"Charlie Brandon's daughter? Very well—saw her at Newport some time ago. Lily-white style—all eyes and hair."

"You ought to remember her. You used to rave about her, and you nearly ruined yourself in roses. You will have another chance; she is going to spend the winter with me."

"Not really?" ejaculated Mr. Vancouver, in some surprise, as he again sat down upon the sofa.

"Yes; you know she is all alone in the world now."

"What? Is her mother dead too?"

"She died last spring, in Paris. I thought you knew."

"No," said Vancouver, thoughtfully. "How awfully sad!"

"Poor girl," said Mrs. Wyndham; "I thought it would do her good to be among live people, even if she does not go out."

"When is she coming?" There was a show of interest about the question. "She is here now," answered Mrs. Sam.

"Dear me!" said Vancouver. "May I have another cup?" His hostess began the usual series of operations necessary to produce a second cup of tea.

"Mrs. Wyndham," began Vancouver again after a pause, "I have an idea—do not laugh, it is a very good one, I am sure."

"I am not laughing."

"Why not marry Sibyl Brandon to John Harrington?"

Mrs. Wyndham stared for a moment.

"How perfectly ridiculous!" she cried at last.

"Why?"

"They would starve, to begin with."

"I doubt it," said Vancouver.

"Why, I am sure Mr. Harrington never had more than five thousand a year in his life. You could not marry on that, you know—possibly."

"No; but Miss Brandon is very well off—rich, in fact."

"I thought she had nothing."

"She must have thirty or forty thousand a year from her mother, at the least. You know Charlie never did anything in his life; he lived on his wife's money, and Miss Brandon must have it all."

Mrs. Wyndham did not appear surprised at the information; she hardly seemed to think it of any importance.

"I knew she had something," she repeated; "but I am glad if you are right. But that does not make it any more feasible to marry her to Mr. Harrington."

"I thought that starvation was your objection," said Vancouver.

"Oh, no; not that only. Besides, he would not marry her."

"He would be very foolish not to, if he had the chance," remarked Vancouver.

"Perhaps he might not even have the chance—perhaps she would not marry him," said Mrs. Wyndham, thoughtfully. "Besides, I do not think John Harrington ought to marry yet; he has other things to do."

Mr. Vancouver seemed about to say something in answer, but he checked himself; possibly he did not speak because he saw some one enter the room at that moment, and was willing to leave the discussion of John Harrington to a future time.

In fact, the person who entered the room should have been the very last to hear the conversation that was taking place, for it was Miss Brandon herself, though Mr. Vancouver had not recognized her at once.

There were greetings and hand-shakings, and then Miss Brandon sat down by the fire and spread out her hands as though to warm them. She looked white and cold.

There are women in the world, both young and old, who seem to move among us like visions from another world, a world that is purer and fairer, and more heavenly than this one in which the rest of us move. It is hard to say what such women have that marks them so distinctly; sometimes it is beauty, sometimes only a manner, often it is both. It is very certain that we know and feel their influence, and that many men fear it as something strange and contrary to the common order of things, a living reproach and protest against all that is base and earthly and badly human.

Most people would have said first of Sybil Brandon that she was cold, and many would have added that she was beautiful. Ill-natured people sometimes said she was deathly. No one ever said she was pretty. Vancouver's description—lily-white, all eyes and hair—certainly struck the principal facts of her appearance, for her skin was whiter than is commonly natural, her eyes were very deep and large and blue, and her soft brown hair seemed to be almost a burden to her from its great quantity. She was dressed entirely in black, and being rather tall and very slight of figure, the dress somewhat exaggerated the ethereal look that was natural to her. She seemed cold, and spread out her delicate hands to the bright flame of the blazing wood-fire. Mrs. Wyndham and Pocock Vancouver looked at her in silence for a moment. Then Mrs. Wyndham rose with a cup of tea in her hand, and crossed to the other side of the fireplace where Sybil was sitting and offered it to her.

"Poor Sybil, you are so cold. Drink some tea." The elder woman sat down by the young girl, and lightly kissed her cheek. "You must not be sad, darling," she whispered sympathetically.

"I am not sad at all, really," answered Miss Brandon aloud, quite naturally, but pressing Mrs. Wyndham's hand a little, as though in acknowledgment of her sympathy.

"No one can be sad in Boston," said Vancouver, putting in a word. "Our city is altogether too wildly gay." He laughed a little.

"You must not make fun of us to visitors, Mr. Vancouver," answered Mrs. Wyndham, still holding Sybil's hand.

"It is Mr. Vancouver's ruling passion, though he never acknowledges it," said Miss Brandon, calmly. "I remember it of old."

"I am flattered at being remembered," said Mr. Vancouver, whose delicate features betrayed neither pleasure nor interest, however. "But," he continued, "I am not particularly flattered at being called a scoffer at my own people—"

"I did not say that," interrupted Miss Brandon.

"Well, you said my ruling passion was making fun of Boston to visitors; at least, you and Mrs. Wyndham said it between you. I really never do that, unless I give the other side of the question as well."

"What other side?" asked Mrs. Sam, who wanted to make conversation.

"Boston," said Vancouver with some solemnity. "It is not more often ridiculous than other great institutions."

"You simply take one's breath away, Mr. Vancouver," said Mrs. Wyndham, with a good deal of emphasis. "The idea of calling Boston 'an institution!'"

"Why, certainly. The United States are only an institution after all. You could not soberly call us a nation. Even you could not reasonably be moved to fine patriotic phrases about your native country, if your ancestors had signed twenty Declarations of Independence. We live in a great institution, and we have every right to flatter ourselves on the success of its management; but in the long run this thing will not do for a nation."

Miss Brandon looked at Vancouver with a sort of calm incredulity. Mrs. Wyndham always quarreled with him on points like the one now raised, and accordingly took up the cudgels.

"I do not see how you can congratulate yourself on the management of your institution, as you call it, when you know very well you would rather die than have anything to do with it."

"Very true. But then, you always say that gentlemen should not touch anything so dirty as politics, Mrs. Wyndham," retorted Vancouver.

"Well, that just shows that it is not an institution at all, and that you are quite wrong, and that we are a great nation supported and carried on by real patriotism."

"And the Irish and German votes," added Vancouver, with that scorn which only the true son of freedom can exhibit in speaking of his fellow-citizens.

"Oh, the Irish vote! That is always the last word in the argument," answered Mrs. Sam.

"I do not see exactly what the Irish have to do with it," remarked Miss Brandon, innocently. She did not understand politics.

Vancouver glanced at the clock and took his hat.

"It is very simple," he said, rising to go. "It is the bull in the china shop—the Irish bull amongst the American china—dangerous, you know. Good evening, Mrs. Wyndham; good evening, Miss Brandon." And he took his leave. Miss Brandon watched his slim figure disappear through the heavy curtains of the door.

"He has not changed much since I knew him," she said, turning again to the fire. "I used to think he was clever."

"And have you changed your mind?" asked Mrs. Wyndham, laughing.

"Not quite, but I begin to doubt. He has very good manners, and looks altogether like a gentleman."

"Of course," said Mrs. "Wyndham." His mother was a Shaw, although his father came from South Carolina. But he is really very bright; Sam always says he is one of the ablest men in Boston."

"In what way?" inquired Sybil.

"Oh, he is a lawyer, don't you know?—great railroad man."

"Oh," ejaculated Miss Brandon, and relapsed into silence.

Mrs. Wyndham rose and stood before the fire, and pushed a log back with her small foot. Miss Brandon watched her, half wondering whether the flames would not catch her dress.

"I have been to see that Miss Thorn," said Sybil presently.

"Oh," exclaimed Mrs. Sam, with sudden interest, "tell me all about her this minute, dear. Is not she the most extraordinary creature?"

"I rather like her," answered Miss Brandon. "She is very pretty."

"What style? Dark?"

"No; not exactly. Brown hair, and lots of eyebrows. She is a little thing, but very much alive, you know."

"Awfully English, of course," suggested Mrs. Sam.

"Well—yes, I suppose so. She is wild about horses, and says she shoots. But I like her—I am sure I shall like her very much. She does not seem very pleased with her aunt."

"I do not wonder," said Mrs. Sam. "Poor little thing—she has nobody else belonging to her, has she?"

"Oh, yes," answered Sybil, with a little tremor in her voice; "she has a mother in England."

"I want to see her ever so much," said Mrs. Sam. "Bring her to luncheon."

"You will see her to-night, I think; she said she was going to that party."

"I hate to leave you alone," said Mrs. Wyndham. "I really think I had better not go."

"Dear Mrs. Wyndham," said Sybil, rising, and laying her hands on her hostess's shoulders, half affectionately, half in protest, "this idea must be stopped from the first, and I mean to stop it. You are not to give up any party, or any society, or anything at all for me. If you do I will go away again. Promise me, will you not?"

"Very well, dear. But you know you are the dearest girl in the world." And so they kissed, and agreed that Mrs. Wyndham should go out, and that Sybil should stay at home.

Mrs. Wyndham was really a very kind-hearted woman and a loving friend. That might be the reason why she was never popular. Popularity is a curious combination of friendliness and indifference, but very popular people rarely have devoted friends, and still more rarely suffer great passions. Everybody's friend is far too apt to be nobody's, for it is impossible to rely on the support of a person whose devotion is liable to be called upon a hundred times a day, from a hundred different quarters. The friendships that mean anything mean sacrifice for friendship's sake; and a man or a woman really ready to make sacrifices for a considerable number of people is likely to be asked to do it very often, and to be soon spent in the effort to be true to every one.

But popularity makes no great demands. The popular man is known to be so busy in being popular that his offenses of omission are readily pardoned. His engagements are legion, his obligations are innumerable, and far more than he can fulfill. But, meet him when you will, his smile is as bright, his greeting as cordial, and his sayings as universally good-natured and satisfactory as ever. He has acquired the habit of pleasing, and it is almost impossible for him to displease. He enjoys it all, is agreeable to every one, and is never expected to catch cold in attending a friend's funeral, or otherwise to sacrifice his comfort, because he is quite certain to have important engagements elsewhere, in which the world always believes. There is probably no individual more absolutely free and untrammeled than the thoroughly popular man.

Chapter II

Fate, the artist, mixes her own colors. She grinds them with a pestle in the fashion of the old masters, and out of the most strange pigments she produces often only soft neutral tints for background and shadow, kneading a vast deal of bright colors away among the grays and browns; but now and then she takes a palette loaded with strong paint, and a great brush, and splashes a startling full length portrait upon the canvas, without much regard for drawing or general composition, but with very startling effect. To paint well needs life-long study; to paint so as merely to attract attention needs courage and a heart hardened against artistic sensitiveness.

John Harrington was a high light against the mezzotint of his surroundings. He was a constant source of interest, and not infrequently of terror, to the good town of Boston. True, he was a Bostonian himself, a chip of the old block, whose progenitors had lived in Salem, and whose very name breathed Pilgrim memories. He even had a teapot that had come over in the Mayflower. This was greatly venerated, and whenever John Harrington said anything more than usually modern, his friends brandished the teapot, morally speaking, in his defense, and put it in the clouds as a kind of rainbow—a promise that Puritan blood could not go wrong. Nevertheless, John Harrington continued to startle his fellow-townsmen by his writings and sayings, so that many of the grave sort shook their heads and swore that he sympathized with the Irish and believed in Chinese labor.

As a matter-of-fact, he did not mince matters. Endowed with unbounded courage and an extraordinary command of language, when he got upon his feet he spoke his mind in a way that was good to hear. Moreover, he had the strong oratorical temperament that forces attention and commands men in a body. He said that things were wrong and should be put right; and when he had said so for half an hour to a couple of thousand people, most of them were ready to follow him out of the hall and go and put things right on the spot, with their own hands. As yet the opportunity had not offered for proceeding in so simple a manner, but the aforesaid Bostonians of the graver sort said that John Harrington would some day be seen heading a desperate mob of socialists in an assault upon the State House. What he had to do with socialism, or to what end he should thus fiercely invade the headquarters of all earthly respectability, was not exactly apparent, but the picture thus evoked in the minds of the solemn burghers satisfactorily defined for them the personality of the man, and they said it and said it again.

It was somewhat remarkable that he had never been called clever. At first he was regarded as a fool by most of his own class, though he always had friends who believed in him. By and by, as it came to be seen that he had a purpose and would be listened to while he stated it, Boston said there was something in him; but he was never said to be clever or "bright"—he was John Harrington, neither more nor less. He was never even called "Jack."

He was a friend of Mrs. Wyndham's; her keen instincts had long ago recognized the true metal in the man, and of all who came and went in her house there was none more welcome than he. Sam Wyndham utterly disagreed with him in politics, but always defended him in private, saying that he would "calm down a lot when he got older," and that meanwhile he was "a very good fellow if you did not stir him up."

He was therefore very intimate at the Sam Wyndham establishment; in fact, at the very hour when Pocock Vancouver was drinking Mrs. Sam's tea, John had intended to be enjoying the same privilege. Unfortunately for his intention he was caught elsewhere and could not get away. He was drinking tea, it is true, but the position in which he found himself was not entirely to his taste.

Old Miss Schenectady, whose niece, Miss Josephine Thorn, had lately come over from England to pass the winter, had asked John Harrington to call that afternoon. The old lady believed in John on account of the Mayflower teapot, and consequently thought him a desirable acquaintance for her niece. Accordingly, John went to the house, and met Miss Sybil Brandon just as she was leaving it; which he regretted, suspecting that her society would have been more interesting than that of Miss Thorn. As it turned out, he was right, for his first impression of the young English girl was not altogether agreeable; and he found himself obliged to stay and talk to her until an ancient lady, who had come to gossip with Miss Schenectady, and was fully carrying out her intentions, should go away and make it possible for him to take his leave without absolutely abandoning Miss Thorn in the corner of the room she had selected for the tête-à-tête.

"All that, of course, you know," said Miss Thorn, in answer to some remark of John's, "but what sort of things do you really care for?"

"People," answered John without hesitation.

"Of course," returned his companion, "everybody likes people. It is not very original. One could not live without lots of society, could one?"

"That depends on the meaning of society."

"Oh, I am not in the least learned about meanings," answered Miss Thorn. "I mean what one means by society, you know. Heaps of men and women, and tea-parties, and staying in the country, and that."

"That is a sketch indeed," said John, laughing. "But then it is rather different here. We do not relapse into the country as you do in England, and then come back to town like lions refreshed with sleep."

"Why not?"

"Because once in society here one is always in it. At least, most people are. As soon as heat begins Boston goes to New York; and by-and-by New York goes to Saratoga, and takes Boston with it; and then all three go to Newport, and the thing begins again, until there is a general rush to Lenox, to see the glories of the autumn; and by the time the glories are getting a little thin it is time to be in Beacon Street again."

"But when do people shoot and ride?—do they ever hunt?" asked Miss Thorn, opening her wide brown eyes in some astonishment at John Harrington's description of society life in America.

"Oh yes, they hunt at Newport with a drag and a bagged fox. They do it in July and August, when it is as hot as it can be, and the farmers turn out with pitchforks and stones to warn them off the growing crops."

"How ridiculous!" exclaimed Miss Josephine.

"It is absurd, of course," said Harrington, "and cruel. But I must say they ride as though there were no hereafter, and it is a stiff country."

"They must, I should think; no one who believed in a hereafter would hunt in summer."

"I will wager that if you go to Newport this summer you will hunt, just like everybody else," said John boldly.

Josephine Thorn knew in her heart that it was true, but she did not like the tone in which John said it. There was an air of certainty about his way of talking that roused her opposition.

"I would do nothing so foolish," said she. "You do not know me. And do you mean to tell me that you like these people who rush madly about the country and hunt in summer, and those sort of things?"

"No," said John, "not always."

"But you said you liked people. How awfully inconsistent you are!"

"Excuse me, I think not. I meant that I liked people and having to do with them—with men and women—better than I like things."

"What are 'things'?" inquired Josephine, sarcastically. "You are not very clear in your way of expressing yourself."

"I will be as clear as you please," answered John, looking across the room at Miss Schenectady and her ancient friend, and devoutly wishing he could get away. "I mean by 'things' the study of the inanimate part of creation, of such sciences as are not directly connected with man's thoughts and actions, and such pursuits as hunting, shooting, and sporting of all kinds, which lead only to the amusement of the individual. I mean also the production of literature for literature's sake, and of works of art for the mere sake of themselves. When I say I like 'people,' I mean men and women, their opinions and their relations to each other."

"I should think you would get very tired of them," said Miss Thorn scornfully. "They are all dreadfully alike."

She never forgot the look Harrington turned upon her as he answered. His calm, deep-set gray eyes gazed steadily at her, and his square features assumed an air of gravity that almost startled her.

"I am never tired of men and women," he said. "Has it ever struck you, Miss Thorn, that the study of men and women means the study of government, and that a knowledge of men and women may give the power to influence the destiny of mankind?"

"I never thought of it like that," said Josephine, very quietly. She was surprised at his manner, and she suddenly felt that he was no ordinary man.

To tell the truth, her aunt had informed her that John Harrington was coming that afternoon, and had told her he was an exceedingly able man, a statement which at once roused Josephine's opposition to its fiercest pitch. She thoroughly hated to be warned about people, to be primed as it were with a dose of their superiority beforehand. It always prepared her to dislike the admirable individual when he appeared. It seemed as though it were taken for granted that she herself had not enough intelligence to discover wit in others, and needed to be told of it with great circumstance in order to be upon her good behavior. Consequently Josephine began by disliking John. She thought he was a Philistine; his hair was too straight, and besides, it was red; he shaved all his face, whereas the men she liked always had beards; she liked men with black eyes, or blue— John's were gray and hard; he spoke quietly, without expression, and she liked men who were enthusiastic. After all, too, the things he said were not very clever; anybody could have said them.

She meant to show her Boston aunt that she had no intention of accepting Boston genius on faith. It was not her way; she liked to find out for herself whether people were able or not, without being told, and if she ascertained that John Harrington enjoyed a fictitious reputation for genius it would amuse her to destroy it—or at all events to write a long letter home to a friend, expressing her supreme opinion on that and other matters.

John, on his part, did not very much care what impression he produced. He never did on such occasions, and just now he was rendered doubly indifferent by the fact that he was wishing himself somewhere else. True, there was a certain novelty in being asked point-blank questions about his tastes. Boston people knew what he liked, and generally only asked him about what he did. Perhaps, if he had met Josephine by daylight, instead of in the dim shadows of Miss Schenectady's front drawing-room, he might have been struck by her appearance and interested by her manner. As it was, he was merely endeavoring to get through his visit with a proper amount of civility, in the hope that he might get away in time to see Mrs. Sam Wyndham before dinner.

Josephine thought John dull, probably well informed, and utterly without interest in anything. She felt inclined to do something desperate—to throw the cushions at him, to do anything, in short, to rouse him from his calmness. Then he made that remark about government, and his voice deepened, and his gray eyes shone, and she was aware that he had a great and absorbing interest in life, and that he could be roused in one direction at least. To do her justice, she had quick perceptions, and the impression on her mind was instantaneous.

"I never thought of it like that," she said. "Do you know?" she added in a moment, "I should not have thought you took much interest in anything at all."

John laughed. He was amused at the idea that he, who knew himself to be one of the most enthusiastic of mortals, should be thought indifferent; and he was amused at the outspoken frankness of the girl's remark.

"You know that is just like me," continued Miss Thorn quickly. "I always say what I think, you know. I cannot help it a bit."

"What a pity all the world is not like you!" said John. "It would save a great deal of trouble, I am sure."

"The frump is going at last," said Josephine, in an undertone, as the ancient friend rose and showed signs of taking leave of Miss Schenectady.

"There is certainly no mistake about the frankness of that speech," said John, rising to his feet and laughing again.

"There is no mistaking its truth," answered Josephine. "She is the real thing—the real old-fashioned frump—we have lots of them at home."

"You remind me of Heine," said John. "He said he called a spade a spade, and Herr Schmidt an ass."

Miss Thorn laughed. "Exactly," she answered, "that is the knowledge of men which you say leads to power."

She rose also, and there was a little stir as the old lady departed. Josephine watched John as he bowed and opened the door of the room to let the visitor out. She wondered vaguely whether she would like him, whether he might not really be a remarkable man—a fact she doubted in proportion as her aunt assured her of its truth; she liked his looks and tried to determine whether he was handsome or not, and she watched closely for any awkwardness or shyness of manner, that being the fault in a man which she never pardoned.

He was very different from the men she had generally known, and most completely different from those she had known as her admirers. In fact she had never admired her admirers at all,—except dear Ronald, of course. They competed with her on her own ground, and she knew well enough she was more than a match for any of them. Ronald was different; she had known him all her life. But all those other men! They could ride—but she rode as well, or better. They could shoot, but so could she, and allowing for the disadvantages of a woman in field sports, she was as good a shot as they. She knew she could do anything they could do, and understood most things they understood. All in all, she did not care for the average young Englishman. He was great fun in his own way, but there were probably more interesting things in the world than pheasants and fences. Politics would be interesting, she thought; she had known three or four men who were young and already prominent in Parliament, and they were undeniably interesting; but they were generally either ugly or clumsy,—the unpardonable sin,—or perhaps they were vain. Josephine could not bear vain men. John Harrington probably had some one or more of these defects. He was certainly no "beauty man," to begin with, nevertheless, she wondered whether he might not be called handsome by stretching a point. She rather hoped, inwardly and unconsciously, that her ultimate judgment would decide in favor of his good looks. She always judged; it was the first thing she did, and she was surprised, on the present occasion, to find her judgment so slow. People who pride themselves on being critical are often annoyed when they find themselves uncertain of their own opinion. As for his accomplishments, they were doubtful, to say the least. Miss Thorn was not used to considering American men as manly. She had read a great many books which made game of them, and showed how unused they were to all those good things which make up the life of an English country gentleman; she had met one or two Americans who turned up their noses in impotent scorn of all field sports except horse-racing, which they regarded from a financial point of view. Probably John Harrington had never killed a pheasant in his life. Lastly, he might be vain. A man with such a reputation for ability would most likely be conceited.

And yet, despite probability, she could not help thinking John interesting. That one speech of his about government had meant something. He was a man with a strong personality, with a great interest in the world led by a dominant aspiration of some sort; and Josephine, in her heart, loved power and admired those who possessed it. Political power especially had that charm for her which it has for most English people of the upper class. There is some quality in the English race which breeds an inordinate admiration for all kinds of superiority: it is certain that if one class of English society can be justly accused of an over-great veneration for rank, the class which is rank itself is not behindhand in doing homage to the political stars of the day. In favor of this peculiarity of English people it may fairly be said that they love to associate with persons of rank and power from a disinterested love of those things themselves, whereas in most other countries the society of noble and influential persons is chiefly sought from the most cynical motives of personal advantage.

Politics—that is, the outward and appreciable manifestations of political life—must always furnish abundant food for the curiosity of the many and the intelligent criticism of the few. There is no exception to that rule, be the state great or small. But politics in England and politics in America, so far as the main points are concerned, are as different as it is possible for any two social functions to be. Roughly, Government and the doings of Government are centripetal in England, and centrifugal in America. In England the will of the people assists the workings of Providence, whereas in America devout persons pray that Providence may on occasion modify the will of the people. In England men believe in the Queen, the Royal Family, the Established Church, and Belgravia first, and in themselves afterwards. Americans believe in themselves devoutly, and a man who could "establish" upon them a church, a royalty, or a peerage, would be a very clever fellow.

Josephine Thorn and John Harrington were fair examples of their nationalities. Josephine believed in England and the English; John Harrington believed in America and the Americans. How far England and America are ever likely to believe in each other, however, is a question of future history and not of past experience, and any reasonable amount of doubt may be cast upon the possibility of such mutual confidence.

But as Josephine stood watching John Harrington while he opened the drawing-room door for the visitor to go out, she thought of none of these things. She certainly did not consider herself a type of her nation—a distinction to which few English people aspire—and she as certainly would have denied that the man before her was a type of the modern American.

John remained standing when the lady was gone.

"Do sit down," said Miss Schenectady, settling herself once more in her corner.

"Thank you, I think I must be going now," answered John. "It is late." As he spoke he turned toward Miss Thorn, and for the first time saw her under the bright light of the old-fashioned gas chandelier.

The young girl was perhaps not what is called a great beauty, but she was undeniably handsome, and she possessed that quality which often goes with quick perceptions and great activity, and which is commonly defined by the expression "striking." Short, rather than tall, she was yet so proportioned between strength and fineness as to be very graceful, and her head sat proudly on her shoulders—too proudly sometimes, for she could command and she could be angry. Her wide brown eyes were bright and fearless and honest. The faint color came and went under the clear skin as freely as the heart could send it, and though her hair was brown and soft, there were ruddy tints among the coils, that flashed out unexpectedly here and there like threads of red gold twined in a mass of fine silk.

John looked at her in some astonishment, for in his anxiety to be gone and in the dimness of the corner where they had sat, he had not realized that Josephine was any more remarkable in her appearance than most of the extremely young women who annually make their entrance into society, with the average stock of pink and white prettiness. They call them "buds" in Boston—an abbreviation for rosebuds.

Fresh young roses of each opening year, fresh with the dew of heaven and the blush of innocence, coming up in this wild garden of a world, what would the gardener do without you? Where would all beauty and sweetness be found among the thorny bushes and the withering old shrubs and the rotting weeds, were it not for you? Maidens with clean hands and pure hearts, in whose touch there is something that heals the ills and soothes the pains of mortality, roses whose petals are yet unspotted by dust and rain, and whose divine perfume the hot south wind has not scorched, nor the east wind nipped and frozen—you are the protest, set every year among us, against the rottenness of the world's doings, the protest of the angelic life against the earthly, of the eternal good against the eternal bad.

John Harrington looked at Miss Thorn, and looked at her with pleasure, for he saw that she was fair—but in spite of her newly discovered beauty he resisted Miss Schenectady's invitation to sit down again, and departed. Any other man would have stayed, under the circumstances.

"Well, Josephine," said Miss Schenectady, when he was gone, "now you have seen John Harrington."

Josephine looked at her aunt and laughed a little; it seemed to her a very self-evident fact, since John had just gone.

"Exactly," said she. "Won't you call me Joe, aunt Zoruiah? They all do at home—even Ronald."

"Joe? Boy's name. Well, if you insist upon it. As I was saying, you have seen John Harrington, now."

"Exactly," repeated Joe.

"But I mean, how does he strike you?"

"Clever I should think," answered the young lady. "Clever, you know—that sort of thing. Not bad looking, either."

"I told you so," said Miss Schenectady.

"Yes—but I expected ever so much more from what you said," returned Joe, kneeling on the rug before the fire and poking the coals with the tongs. Miss Schenectady looked somewhat offended at the slight cast upon her late guest.

"You are very difficile, Josephi—I mean Joe, I forgot."

"Ye—es, very diffyseal—that sort of thing," repeated Josephine, mimicking her aunt's pronunciation of the foreign word, "I know I am, I can't possibly help it, you know." A dashing thrust with the tongs finally destroyed the equilibrium of the fire, and the coals came tumbling down upon the hearth.

"Goodness gracious me!" exclaimed the old lady in great anxiety, "you will have the house on fire in no time! Give me the tongs right away, my dear. You do not understand American fires!"

Chapter III

"Dear Ronald,—You can't imagine what a funny place Boston is. I wish you were here, it would be so nice to talk about them together—I mean the people, of course, for they are much funnier than the place they live in. But I think they are very nice, too, particularly some of the men. I don't understand the women in the least—they go in awfully for sets, if you understand that kind of thing—and art, too, and literature. The other day at a lunch party—that is what they call it here—they sat and talked about pictures for ever so long. I wonder what you would have said if you had been there! but then there were no men, and so you couldn't have been, could you? And the sets, too. The girls who come out together, all in a batch, like a hive of bees swarming, spend the rest of their lives together; and they have what they call sewing circles, that go on all their lives. There are sewing circles of old frumps sixty years old who have never been parted since they all went to their first ball together. They sew for the poor; they don't sew so very much, you know; but then they have a tremendous lunch afterwards. I sewed for the poor the other day, because one of the sewing circles asked me to their meeting. I sewed two buttons on to the end of something, and then I ate six kinds of salad, and went to drive with Mr. Vancouver. I dare say it does a lot of good in its way, but I think the poor must be awfully good-natured.

"It is quite too funny about driving, too. You may go out with a man in a sleigh, but you couldn't possibly go with him on wheels—on the same road, at the same hour, same man, same everything, except the wheels. You agree to go out next week in a sleigh with Mr. Vancouver; but when the day comes, if it has happened to thaw and there is no snow, and he comes in a buggy, you couldn't possibly go with him, because it would be quite too improper. But I mean to, some day, just to see what they will say. I wish you would come! We would do a lot of driving together, and by and by, in the spring, they say one can ride here, but only along the roads, for everything else is so thick with steam-engines and Irishmen that one could not possibly go across country.

"But although they are so funny, they are really very nice, and awfully clever. I don't think there are nearly so many clever men anywhere else in society, when once you have got over their Americanisms. Most of them would be in Parliament at home; but nobody goes into Parliament here, except Mr. Harrington—that is, into Congress, which is the same thing, you know. They say politics in America are not at all fit for gentlemen, and they spend an hour or two every day in abusing all the politicians, instead of turning them out and managing things themselves. But Mr. Harrington is going to be a senator as soon as he can, and he is so clever that I am sure he will make a great reform.

"I don't think of anything else to say just now, but if I do I will write again—only it's unfeminine to write two letters running, so you must answer at once. And if you should want to travel this winter you can come here; they will treat you ever so much better than you deserve. So good-by. Yours ever sincerely,

"Joe Thorn."

The precise nature of the friendship that existed between Josephine Thorn and Ronald Surbiton could not be accurately inferred from the above specimen of correspondence; and indeed the letter served rather to confuse than to enlighten the recipient as to the nature of his relations with the writer. He was, of course, very much in love with Joe Thorn; he knew it, because he had always been in love with her since they were children together, so there could be no possible doubt in the matter. But whether she cared a jot for him and his feelings he could not clearly make out, from the style of the hurried, ungrammatical sentences, crammed with abbreviations and unpermissible elisions. True, she said three times that she hoped he would come to America; but America was a long way off, and she very likely reckoned on his laziness and dislike to foreign traveling. It is so easy for a young woman writing from Boston to say to a young man residing in Scotland, "Do come over for a few days"—Surbiton thought it would be a good joke to take her at her word and go. The idea of seeing her again so much sooner than he had expected was certainly uppermost in his mind as he began to make his resolution; but it was sustained and strengthened by a couple of allusions Joe had made to men of her acquaintance in

Boston, not to say by the sweeping remark that there were more clever men in Boston society than anywhere else, which made his vanity smart rather unpleasantly. When Josephine used to tell him, half in earnest, half in jest, that he was "so dreadfully stupid," he did not feel much hurt; but it was different when she took the trouble to write all the way from America to tell him that the men there were much cleverer than at home. He had a great mind to go and see for himself whether it were true. Nevertheless, the hunting was particularly good just at the time when he got the letter, and being rather prudent of counsel, Ronald determined to wait until a hard frost should spoil his temper and give the necessary stimulus to his activity, before he packed his boxes for a western voyage.

As for Josephine, it was very natural that she should feel a little homesick, and wish to have some one of her own people with her. In spite of the favorable views she expressed about America, Boston, and her new acquaintances, her position was not without some drawbacks in her own eyes. She felt herself out of her natural element, and the very great admiration she received in society, though pleasant enough in itself, was not to her so entirely satisfactory as it would have been to a woman older or younger than she, or to a more thorough flirt. An older woman would have enjoyed more keenly the flattery of it; a younger girl would have found it more novel and fresh, and the accomplished professional society flirt— there is no other word to express her—would have rejoiced exceedingly over a great holocaust of victims.

In writing to Surbiton and suggesting to him to come to Boston, Joe had no intention of fanning his hopes into flame. She never thought much about Ronald. She had long been used to him, and regarded him in the light of a marriage fixture, though she had never exactly promised to marry him; she had been brought up to suppose she would, and that was all. When or where the marriage would actually take place was a question she did not care to raise, and if ever Surbiton raised it she repressed him ruthlessly. For the present she would look about the world, seeing she had been transported into a new part of it, and she found it amusing. Only she would like to have a companion to whom she could talk. Ronald would be so convenient, and after all it was a great advantage to be able to make use of the man to whom she was engaged. She never had known any other girl who could do that, and she rather prided herself on the fact that she was not ridiculous, although she was in the most traditionally absurd position, that of betrothal. She would like to compare Ronald with the men she had met lately.

The desire for comparison had increased of late. A fortnight had passed since she had first met John Harrington, and she had made up her mind. He was handsome, though his hair was red and he had no beard, and she liked him; she liked him very much; it was quite different from her liking for Ronald. She liked Ronald, she said to herself that she loved him dearly, partly because she expected to marry him, and partly because he was so good and so much in love with herself. He would take any amount of trouble for anything she wanted. But John was different. She knew very well that she was thinking much more of him than he of her, if indeed he thought of her at all. But she was a little ashamed of it, and in order to justify herself in her own eyes she was cold and sarcastic in her manner to him, so that people noticed it, and even John Harrington himself, who never thought twice whether his acquaintances liked him or disliked him, remarked one day to Mrs. Wyndham that he feared he had offended Miss Thorn, as she took such particular pains to treat him differently from others. On the other hand Joe was always extremely candid to Pocock Vancouver.

It was on a Monday that John made the aforesaid remark. All Boston was at Mrs. Wyndham's, excepting all the other ladies who lived in Beacon Street, and that is a very considerable portion of Boston, as every schoolboy knows. John was standing near the tea-table talking to Mrs. Sam, when Joe entered the room and came up to the hostess, who welcomed her warmly. She nodded coldly to John without shaking hands, and joined a group of young girls near by.

"It is very strange," said John to Mrs. Wyndham. "I wonder whether I can have done anything Miss Thorn resents. I am not sensitive, but it is impossible to mistake people when they look at one like that. She always does it just in that way."

Mrs. Wyndham looked inquiringly at John for a moment, and the quick smile of ready comprehension played on her sensitive mouth.

"Are you really quite sure you have not offended her?" she asked.

"Quite sure," John answered, in a tone of conviction. "Besides, I never offend any one, certainly not ladies. I never did such a thing in my whole life."

"Not singly," said Mrs. Wyndham, laughing. "You offend people in large numbers when you do it at all, especially newspaper people. Sam read that ridiculous article in the paper to me last night."

"Which paper?" asked John, smiling. "They have most of them been at me this week."

"The paper," answered Mrs. Sam, "the horrid paper. You do not suppose I would mention such a publication in my house?"

"Oh, my old enemy," laughed John. "I do not mind that in the least. One might almost think those articles were written by Miss Thorn."

"Perhaps they are," answered Mrs. Wyndham. "Really," she added, glancing at Josephine, whom Pocock Vancouver had just detached from her group of girls, "really you may not be so very, very far wrong." John's glance followed the direction of her eyes, and he saw Vancouver. He looked steadily at the man's delicate pale features and intellectual head, and at the end of half a minute he and Mrs. Wyndham looked at each other again. She probably regretted the hint she had carelessly dropped, but she met Harrington's gaze frankly.

"I did not mean to say it," she said, for John looked so grave that she was frightened. "It was only a guess."

"But have you any reason to think it might be the truth?" asked John.

"None whatever—really none, except that he differs so much from you in every way, politically speaking."

She knew very well that Vancouver hated John, and she had often thought it possible that the offensive articles in question came from the pen of the former. There was a tone of superior wit and a ring of truer English in them than are generally met with in the average office work of a daily newspaper.

"I do not believe Vancouver writes them," said John, slowly. "He is not exactly a friend, but he is not an enemy either."

Mrs. Wyndham, who knew better than that, held her peace. She was not a mischief-maker, and moreover she liked both the men too well to wish a quarrel between them. She busied herself at the tea-table for a moment, and John stood near her, watching the moving crowd. Now and then his eyes rested on Josephine Thorn's graceful figure, and he noticed how her expressive features lighted up in the conversation. John could hear something of their conversation, which was somewhat noisy. They were talking in that strain of objectless question and answer which may be stupid to idiocy or clever to the verge of wit, according to the talkers. Joe called it "chaff."

"I have learned America," said Joe.

"Indeed!" said Vancouver. "You have not been long about it; but then, you will say there is not much to learn."

"I never believe in places till I have lived in them," said Joe.

"Nor in people till you have seen them, I suppose," returned Vancouver. "But now that you have learned America, of course you believe in us all without exception. We are the greatest nation on earth—I suppose you have heard that?"

"Yes; you told me so the other day; but it needs all the faith I have in your judgment to believe it. If any one else had said it, you know, I should have thought there was some mistake."

"Oh no; it is pretty true, taking it all round," returned Vancouver, with a smile. "But I am tremendously flattered at the faith you put in my sayings."

"Oh, are you? That is odd, you know, because if you are so much flattered at my believing you, you would not be much disappointed if I doubted you."

"I beg to differ. Excuse me"—

"Not at all," answered Joe, laughing. "Only we have old-fashioned prejudices at home. We begin by expecting to be believed, and are sometimes a good deal annoyed if any one says we are telling fibs."

"Of course, if you put it in that way," said Vancouver. "But I suppose it is not a very bad fib to say one's country is the greatest on earth. I am sure you English say it quite as often and as loudly as we do, and, you see, we cannot both be right, possibly."

"No, not exactly. But suppose two men, any two, like you and Mr. Harrington for instance, each made a point of telling every one you met that you were the greatest man on earth."

"It is conceivable that we might both be wrong," said Vancouver, laughing at the idea.

"But one of you might be right," objected Joe.

"No—that is not conceivable," retorted Vancouver.

"No? Let us ask Mr. Harrington. Mr. Harrington!"

Joe turned towards John and called him. He was only a step from her, and joined the two instantly. He looked from one to the other inquiringly.

"Here is a great question to be decided, Mr. Harrington," said Joe. "I was saying to Mr. Vancouver that, supposing each of you asserted that he was the greatest man on earth, it would—I mean, how could the point be settled?" John stared for a moment.

"If you insist upon raising such a very remarkable point of precedence, Miss Thorn," he answered calmly, "I am sure Vancouver will agree with me to leave the decision to you also."

Joe looked slightly annoyed. She had brought the retort on herself.

"Pardon me," said Vancouver, quickly, "I object to the contest. The match is not a fair one. Mr. Harrington means to be the greatest man on earth, or in the water under the earth, whereas I have no such aspiration."

Instead of being grateful to Vancouver for coming to her rescue in the rather foolish position in which she was placed, Joe felt unaccountably annoyed. She was willing to make sure of John herself, if she could, but she was not prepared to allow that privilege to any one else. Accordingly she turned upon Vancouver before John could answer. "The question began in a foolish comparison, Mr. Vancouver," she said coldly. "I think you are inclined to make it personal?"

"I believe it became personal from the moment you hit upon Mr. Harrington and me as illustrations of what you were saying, Miss Thorn," retorted Vancouver, very blandly, but with a disagreeable look in his eyes. He was angry at Joe's rebuke.

John stood calmly by without exhibiting the least shade of annoyance. The chaff of a mere girl, and the little satirical thrusts of a lady's man like Vancouver, did not seem to him of much importance. Joe, however, did not vouchsafe any answer to Vancouver's last remark, and it devolved on John to say something to relieve the awkwardness of the situation.

"Have you become reconciled to our methods of amusement, Miss Thorn?" he asked, "or shall we devise something different from the everlasting sleighing and five o'clock tea, and dinner parties and 'dancing classes'?"

"Oh, do not remind me of all that," said Joe. "I did not mean half of it, you know." She turned to John, and Vancouver moved away in pursuit of Sybil Brandon, who had just entered the room.

"Tell me," said Joe, when Pocock was gone, "do you like Mr. Vancouver? You are great friends, are you not?" John looked at her inquiringly.

"I should not say we were very great friends," he answered, "because we are not intimate; but we have always been on excellent terms, as far as I know. Vancouver is a very clever fellow."

"Yes," said Joe, thoughtfully, "I fancy he is. You do not mind my having asked, do you?"

"Not in the least," said John, quietly. His face had grown very grave again, and he seemed suddenly absorbed by some thought. "Let us sit down," he said presently, and the two installed themselves on a divan in a corner.

"You are not in the least inquisitive," remarked Joe, as soon as they were settled.

"What makes you say that?" asked John.

"It was such a silly thing, you know, and you never asked what it was all about."

"When you called me? No—I did not hear what led up to it, and I supposed from what you said afterwards that I understood."

"Did you? What did you think?" asked Joe.

"I thought from the question about Vancouver that you wanted to put us into an awkward position in order to find out whether we were friends."

"No," said Joe, with a little laugh, "I am not so clever as that. It was pure silliness—chaff, you know—that sort of thing."

"Oh," ejaculated John, still quite unmoved, "then it was not of any importance."

"Very silly things sometimes turn out to be very important. Saul, you know—was not it he?—was looking for asses and he found a kingdom."

John laughed suddenly. "And so it is clear which part Vancouver and I played in the business," he said. "But where is the kingdom?"

"I did not mean that," said Joe, seriously. "I am not making fun any more. I have not been successful in my chaff to-day. I should think that in your career it would be very important for you to know who are your friends. Is it not?"

"Certainly," said John, looking at her curiously. "It is very important; but I think political life is generally much simpler than people suppose. It is rather like fighting. The man who hits you is your enemy. The man who does not is practically your friend. Do you mean in regard to Vancouver?"

"Yes."

"Vancouver never hit me, that I can swear," said John, "and I am very sure I never hit him."

"I dare say I am mistaken," said Joe. "You ought to know best. Let us leave him alone."

"With all my heart," answered John.

"Tell me what you have been doing, Mr. Harrington," said Joe, after a moment's pause; "all the papers are full of you."

"Yes, I have been rather in the passive mood during the last week. I have been standing up to be shot at."

"Without shooting back? What are they so angry about?"

"The truth," said John, calmly. "They do not like to hear it."

"What is truth—in this instance?"

"Apparently something so unpleasant that the mere mention of it has roused the bile of every penny-a-liner in the Republican press. I undertook to demonstrate that one of the fifteen millions of the 'ablest men in the country,' whom you are always hearing about, is a swindler. He is, but he does not like to be told so."

"I suppose not," said Joe. "I wonder if any one likes unpleasant truths. But what do you mean to do now? Are you going to fight it out? I hope so!"

"Of course, in good time. One can hardly retire from such a position as mine; they would make an end of me in a week and quarrel over my bones. But the real fight will be fought by and by, when the elections come on."

"How exciting it must all be," said Joe. "I wish I were a man!"

"And an American?" asked John, smiling. "How are the mighty fallen! You were laughing at us and our politics the day before yesterday, and now you are wishing you were one of us yourself. I think you must be naturally fond of fighting"—

"Fond of a row?" suggested Miss Thorn, with a laugh. "Yes, I fancy I am. I am fond of all active things. Are not you?"

"I do not know," said John. "I never thought much about it. But I suppose I should be called rather an active person."

"Is not she beautiful?" ejaculated Miss Thorn, looking across the room at Sybil Brandon, whose fair head was just visible between two groups of people.

"Who?" asked John, who was looking at his companion.

"Miss Brandon," said Joe. "Look at her, over there. I think she is the most beautiful thing I ever saw."

"Yes," said John, "she is very beautiful."

Chapter IV

All sorts and conditions of men and women elbowed and crowded each other under the dim gaslight at the three entrances to the Boston Music Hall. The snow was thick on the ground outside, and it had been thawing all the afternoon. The great booby sleighs slid and slipped and rocked through the wet stuff, the policemen vociferated, the horse-car drivers on Tremont Street rang their bells furiously, and a great crowd of pedestrians stumbled and tumbled about in the mud and slush and snow of the crossings, all bent on getting inside the Music Hall in time for the beginning of the lecture.

The affair was called a "lecture" in accordance with the time-honored custom of Boston, and unless it were termed an oration, it would be hard to find a better name for it. A "meeting" implies a number of orators, or at least a well-filled row of chairs upon the platform. A "lecture," on the other hand, does not convey to the ordinary mind the idea of a political speech, and critical persons with a taste for etymology say that the word means something which is read.

John Harrington had determined to speak in public on certain subjects connected with modern politics, and had caused the fact to be extensively made known. His name alone would have sufficed to draw a large audience, but the great attention he had attracted by his doings for some time past, and the severe criticisms lately made upon him by the local press, rendered the interest even greater than it would otherwise have been. Moreover, the lecture was free. Harrington was a poor man, as fortunes go in Boston, but it was his chiefest principle that a man had no right to be paid for speaking the truth, even though it might sometimes be just that people should pay something for hearing it. Accordingly the lecture was free, and at the appointed hour the house was full to overflowing.

In the front row of the first gallery sat old Miss Schenectady, and by her side was Josephine Thorn. A little colony of "Beacon Street" had collected there, and Pocock Vancouver was not far off. It is not often that Beacon Street goes to such lectures, but John was one of themselves, and had too many friends and enemies among them not to be certain of a large attendance.

Miss Schenectady was there, partly because she believed in John Harrington, and partly because Joe insisted upon going; and, generally speaking, what Joe insisted upon was done. The old lady did not understand why her niece was so very anxious to be present, but as the proposition fell in with her own desires, she made no objection. The fact was that Joe's interest in John had very greatly increased of late, and her curiosity to hear the man she met so often speak to a great audience was excited to its highest pitch. She fancied, too, from many things she had heard said, that a large proportion of his audience would be hostile to him, and that she would see him roused to his greatest strength and eloquence. She did not consider her impulse in the least, for though she felt a stronger interest in Harrington than she had ever before felt in any individual, it had not struck her that she was beginning to care overmuch for the sight of his face and the sound of his voice. She could not have believed she was beginning to love him; and if any secret voice had suggested to her conscience that it was so, she could have silenced it at once to her own satisfaction by merely remembering the coldness with which she generally treated him. She had got into the habit of treating him in that way from the first, when she had been prejudiced against him and the annoyance she often felt at his indifference made her think that she ought to be consistent and never allow her formal manner to change. Unfortunately she now and then forgot herself, as she had done after the little skirmish with Vancouver at Mrs. Wyndham's, and then she talked to him and asked him questions of himself almost as though he were an intimate friend.

John, who was a man of the world as well as a man of talent, thought she was capricious, and since he was infinitely removed from falling in love with her, or indeed with any other woman, he found it agreeable to talk to her when she was in a good humor, and when she was ungracious he merely kept out of her way. If he had deliberately made up his mind to attract her attention and interest, he could have chosen no surer way than this. But although he admired her beauty and vivacity, and now and then took a real pleasure in her conversation, his mind was too full of other matters to receive any lasting impression of such a kind. Besides, she was capricious, and he hated mere caprice.

And now there was a hush in the house, and then a short burst of applause, and Josephine, looking down, saw John standing alone upon the platform in front of the great bronze statue of Beethoven. He looked exactly as he did when she met him in society; there was no change in the even color of his face, nor any awkwardness or self-consciousness in his easy attitude as he stood there, broad-shouldered and square, his strong hand just resting on the plain desk that had been placed in the middle of the stage. He waited a few seconds for silence in the audience, and then began to speak. His voice sounded as natural and his accent as unaffected as though he were talking alone with a friend, saving only that every syllable he uttered was audible in the furthest gallery. Josephine leaned forward upon the red leather cushion of the railing before her, watching and listening intently.

She did not understand the subject well. John Harrington was a reformer, she knew; or, to speak more accurately, he desired to be one. He believed great changes were necessary. He believed in an established Civil Service, in something which, if not exactly Free Trade, was much nearer to it than the existing tariff. Above all, he believed in truth and freedom instead of lying and bribery. As he spoke and cleared the way to his main points, his voice never quavered or faltered. He was perfectly sure of himself, and he reserved all his strength for the time when it should be most required. For a quarter of an hour he proceeded, and the people sat in dead silence before him. Then he paused a moment, and shifted his position a little, moving a step forward as though to gain a better hearing.

"I am coming to the point," he said,—"the point that I must come to sooner or later. I am a Democrat, as perhaps some of you know."

Here there was an uneasy movement in the house. "Yes, I guess you are!" cried a voice from somewhere, in a tone of high nasal irony. Some one laughed, and some one hissed, and then there was silence again.

"Exactly," continued John, unmoved by the interruption. "I am a Democrat, and though the sight does not astonish you so much as it might have done twenty years ago, it is worthy of remark, nevertheless. But I have a peculiarity which I think you will allow to be extremely novel. I do not begin by saying that salvation is only to be found with Democrats, and I will not believe any man who says it belongs exclusively to Republicans. If we were suddenly put in great danger of any kind, war, famine, or revolution, I think that in some way or other we should manage to save the country between us, Republicans and Democrats, for the common good."

"That's so!" said more than one voice.

"Of course we should. Is there any one among us all who would not give up his individual views about a local election rather than see the country go to pieces? Would any man be such a coward as to be afraid to change his mind in order to prevent another Rebellion, another Civil War? No, no, we are more civilized than that. We want our own men in Congress, our own friends in office, just so long as they are serviceable—just so long as the country can stand it, if you like it in that way. But if it comes to be a question between the public good and having your cousin made postmaster in a country village, I think there is enough patriotism in the average Democrat or Republican to send the country cousin about his business. If worst comes to worst, we can save the country between us, depend upon it. We have done it before."

Here there was a burst of willing applause. It is a great point to bring an audience into the position of applauding themselves.

Joe watched John's every gesture, and listened intently to every word. His voice rang clear and strong through the great hall, and he was beginning to be roused. He had gained a decided advantage in the success of his last words, and as he gathered his strength for the real effort which was to come, his cheek paled and his gray eyes grew brighter. He spoke out again through the subsiding clamor.

"Now I say that the country is in danger. It is in very great danger, the greatest danger that can threaten any community. The institutions of a nation are like the habits of a man, except that they are harder to improve and easier to spoil. We have got into bad habits, and if we do not mend them they will take us to a more certain destruction than revolution, famine, or war,—or all three together. It is easier to fight a thing that has a head to it and a name, than a thing that is everywhere and has no name, because no one has the courage to christen it.

"We are like a man who has grown from being a peddler of tape and buttons to be the greatest dry-goods-man in his town, and then to being a great dealer for many towns. When he was a peddler he could carry the profit and loss on his buttons and tape in his head, because the profits were literally in his pocket, and the losses were literally out of it. But when he has grown into a great merchant he must keep books, and he must keep a great many of them, and they must be kept accurately, or he will get into trouble and go to ruin. That is true, is it not? And when he was a peddler he could buy his stock-in-trade himself, and be sure that it was what he wanted; but when he is one of the great merchants he must employ other people to help him, and unless they are the right people and understand the business, he will be ruined. Nobody can deny that.

"Very well. We began in a small way as a nation, without much stock-in-trade, and we kept our accounts by rule of thumb. But it seems to me we are doing a pretty large business as a nation just now."

There was a laugh, and sundry remarks to the effect that the audience understood what John was driving at.

"Yes, we are doing a great business, and to all intents and purposes we are doing it on false business principles, and with an absolutely incompetent staff of clerks. What would you think of a merchant who dismissed all his book-keepers every four years, and engaged a set of shoemakers, or tailors, or artists, or musicians to fill up the vacancies?"

A low murmur ran through the hall, a murmur of disapprobation. Probably a large number out of the three thousand men and women present had cousins in country post offices. But John did not pause; his voice grew full and clear, ringing high above the dull sounds in the house. From her place in the gallery Josephine looked down, never taking her eyes from the face of the orator. She too was pale with excitement; had she been willing to acknowledge it, it was fear. That deep-toned beginning of a protest from the great concourse was like an omen of failure to her sensitive ear. She longed to see John Harrington succeed and carry his hearers with him into an access of enthusiasm. John expected no such thing. He only wanted the people to understand thoroughly what he meant, for he was sure that if once they knew the truth clearly they would feel for it as he himself did.

"Nevertheless," he continued, "I tell you that is what we are doing, what we have been doing for years, from the very beginning. And if we go on doing it we shall get into trouble. We choose schoolboys to do the work of men, we expect that by the mere signature of the head of the executive any man can be turned into an accomplished public officer fit to be compared with one whose whole life has been spent in the public service. We wish to be represented abroad among foreign nations in a way becoming to our dignity and very great power, and we select as our ministers a number of gentlemen who in most cases have never read a diplomatic dispatch in their lives, and who sometimes are not even acquainted with any language save their own. Perhaps you will say that our dignity is not of much importance provided our power is great enough. I do not think you will say it, but there are communities in our country where it would most certainly be said. Very well, so be it. But where do you think our power comes from? Do you think there is a boundless store of some natural product called power, of which we need only take as much as we want in order to stand a head and shoulders higher than any other nation in the world? What is power? Can a man be strong if he has an internal disease, or is his strength any use to him if his arms and legs are out of joint? Would you believe in the strength of a great firm that hired a company of actors from a theatre, and made the tragedian cashier and the low-comedy man head book-keeper?

"The sick man may live for years with his sickness, and the man whose limbs are all distorted may still deal a formidable blow with his head, if it is thick enough. The firm may prosper for a time with its staff of theatrical clerks, provided there is enough business to pay for all their mistakes and leave a margin of profit. But the sick man does not live because he is diseased, but in spite of it. The distorted joints of the cripple do not help him to fight. The firm is not rich because its business is done by tragedians and walking-gentlemen, but in spite of them. If the doctor fails to give his medicine, if the fighting grows too rough for the cripple, if business grows slack, or if some good business man with competent assistants starts a strong opposition—what happens? What must inevitably happen? Why, the sick man dies, the cripple gets the worst of it, and the theatrical firm of merchants goes straight into bankruptcy.

"And so I tell you that we are in danger. We are sick with the foul disease of office seeking; we are crippled hand and foot not only for fighting but for working, because our public officers are inexperienced men who spend four years in learning a trade not theirs, and are very generally turned out before they have half learnt it; we are doing a political business which will succeed fairly well just so long as we are rich enough to provide funds for any amount of extravagance and keep enough in our pockets to buy bread and cheese with afterwards. Just so long.

"When we have been lanced here in Boston and the blood is running freely, we can still cut a slice out of the West and use it like court-plaster to stop the bleeding. Some day there will be no more slices to be had. It will be a bad day in State Street."

This remark raised a laugh and a good deal of noise for a moment. But the audience were soon silent again. Whether they meant to approve or disapprove, they kept their opinions to themselves. Miss Thorn did not comprehend the allusion, but she was listening with all her ears.

"You understand that," John went on. "Then understand it about the rest of the country as well. Understand that we are all the time patching our income with our capital; and it answers pretty well because there is a good deal of capital and not so very many of ourselves, as yet. There will be twice as many of us in a few years, and very much less than half as much capital. Understand above all that we are getting into bad habits—habits we should despise in a corporation, and condemn by very bad names in any individual man of our acquaintance.

"And when you have understood it, look at matters as they stand. Look at the incompetence of our public officers, look at our ruined carrying trade, at those vile enactions of fools, and worse than fools, the Navigation Laws of the United States, and tell me whether things are as they should be. Tell me what has become of liberty if you cannot buy a ship where you can get her best and cheapest, and hoist your own flag upon her, and call her your own? You may pay for her and bring her home with you, but though she were ten times paid for, you cannot hoist the American flag, nor register her in your own port, nor claim the protection of your country for your own property—because, forsooth, the ship was not built on American stocks, where she would cost three times her value, and put a job into the hands of a set of builders of river steamboats and harbor mudscows."

Loud murmurs ran through the audience, and cries of "That's so!" and counter cries of "Freetrader!" were heard on all sides. John's great voice rang out like a trumpet. He knew the sensitiveness of his townsmen on the point.

"I am not speaking against protection," he said, and at the magic word "protection" a dead silence again fell over the vast crowd. "I say to you, 'Protect!' Protect, all of you, merchants, tradesmen, the great body of the commerce of this country; protect whatever you all decide together needs protection. But by the greatness and the power you have, by the Heaven that gave us this land of ours to till and to enjoy, protect also yourselves and your liberties."

A patriotic phrase in the mouth of a man who has the golden gift of speech, coupled with the statement of a principle popular with his audience, is a sure point in an oration. Something in John's tone and gesture touched the sympathetic chord, and the house broke out in a great cry of applause.

An orator cannot always talk in strict logical sequence. He must search about for the right nail till he has found it, and then drive it home.

"Aye, that is the point," he said. "You men of Boston here, look to your harbors, crowded with English craft, and think of what is gone, lost to you forever, unless you will strike a blow for it. Many of you are old enough to remember how it used to be. Look at Salem Harbor, at Marblehead. Where are the fleets of noble ships that lay side by side along the great docks, the ships that did half the carrying trade of the world? Where are the great merchantmen that used to sail so grandly away to the East and that came home so richly laden? They are sunk or gone to pieces, or sold as old timber and copper and nails to the gentlemen who build mudscows. What are the great merchants doing who owned those fleets? They are employing their time in building railroads with English iron and foreign labor into desolate deserts in the West, which they hope to sell for a handsome profit, and probably will. But when there are no more desolate deserts and English iron and foreign labor to be had, they will wish they had their ships again, and that in all these years they had got possession of the carrying trade of the world, as they might have done.

"That is what I am here to say. The time is come to give up the shifts and unstable expedients that we needed, or thought we needed, in our early beginnings. Let us pull down all these scaffoldings and stages that have helped us to build, and let us see whether our fabric will stand upon its base, erect, without the paltry support of a few rotting timbers. Let us substitute the permanent for the transitory, the stable for the unstable, and the reality for the sham. Let us have a Civil Service in fact as well as in name, a service of men trained to their duties, and who shall spend their lives in fulfilling them; a service of competent men to represent us abroad, and a service of honest men to do the country's business at home, instead of making the country do theirs and being paid for it into the bargain. Let us put men into Congress who will cover the seas with our ships again, as well as make our harbors impassable with a competition of cheap ferry-boats. Begin here, as you began here more than a hundred years ago, and as you succeeded then you will succeed now.

"Begin, and go on, and God prosper you; and when the work is done, when bribery and extortion and all corruption are crushed forever out of our public life, when the Navigation Act is a thing of the past, and you are again the carriers of the world's commerce as well as the greatest sharers in it, then it will be time enough to give a name to the men who shall have done all these things, Republicans and Democrats together, a new party, the last and the greatest of all parties that the country has ever seen. You will find a name, surely enough, that will answer the purpose then; but whatever that name may be, it will not be forgotten that, for the third time in the history of our land, Massachusetts has struck the first and the strongest blow in the struggle for liberty, honor, and truth."

Few men in public life had as good a right as John Harrington to denounce all manner of dishonesty. Many a speaker would have raised a sneering laugh by that last phrase, but even John's enemies admitted that his hands were clean. Coming from one of themselves it was a strong appeal, and the applause was long and loud. With a courteous inclination John turned and left the platform through the door at the back.

He was well enough satisfied. His hearers had been moved for a moment to enthusiasm. They would go home and on mature reflection would not agree with him; but a blow struck is a point in the fight so long as it is felt at all, and John was well pleased at the reception he had met with. He had avoided every detail, and had confined himself to the widest generalities, but his homely illustrations would not be forgotten, and his strong individuality had created a sincere desire in many who had been there that night to hear him speak again.

For some minutes after John had left the platform, Josephine sat unmoved in her seat beside her aunt, lost in thought as she watched the surging crowd below.

"Well," said Miss Schenectady, "you have heard John Harrington now." Joe started. She had grown used to the implied interrogation her aunt usually conveyed in that way.

"He is a great man, Aunt Zoë," she said quietly, and looked round. There was a moisture in her beautiful brown eyes that told of great excitement. She was very pale too, and looked tired.

"Yes, my dear," said Aunt Zoruiah. "But we had better go home right away, Joe darling. You are so pale, I suppose you must be a good deal used up."

"Allow me to see you to your carriage," said Pocock Vancouver in dulcet tones, coming up to the two ladies as they rose.

Chapter V

"Why can't you get in, Mr. Vancouver?" inquired Miss Schenectady, when she and Joe were at last packed into the deep booby. It was simply a form of invitation. There was no reason why Mr. Vancouver should not get in, and with a word of thanks he did so. Ten minutes later the three were seated round the fire in Miss Schenectady's drawing-room.

"It was very fine, was it not, Miss Thorn?" said Vancouver.

"Yes," said Joe, staring at the fire.

"There are some people," said Miss Schenectady, "it does not seem to make much difference what they say, but it is always fine."

"Is that ironical?" asked Vancouver.

"Why, goodness gracious no! Of course not! I am John Harrington's very best friend. I only mean to say."

"What, Aunt Zoë?" inquired Joe, not yet altogether accustomed to the peculiar implications of her aunt's language.

"Why, what I said, of course; it sounds very fine."

"Then you do not believe it all?" asked Vancouver.

"I don't understand politics," said the old lady. "You might ring the bell, Joe, and ask Sarah for some tea."

"Nobody understands politics," said Vancouver. "When people do, there will be an end of them. Politics consist in one half of the world trying to drive paradoxes down the throats of the other half."

Joe laughed a little.

"I do not know anything about politics here," she said, "though I do at home, of course. I must say, though, Mr. Harrington did not seem so very paradoxical."

"Oh no," answered Vancouver, blandly, "I did not mean in this case. Harrington is very much in earnest. But it is like war, you see. When every one understands it thoroughly, it will stop by universal consent. Did you ever read Bulwer's 'Coming Race'?"

"Yes," said Joe. "I always read those books. Vril, and that sort of thing, you mean? Oh yes."

"Approximately," answered Vancouver. "It was an allegory, you know. A hundred years hence people will write a book to explain what Bulwer meant. Vril stands for the cumulative power of potential science, of course."

"I think Bulwer's word shorter, and a good deal easier to understand," said Joe, laughing.

"It is a great thing to be great," remarked Miss Schenectady. "Sarah, I think you might bring us some tea, please, and ask John if he couldn't stir the furnace a little. And then to have people explain you. Goethe must be a good deal amused, I expect, when people write books to prove that Byron was Euphorion." Miss Schenectady was fond of German literature, and the extent of her reading was a constant surprise to her niece.

"What a lot of things you know, Aunt Zoë!" said Joe. "But what had Bulwer to do with war, Mr. Vancouver?"

"Oh, in the book—the 'Coming Race,' you know—they abolished war because they could kill each other so easily."

"How nice that would be!" exclaimed Joe, looking at him.

"Why, you perfectly shock me, Joe," cried Miss Schenectady.

"I mean, to have no war," returned Joe, sweetly.

"Oh; I belonged to the Peace Conference myself," said her aunt, immediately pacified. "Well, yes. Perhaps you could bring us a little cake, Sarah? War is a terrible thing, my dear, as Mr. Vancouver will tell you."

Vancouver, however, was silent. He probably did not care to have it remembered that he was old enough to carry a musket in the Rebellion. Joe understood and asked no Questions about it, and Vancouver was grateful for her tact. She rose and began to pour out some tea.

"You began talking about Mr. Harrington's speech," said she presently, "but we got away from the subject. Is it all true?"

"That is scarcely a fair question, Miss Thorn," answered Vancouver. "You see, I belong to the opposite party in politics."

"But Mr. Harrington said he wanted both parties to combine. Besides, you do not take any active part in it all."

"I have very strong opinions, nevertheless," replied Pocock.

"Strong opinions and activity ought to go together," said Joe.

"Not always."

"But if you have strong opinions and disagree with Mr. Harrington," persisted Miss Thorn, "then you have a strong opinion against your two parties acting together for the common good."

"Not exactly that," said Vancouver, embarrassed between the directness of Joe's question and a very strong impression that he had better not say anything against John Harrington.

"Then what do you believe? Will you please give this cup to Miss Schenectady?"

Vancouver rose quickly to escape.

"Cream and sugar, Miss Schenectady?" he said. "Ah, Miss Thorn has already put them in. It is such celebrated tea of yours! Do you know, I always look forward to a cup of it as one of the greatest pleasures in life!"

"When you have quite done praising the tea, will you please tell me what you believe about Mr. Harrington's speech?" said the inexorable Joe, drowning her aunt's reply to Vancouver's polite remark.

Thus cornered, Vancouver faced the difficulty.

"I believe it was a very good speech," he said mildly.

"Do you believe what he said was true?"

"A great deal of it was true, but I assure you that Harrington is very enthusiastic. Much of it was extremely imaginative."

"I dare say; all that about making a Civil Service, I suppose?"

"Well, not exactly. I think all good Republicans hope to have a regular Civil Service some day. It is necessary, or will be so before long."

"But then it is what he said about that ridiculous Navigation Act that you object to?" pursued Joe, without mercy.

"Really, I think it would be an advantage to repeal it. It is only kept up for the sake of a few builders who have influence."

"Ah, I see," exclaimed Joe triumphantly, "you think the hope he expressed that bribery and that sort of thing might be suppressed was altogether imaginary?"

"I hope not, Miss Thorn. But I am sure there is not nearly so much of it as he made out. It was a very great exaggeration."

"Was there? Really, he only used the word once in the most general way. I remember very well, at the end; he said, 'when bribery, corruption, and all extortion are crushed forever;' anybody might say that!"

"You make out a wonderfully good case, Miss Thorn," said Vancouver, who was not altogether pleased; "was the speech printed before Harrington spoke it this evening?"

"No!" exclaimed Joe. "I have a very good memory, in that way, just to remember what I hear. I could repeat word for word everything he said, and everything you have said since during the evening."

"What a terrible person you are!" said Vancouver, smiling pleasantly. "Well, then, now that you have proved every word of Harrington's speech out of an opponent's evidence, I will tell you frankly how it is that I do not agree with him. He is a Democrat, I am a Republican. That is the whole story. I do not believe, nor shall I ever believe, that any large number of the two parties can work together. I cannot help my belief in the least; it is a matter of conscience. Nevertheless, I have a very great respect for

Harrington, and as I take no active part whatever in any political contest, my opinion of his politics will never interfere with my personal feeling for him."

Frankness seemed to be Mr. Vancouver's strong point. Joe was obliged to admit that he spoke clearly, even if she did not greatly respect his logic. During all this time, Miss Schenectady had been sipping her tea in silence.

"Joe," she said at last, "you are a perfect Socrates for questions. You ought to have been a lawyer."

"I wish I were," said Joe, laughing, "or Socrates himself."

"Yes, you ought to have been. Here you know nothing at all about this thing, and you have been talking like anything for half an hour. I think Socrates was perfectly horrid."

"So do I," said Vancouver, laughing aloud.

"Why?" Joe asked, turning to her aunt.

"To be always stopping people in the street, and button-holing them with his questions. Of course it was very clever, as Plato makes it out; but I do wish he could have met me—when I was young, my dear. I would have answered him once and for all!"

"Try me, Aunt Zoë, for practice," said Joe, "until you meet him."

"Really, I expect you would do almost as well. Look at Mr. Vancouver, he is quite used up."

The case was not so serious with Mr. Vancouver as the old lady made it out to be. He was silent and to all intents vanquished for the present, but it was not long before he turned the conversation to other things, and succeeded in making himself very agreeable. He admired Josephine very much, and though she occasionally made him feel very uncomfortable, he always returned to the charge with renewed intelligence and sweetness. Joe liked him too, in spite of an unfounded suspicion she felt that he was dangerous. He was always ready when she needed anything at a party; he never bored her, but whenever he saw she was wearied by any one else he came up and saved her, clearing a place for himself at her side with an ease that bespoke long and constant experience of the world. Women, especially young women, always like men of that description; they are flattered at the attention of a man who is so evidently able to choose, and they enjoy the immunity from all annoyance and weariness that such men are able to carry with them.

Consequently Joe accepted the attentions of Pocock Vancouver with a certain amount of satisfaction, and she had not been displeased that he should come to Miss Schenectady's house for tea. The evening passed quickly, and Vancouver took his leave. As he opened the front door to let himself out he nearly fell over a small telegraph messenger.

"Thorn here?" inquired the boy, laconically.

"Yes, I'll take it in," said Vancouver quickly. He went back with the telegram, and the boy stood inside the door waiting for the receipt. He noticed the stamp of the Cable Office on the envelope.

"Miss Thorn," said Vancouver, entering the drawing-room again, hat in hand, "I just met this telegram on the steps, so I brought it in. It may need an answer, you know."

"Thanks, so much," said Joe, tearing open the pale yellow cover. She was startled, not being accustomed to receive telegrams. Her brow contracted as she read the contents, and she tapped her small foot on the carpet impatiently.

Thorn, care Schenectady,
Beacon, Boston.
Sailed to-day.
Ronald.

Josephine crushed the paper in her hand and signed the receipt with the pencil Vancouver offered her.

"Thanks, so much," she said again, but in a different tone of voice.

"Any answer?" suggested Vancouver.

"Thanks, no," answered Joe. "Good-night again."

"Good-night." And Vancouver departed, wondering what the message could have been.

Miss Schenectady had looked on calmly throughout the little scene, and nodded to Pocock as he left the room; her peculiarities were chiefly those of diction; she was a well-bred old lady, not without wisdom.

"Nothing wrong, Joe?" she inquired, when alone with her niece.

"I hardly know," answered Joe. "Ronald has just sailed from England. I suppose he will be here in ten days."

"Business here?" asked Miss Schenectady.

"Oh dear, no! He knows nothing about business. I wish he would stay at home. What a bore!"

It was evident that Joe had changed her mind since she had written to Ronald a fortnight before. It seemed to her now, when she looked forward to Surbiton's coming, that he would not find his place in Boston society so easily as she had done. Of course he would expect to see her every day, and to spend all his leisure hours at Miss Schenectady's house. Whatever she happened to be doing, it would always be necessary to take Ronald into consideration, and the prospect did not please her at all.

Ronald was a dear good fellow, of course, and she meant to marry him in the end—at least, she probably would. But then, she intended to marry him at a more convenient season, some time in the future. She knew him well, and she was certain that when he saw her surrounded by her Boston acquaintances, his British nature would assert itself, and he would claim her, or try to claim her, and persuade her to go away. She bid Miss Schenectady good night, and went to her room; and presently, when she was sure every one was in bed in the house, she stole down to the drawing-room again, and sat alone by the remains of the coal-fire, thinking what she should do.

Josephine Thorn was young and more full of life and activity than most girls of her age. She enjoyed what came in her way to enjoy with a passionate zest, and she had the reputation of being somewhat capricious and changeable. But she was honest in all her thoughts, and very clear-sighted. People often said she spoke her mind too freely, and was not enough in awe of the veiled deity known in society as "The Thing." How she hated it! How many times she had been told that what she said and did was not quite "The Thing." She knew now what Ronald would say when he came, if he found her worshiped on all sides by Pocock Vancouver and his younger and less accomplished compeers. Ronald would say "it was rather rough, you know."

She sat by the fire and thought the matter over, and when she came to formulating in her mind the exact words that Ronald would say, she paused to think of him and how he would look. He was handsome—far handsomer than Vancouver or—or John Harrington. He was very nice; much nicer than Vancouver. John Harrington was different, "nice" did not describe him; but Ronald was nicer than all the other men she knew. He would make a charming husband. At the thought Joe started.

"My husband!" she repeated aloud to herself in the silence. Then she rose quickly to her feet and leaned against the smooth white marble mantelpiece, and buried her face in her small white hands for an instant.

"Oh no, no, no, no!" she cried aloud. "It is impossible; oh no! never! I never really meant it; did I?" She stared at herself in the glass for a few seconds, and her face was very pale. Then she bent over her hands again, and the tears came and wetted them a little, and at last she sat down as she had sat before, and stared vacantly at the fire.

It would be very wrong to break Ronald's heart, she thought. He would come to her so full of hope and gladness; how could she tell him she did not love him?

But how was it possible that in all these years she had never before understood that she could not marry him? It had always seemed so natural to marry Ronald. And yet she must have always really felt just as she did to-night; only she had never realized it, never at all. Why had it come over her so suddenly too? It would have been so much better if she could have seen the truth at home, before she parted from him; for it would be so hard for him to bear it now, after coming across the ocean to see her —so cruelly hard. Dear Ronald; and yet he must be told.

Yes, there was no doubt about it, the very first meeting must explain it to him. He would say—what would he say? He would tell her she liked some one else better.

Some one else! Some one who had stolen away her heart; of course he would say that. But he would be wrong, for there was no one else, not one of all these men she had seen, who had so much as breathed a word of love to her. None whom she liked nearly so much as Ronald, no, not one.

For a long time she sat very quietly, following a train of thought that was half unconscious. Her lips moved now and then, as though she were repeating something to herself, and gradually the pained and anxious expression of her face melted away into a look of peace.

The old gilt clock upon the chimney-piece struck twelve in its shrill steel tones. Josephine started at the sound, and passed one hand over her eyes as though to rouse herself, and at the same time a deep blush spread over her delicate cheek. For with the voice of midnight there was also the voice of a man ringing in her ears, and she heard the two together, so that it seemed as though all the world must hear them also, and her gentle maiden's soul was shamed at the thought.

So it is that our loves are always with us, and though we search ourselves diligently to find them and rebuke them, we find them not; but if we give up searching they come upon us unawares, and speak very soft words. Love also is a gentle thing, full of sweetness and peace, when he comes to us so; and though the maiden blushes at his speaking, she would not stop the ears of her heart against him for all the world; and although the boy trembles and turn pale, and forgets to be boyish when, the fit is on him, nevertheless he goes near and worships, and loses his heart in learning a new language. So kind and soft is love, so tender and sweet-spoken, that you would think he would not so much as ruffle the leaf of a rose, nor breathe too sharply on a violet, lest he should hurt the flower-soul within; and if you treat him hospitably he is kind to the last, so that when he is gone there is still a sweet savor of him left. But if you would drive him roughly away with scorn and rude language, he will stand at your door and will not leave you. Then his wings drop from him, and he grows strong and fierce, and deadly and beautiful, as the fallen archangel of heaven, crying aloud bitter things to you by day and night; till at the last he will break down bolt and bar and panel, and enter your chamber, and drag you out with him to your death in the wild darkness.

But Josephine blushed deeply there in the old-fashioned drawing-room at midnight, and as she turned away she wondered at herself, for she could not believe nor understand what was happening.

Poor girl! She had talked of love so often as an abstract thing, she had seen so many love-makings of others, and so many men had tried to make love to her in her short brilliant life, and she had always thought it could not come near her, because, of course, she really loved Ronald. She had marveled, indeed, at what people were willing to do, and at what they were ready to sacrifice, for a feeling that seemed to her of such little importance as that. It had been an illusion, and the waking had come at last very suddenly. Whoever it might be whom she was destined to take, it was not Ronald. It was madness to think she could be bound forever to him, however much she might admire him and desire him as a friend.

When the clock struck she was thinking of John, and the words he had said that night to his great audience were ringing again in her ears. She blushed indeed at the idea that she was thinking so much of him, but it was not that she believed she loved him. If as yet she really did, she was herself most honestly unconscious of it; and so the blush was not accounted for in the reckoning she made.

She lay awake long, trying to determine what was best to be done, but she could not. One thing she must do; she must explain to Ronald, when he came, that she could never, never marry him.

If only she had a sister, or some one! Dear Aunt Zoruiah was so horrid about such things that it was impossible to talk to her!

Chapter VI

"Do you know how to skate?" Sybil Brandon asked of Joe as the two young girls, clad in heavy furs, walked down the sunny side of Beacon Street two days later. They were going from Miss Schenectady's to a "lunch party"— one of those social institutions of Boston which had most surprised Joe on her first arrival.

"Of course," answered Joe. "I do not know anything, but I can do everything."

"How nice!" said Sybil. "Then you can go with us to-night. That will be too lovely!"

"What is it?"

"We are all going skating on Jamaica Pond. Nobody has skated for so long here that it is a novelty. I used to be so fond of it."

"We always skate at home, when there is ice," said Joe. "It will be enchanting though, with the full moon and all. What time?"

"Mrs. Sam Wyndham will arrange that," said Sybil. "She is going to matronize us."

"How dreadful, to have to be chaperoned!" ejaculated Joe. "But Mrs. Wyndham is very jolly after all, so it does not much matter."

"I believe they used to have Germans here without any mothers," remarked Sybil, "but they never do now."

"Poor little things, how awfully lonely for them!" laughed Joe.

"Who?"

"The Germans—without their mothers. Oh, I forgot the German was the cotillon. You mean cotillons, without tapestry, as we say."

"Yes, exactly. But about the skating party. It will be very select, you know; just ourselves. You know I never go out," Sybil added rather sadly, "but I do love skating so."

"Who are 'ourselves'—exactly?"

"Why, you and I, and the Sam Wyndhams, and the Aitchison girls, and Mr. Topeka, and Mr. Harrington, and Mr. Vancouver—let me see—and Miss St. Joseph, and young Hannibal. He is very nice, and is very attentive to Miss St. Joseph."

"Is it nice, like that, skating about in couples?" asked Joe.

"No; that is the disagreeable part; but the skating is delicious."

"Let us stay together all the time," said Joe spontaneously, "it will be ever so much pleasanter. I would not exactly like to be paired off with any of those men, you know."

Sybil looked at Joe, opening her wide blue eyes in some astonishment. She did not think Joe was exactly one of those young women who object to a moonlight tête-à-tête, if properly chaperoned.

"Yes, if you like, dear," she said. "I would like it much better myself, of course."

"Do you know, Sybil," said Joe, looking up at her taller companion, "I should not think you would care for skating and that sort of thing."

"Why?" asked Sybil.

"You do not look strong enough. You are not a bit like me, brought up on horseback."

"Oh, I am very strong," answered Sybil, "only I am naturally pale, you see, and people think I am delicate."

But the north wind kissed her fair face and the faint color came beneath the white and through it, so that Joe looked at her and thought she was the fairest woman in the world that day.

"When I was a little girl," said Joe, "mamma used to tell me a story about the beautiful Snow Angel: she must have been just like you, dear."

"What is the story?" asked Sybil, the delicate color in her cheek deepening a little.

"I will tell you to-night when we are skating, we have not time now. Here we are." And the two girls went up the steps of the house where they were going to lunch.

On the other side of the street Pocock Vancouver and John Harrington met, and stopped to speak just as Joe and Sybil had rung the bell, and stood waiting at the head of the steps.

"Don't let us look at each other so long as we can look at them," said Vancouver, shaking hands with John, but looking across the street at the two girls. John looked too, and both men bowed.

"They are pretty enough for anything, are they not?" continued Vancouver.

"Yes," said John, "they are very pretty."

With a nod and a smile Joe and Sybil disappeared into the house.

"Why don't you marry her?" asked Vancouver.

"Which? The English girl?"

"No; Sybil Brandon."

"Thank you, I am not thinking of being married," said John, a half-comic, half-contemptuous look in his strong face. "Miss Brandon could do better than marry a penniless politician, and besides, even if I wanted it, I care too much for Miss Brandon's friendship to risk losing it by asking her to marry me."

"Nonsense, my dear fellow," said Vancouver, "she would accept you straight off. So would the other."

"You ought to know," said John, eyeing his companion calmly.

Vancouver looked away; it was generally believed that he had been refused by Miss Brandon more than a year previous.

"Well, you can take my word for it, you could not do better," he answered, ambiguously. "There is no knowing how the moonlight effects on Jamaica Pond may strike you this evening. I say, though, you were pretty lucky in having such warm weather the night before last."

"Yes," said John. "The house was full. Were you there?"

"Of course. If I were not a Republican I would congratulate you on your success. It is a long time since any one has made a Boston audience listen to those opinions. You did it surprisingly well; that sentence about protection was a masterpiece. I wish you were one of us."

"It is of no use arguing with you," said John. "If it were, I could make a Democrat of you in an afternoon."

"I make a pretty good thing of arguing, though," answered the other. "It's my trade, you see, and it is not yours. You lay down the law; it is my business to make a living out of it."

"I wish I could lay it down, as you say, and lay it down according to my own ideas," said John. "I would have something to say to you railroad men."

"As for that, I should not care. Railroad law is stronger than iron and more flexible than india-rubber, and the shape of it is of no importance whatever. So long as there is enough of it to work with, you can twist it and untwist it as much as you please."

John laughed.

"It would simplify matters to untwist it and cut it up into lengths," he said. "But then your occupation would be gone."

"I think my occupation will last my life-time," answered Vancouver, laughing in his turn.

"Not if I can help it," returned John. "But we can provide you with another. Good-by. I am going to Cambridge."

They shook hands cordially, and John Harrington turned down Charles Street, while Vancouver pursued his way up the hill. He had been going in the opposite direction when he met Harrington, but he seemed to have changed his mind. He was not seen again that day until he went to dine with Mrs. Sam Wyndham.

There was no one there but Mr. Topeka and young John C. Hannibal, well-dressed men of five-and-thirty and five-and-twenty respectively, belonging to good families of immense fortune, and educated regardless of expense. No homely Boston phrase defiled their anglicized lips, their great collars stood up under their chins in an ecstasy of stiffness, and their shirt-fronts bore two buttons, avoiding the antiquity of three and the vulgarity of one. Well-bred Anglo-maniacs both, but gentlemen withal, and courteous to the ladies. Mr. Topeka was a widower, John C. Hannibal was understood to be looking for a wife.

They came, they dined, and they retired to Sam Wyndham's rooms to don their boots and skating clothes. At nine o'clock the remaining ladies arrived, and then the whole party got into a great sleigh and were driven rapidly out of town over the smooth snow to Jamaica Pond. John Harrington had not come, and only three persons missed him—Joe Thorn, Mrs. Sam, and Pocock Vancouver.

The ice had been cut away in great quantities for storing and the thaw had kept the pond open for a day or two. Then came the sharpest frost of the winter, and in a few hours the water was covered with a broad sheet of black ice that would bear any weight. It was a rare piece of good fortune, but the fashion of skating had become so antiquated that no one took advantage of the opportunity; and as the party got out of the sleigh and made their way down the bank, they saw that there was but one skater before them, sweeping in vast solitary circles out in the middle of the pond, under the cold moonlight. The party sat on the bank in the shadow of some tall pine trees, preparing for the amusement, piling spare coats and shawls on the shoulders of a patient groom, and screwing and buckling their skates on their feet.

"What beautiful ice!" exclaimed Joe, when Vancouver had done his duty by the straps and fastenings. She tapped the steel blade twice or thrice on the hard black surface, still leaning on Vancouver's arm, and then, without a word of warning, shot away in a long sweeping roll. The glorious vitality in her was all alive, and her blood thrilled and beat wildly in utter enjoyment. She did not go far at first, but seeing the others were long in their preparations, she turned and faced them, skating away backwards, leaning far over to right and left on each changing stroke, and listening with intense pleasure to the musical ring of the clanging steel on the clean ice. Some pride she felt, too, at showing the little knot of Bostonians how thoroughly at home she was in a sport they seemed to consider essentially American.

Joe had not noticed the solitary skater, and thought herself alone, but in a few moments she was aware of a man in an overcoat bowing before her as he slackened his speed. She turned quickly to one side and stopped herself, for the man was John Harrington.

"Why, where did you come from, Mr. Harrington?" she asked in some astonishment. "You were not hidden under the seats of the sleigh, were you?"

"Not exactly," said John, looking about for the rest of the party. "I was belated in Cambridge this afternoon, so I borrowed a pair of skates and walked over. Splendid ice, is it not?"

"I am so glad you came," said Joe. She was in such high spirits and was so genuinely pleased at meeting John that she forgot to be cold to him. "It would have been a dreadful pity to have missed this."

"It would indeed," said John, skating slowly by her side.

For down by the pine trees two or three figures began to move on the ice.

"I want to thank you, Mr. Harrington," said Joe.

"What for, Miss Thorn?" he asked.

"For the pleasure you gave me the other night," she answered. "I have not seen you since to speak to. It was splendid!"

"Thanks," said John. "I saw you there, in the gallery on my left."

"Yes; but how could you have time to look about and recognize people? You must have splendid eyes."

"It is all a habit," said John. "When one has been before an audience a few times one does not feel nervous, and so one has time to look about. Do you care for that sort of thing, Miss Thorn?"

"Oh, ever so much. But I was frightened once, when they began to grumble."

"There was nothing to fear," said John, laughing. "Audiences of that kind do not punctuate one's speeches with cabbages and rotten eggs."

"They do sometimes in England," said Joe. "But here come the others!"

Two and two, in a certain grace of order, the little party came out from the shore into the moonlight. The women's faces looked white and waxen against their rich furs, and the moonbeams sparkled on their ornaments. A very pretty sight is a moonlight skating party, and Pocock Vancouver knew what he was saying when he hinted at the mysterious and romantic influences that are likely to be abroad on such occasions. Indeed, it was not long before young Hannibal was sliding away hand in hand with Miss St. Joseph at a pace that did not invite competition. And Mr. Topeka decided which of the Aitchison girls he preferred, and gave her his arm, so that the other fell to the lot of Sam Wyndham, while Mrs. Sam and Sybil Brandon came out escorted by Vancouver, who noticed with some dismay that the party was "a man short." The moment he saw Joe talking to the solitary skater, he knew that the latter must be Harrington, who had gone to Cambridge and come across. John bowed to every one and shook hands with Mrs. Wyndham. Joe eluded Vancouver and put her arm through Sybil's, as though to take possession of her.

Joe would have been well enough pleased at first to have been left with John, but the sight of Vancouver somehow reminded her of the compact she had made in the morning with Sybil, and in a few moments the two girls were away together, talking so persistently to each other that Vancouver, who at first followed them and tried to join their conversation, was fain to understand that he was not wanted, so that he returned to Mrs. Wyndham.

"I want so much to talk to you," Joe began, when they were alone.

"Yes, dear?" said Sybil half interrogatively, as they moved along. "We can talk here charmingly, unless Mr. Vancouver comes after us again. But you do skate beautifully, you know. I had no idea you could."

"Oh, I told you I could do everything," said Joe, with some pride. "Where did you get that beautiful fur, my dear? It is magnificent. You are just like the Snow Angel now."

"In Russia. Everybody wears white fur there, you know. We were in St. Petersburg some time."

"I know. We cannot get it in England. If one could I would have told Ronald to bring me some when he comes."

"Who is Ronald?" asked Sybil innocently.

"Oh, he is the dearest boy," said Joe, with a little sigh, "but I do so wish he were not coming!"

"Because he has not got the white fur?" suggested Sybil.

"Oh no! But because"—Joe lowered her voice and spoke demurely, at the same time linking her arm more closely in Sybil's. "You see, dear, he wants to marry me, and I am afraid he is coming to say so."

"And you do not want to marry him? Is that it?"

Joe's small mouth closed tightly, and she merely nodded her head gravely, looking straight before her. Sybil pressed her arm sympathetically and was silent, expecting more.

"It was such a long time ago, you see," said Joe, after a while. "I was not out when it was arranged, and it seemed so natural. But now—it is quite different."

"But of course, if you do not love him, you must not think of marrying him," said Sybil, simply.

"I won't," answered Joe, with sudden emphasis. "But I shall have to tell him, you know," she added despondently.

"It is very hard to say those things," said Sybil, in a tone of reflection. "But of course it must be done—if you were really engaged, that is."

"Yes, almost really," said Joe.

"Not quite?" suggested Sybil.

"I think not quite; but I know he thinks it is quite quite, you know."

"Well, but perhaps he is not so certain, after all. Do you know, I do not think men really care so much; do you?"

"Oh, of course not," said Joe scornfully. "But it does not seem quite honest to let a man think you are going to marry him if you do not mean to."

"But you did mean to, dear, until you found out you did not care for him enough. And just think how dreadful it would be to be married if you did not care enough!"

"Yes, that is true," answered Joe. "It would be dreadful for him too."

"When is he coming?" asked Sybil.

"I think next week. He sailed the day before yesterday."

"Then there is plenty of time to settle on what you want to say," said Sybil. "If you make up your mind just how to put it, you know, it will be ever so much easier."

"Oh no!" cried Joe. "I will trust to luck. I always do; it is much easier."

"Excuse me, Miss Brandon," said the voice of Vancouver, who came up behind them at a great pace, and holding his feet together let himself slide rapidly along beside the two girls,—"excuse me, but do you not think you are very unsociable, going off in this way?"

"May I give you my arm, Miss Thorn?" asked Harrington, coming up on the other side.

Without leaving each other Joe and Sybil took the proffered arms of the two men, and the four skated smoothly out into the middle of the ice, that rang again in the frosty air under their joint weight. Mrs. Wyndham had insisted that Vancouver and Harrington should leave her and follow the young girls, and they had obeyed in mutual understanding.

"Which do you like better, Miss Brandon, boating in Newport or skating on Jamaica Pond?" asked Vancouver.

"This is better than the Music Hall, is it not?" remarked John to Miss Thorn.

"Oh, Jamaica Pond, by far," Sybil answered, and her hold on Joe's arm relaxed a very little.

"Oh no! I would a thousand times rather be in the Music Hall!" exclaimed Joe, and her hand slipped away from Sybil's white fur. And so the four were separated into couples, and went their ways swiftly under the glorious moonlight. As they parted Sybil turned her head and looked after Joe, but Joe did not see her.

"I would rather be here," said John quietly.

"Why?" asked Joe.

"There is enough fighting in life to make peace a very desirable thing sometimes," John answered.

"A man cannot be always swinging his battle-axe." There was a very slight shade of despondency in the tone of his voice. Joe noticed it at once.

Women do not all worship success, however much they may wish their champion to win when they are watching him fight. In the brilliant, unfailing, all-conquering man, the woman who loves him feels pride; if she be vain and ambitious, she feels wholly satisfied, for the time. But woman's best part is her gentle sympathy, and where there is no room at all for that, there is very often little room for love. In the changing hopes and fears of uncertain struggles, a woman's love well given and truly kept may turn the scale for a man, and it is at such times, perhaps, that her heart is given best, and most loyally held by him who has it.

"I wish I could do anything to help him to succeed," thought Joe, in the innocent generosity of her half-conscious devotion.

"Has anything gone wrong?" she asked aloud.

Chapter VII

"Has anything gone wrong?" There was so much of interest and sympathy in her tone, as Joe put the simple question, that John turned and looked into her face. The magic of moonlight softens the hardest features, makes interest look like friendship, and friendship like love; but it can harden too at times, and make a human face look like carved stone.

"No, there is nothing wrong," John answered presently; "what made you think so?"

"You spoke a little regretfully," answered Joe.

"Did I? I did not mean to. Perhaps one is less gay and less hopeful at some times than at others. It has nothing to do with success or failure."

"I know," answered Joe. "One can be dreadfully depressed when one is enjoying one's self to any extent. But I should not have thought you were that sort of person. You seem always the same."

"I try to be. That is the great difference between people who live to work and people who live to amuse and be amused."

"How do you mean?"

"I mean," said John, "that people who work, especially people who have to do with large ideas and great movements, need to be more or less monotonous. The men who succeed are the men of one idea or at least they are the men who only have one idea at a time."

"Whereas people who live to amuse and be amused must have as many ideas as possible."

"Yes, to play with," said John, completing the sentence. "Their life is play, their ideas are their playthings, and so soon as they have spoiled one toy they must have another. The people who supply ideas to an idle public are very valuable, and may have great power."

"Novel-writers, and that sort of people," suggested Joe.

"All producers of light literature and second-rate poetry, and a very great variety of other people besides. A man who amuses others may often be a worker himself. He raises a laugh or excites a momentary interest by getting rid of his superfluous ideas and imaginations, reserving to himself all the time the one idea in which he believes."

"Not at all a bad theory," said Joe.

"There are more men of that sort with you in Europe than with us. You need more amusement, and you will generally give more for it. You English, who are uncommonly fond of doing nothing, give yourselves vast trouble in the pursuit of pleasure. We Americans, who are ill when we are idle, are content to surround ourselves with the paraphernalia of pleasure when office hours are over; but we make very little use of our opportunities for amusement, being tired out at the end of the day with other things which we think more important. The result is that we have no such thing as what you denominate 'Society,' because we lack the prime element of aristocratic social intercourse, the ingrained determination to be idle."

"You are very hard on us," remarked Joe.

"Excuse me," returned John, "you are compensated by having what we have not. Europeans are the most agreeable people in the world, wherever mutual and daily conversation and intercourse are to be considered. The majority of you, of polite European society, are not troubled with any very large ideas, but you have an immense number of very charming and attractive small ones. In America there are only two ideas that practically affect society, but they are very big ones indeed."

"What?" asked Joe laconically, growing interested in John's queer lecture.

"Money and political influence," answered John Harrington. "They are the two great motors of our machine. All men who are respected among us are in pursuit of one or the other, or have attained to one or the other by their own efforts. The result is, that European society is amusing and agreeable; whereas Americans of the same class are more interesting, less polished, better acquainted with the general laws that govern the development of nations." "Really, Mr. Harrington," said Joe, "you are making us out to be very insignificant. And I think it would be very dull if we all had to understand ever so many general laws. Besides, I do not agree with you."

"About what, Miss Thorn?"

"About Americans. They talk better than Englishmen, as a rule."

"But I am comparing Americans with the whole mass of Europeans," John objected. "The English are a rather silent race, I should say."

"Cold, you think?" suggested Joe.

"No, not cold. Perhaps less cold than we are; but less demonstrative."

"I like that," answered Joe. "I like people to feel more than they show."

"Why?" asked John. "Why should not people be perfectly natural, and show when they feel anything, or be cold when they do not?" "I think when you know some one feels a great deal and hides it, that gives one the idea of reserved strength."

They had reached a distant part of the ice, and were slowly skating round the limits of a little bay, where the slanting moonbeams fell through tall old trees upon the glinting black surface. They were quite alone, only in the distance they could hear the long-drawn clang and ring of the other skaters, echoing all along the lake with a tremulous musical sound in the still bright night. "You must be very cold yourself, Mr. Harrington," Joe began again after a pause, stopping and looking at him.

John laughed a little.

"I?" he cried. "No, indeed, I am the most enthusiastic man alive."

"You are when you are speaking in public," said Joe. "But that may be all comedy, you know. Orators always study their speeches, with all the gestures and that, before a glass, don't they?"

"I do not know," said John. "Of course I know by heart what I am going to say, when I make a speech like that of the other evening, but I often insert a great deal on the spur of the moment. It is not comedy. I grow very much excited when I am speaking."

"Never at any other time?" asked Joe.

"Seldom; why should I? I do not feel other things or situations so strongly."

"In other words," replied Joe, "it is just as I said; you are generally very cold."

"I suppose so," John acquiesced, "since you will not allow the occasions when I am not cold to be counted."

Joe looked down as she stood, and moved her skates slowly on the ice; the shadows hid her face.

"Do you know," she said presently, "you lose a great deal; you must, you cannot help it. You only like people in a body, so as to see what you can do with them. You only care for things on a tremendously big scale, so that you may try to influence them. When you have not a crowd to talk to, or a huge scheme to argue about, you are bored to extinction."

"No," said John; "I am not bored at present, by any means."

"Because you are talking about big things. Most men in your place would be talking about the moonlight, and quoting Shelley."

"To oblige you, Miss Thorn, I could quote a little now and then," said John, laughing. "Would it please you? I dare say you have seen elephants stand upon their hind legs and their heads alternately. I should feel very much like one; but I will do anything to oblige you."

"That is frivolous," said Joe, who did not smile.

"Of course it is. I am heavy by nature. You may teach me all sorts of tricks, but they will not be at all pretty."

"No, you are very interesting as you are," said Joe quietly. "But I do not think you will be happy."

"It is not a question of happiness."

"What is it then?"

"Usefulness," said John.

"You do not care to be happy, you only care to be useful?" Joe asked.

"Yes. But my ideas of usefulness include many things. Some of the people who listen to me would be very much astonished if they knew what I dream."

"Nothing would astonish me," said Joe, thoughtfully. "Of course you must think of everything in a large way—it is your nature. You will be a great man."

John looked at his companion. She had struck the main chord of his nature in her words, and he felt suddenly that thrill of pleasure which comes from the flattery of our pride and our hopes. John was not a vain man, but he was capable of being intoxicated by the grandeur of a scheme when the possibility of its realization was suddenly thrust before him. Like all men of exceptional gifts who are constantly before the public, he could estimate very justly the extent of the results he could produce on any given occasion, but his enthusiastic belief in his ideas could see no limit to the multiplication of those results. His strong will and natural modesty about himself constantly repressed any desire he might have to speak over-confidently of ultimate success, so that the prediction of ultimate success by some one else was doubly sweet to him. We Americans have said of ourselves that we are the only nation who accomplish what we have boasted of. Rash speech and rash action are our national characteristics, and lead us into all manner of trouble, but in so far as such qualifications or defects imply a positive conviction of success, they contribute largely to the realization of great schemes. No one can succeed who does not believe in himself, nor can any scheme be realized which has not gained the support of a sufficient number of men who believe in it and in themselves.

John was gratified by Miss Thorn's speech, for he saw that it was spontaneous.

"I will try to be great," he said, "for the sake of what I think is great."

There was a short pause, and the pair by common consent skated slowly out of the shadow into the broad moonlight.

"Not that I believe you will be happy if you think of nothing else," said Joe presently.

"In order to do anything well, one must think of nothing else," answered John.

"Many great men find time to be great and to do many other things," said Joe. "Look at Mr. Gladstone; he has an immense private correspondence about things that interest him, quite apart from the big things he is always doing."

"When a man has reached that point he may find plenty of time to spare," answered Harrington. "But until he has accomplished the main object of his life he must not let anything take him from his pursuit. He must form no ties, he must have no interests, that do not conduce to his success. I think a man who enters on a political career must devote himself to it as exclusively as a missionary Jesuit attacks the conversion of unbelievers, as wholly as a Buddhist ascetic gives himself to the work of uniting his individual intelligence with the immortal spirit that gives it life."

"I do not agree with you," said Joe decisively, and in her womanly intelligence of life she understood the mistake John made. "I cannot agree with you. You are mixing up political activity, which deals with the government of men, with spiritual ideas and immortality, and that sort of thing."

"How so?" asked John, in some surprise.

"I am quite sure," said Joe, "that to govern man a man must be human, and the imaginary politician you tell me of is not human at all."

"And yet I aspire to be that imaginary politician," said John.

"Do not think me too dreadfully conceited," Joe answered, "in talking about such things. Of course I do not pretend to understand them, but I am quite sure people must be like other people—I mean in good ways—or other people will not believe in them, you know. You are not vexed, are you?" She looked up into John's face with a little timid smile that might have done wonders to persuade a less prejudiced person than Harrington.

"No indeed! why should I be vexed? But perhaps some day you will believe that I am right."

"Oh no, never!" exclaimed Joe, in a tone of profound conviction. "You will never persuade me that people are meant to shut themselves from their fellow-creatures, and not be human, and that."

"And yet you were so good as to say that you thought I might attain greatness," said John, smiling.

"Yes, I think you will. But you will change your mind about a great many things before you do."

John's strong face grew thoughtful, and the white moonlight made his features seem harder and sterner than ever. Slowly the pair glided over the polished black ice, now marked here and there with clean white curves from the skates, and in a few minutes they were once more within hail of the remainder of their party.

Chapter VIII

Eight days after the skating party, Ronald Surbiton telegraphed from New York that he would reach Boston the next morning, and Josephine Thorn knew that the hour had come. She was not afraid of the scene that must take place, but she wished with all her heart that it were over.

As Sybil Brandon had told her, there had been time to think of what she should say, and although she had answered recklessly that she would "trust to luck," she knew when the day was come that she had in reality thought intensely of the very words which must be spoken. To Miss Schenectady she had said nothing, but on the other hand she had become very intimate with Sybil, and to tell the truth, she hoped inwardly for the support and sympathy of her beautiful friend.

Meanwhile, since her long evening with John Harrington on the ice, she had made every effort to avoid his society. Like many very young women with a vivid love of enjoyment and a fairly wide experience, she was something of a fatalist. That is to say, she believed that her evil destiny might spring upon her unawares at any moment, and she felt something when she was with Harrington that warned her. For the first time in her life she knew what it was to have moods of melancholy; she caught herself asking what was really the end and object of her gay life, whether it amounted to anything worthy in comparison with the trouble one had to take to amuse one's self, whether it would not be far better in the end to live like Miss Schenectady, reading and studying and caring nothing for the world.

Not that Josephine admired Miss Schenectady, or thought that she herself could ever be like her. The old lady was a type of her class; intelligent and well versed in many subjects—even learned she might have been called by some. But to Joe's view, essentially European by nature and education, it seemed as though her aunt, like many Bostonians, judged everything—literature, music, art of all kinds, history and the doings of great men— by one invariable standard. Her comments on what she heard and read were uniformly delivered from the same point of view, in the same tone of practical judgment, and with the same assumption of original superiority. It was the everlasting "Carthago delenda" of the Roman orator. Whatever the world wrote, sang, painted, thought, or did, the conviction remained unshaken in Miss Schenectady's mind that Beacon Street was better than those things, and that of all speeches and languages known and spoken in the world's history, the familiar dialect of Boston was the one best calculated by Providence and nature to express and formulate all manner of wisdom.

It is a strange thing that where criticism is on the whole so fair, and cultivation of the best faculties so general, the manner of expressing a judgment and of exhibiting acquired knowledge should be such as to jar unpleasantly on the sensibilities of Europeans. Where is the real difference? It probably lies in some subtle point of proportion in the psychic chemistry of the Boston mind, but the analyst who shall express the formula is not yet born; though there be those who can cast the spectrum of Boston existence and thought upon their printed screens with matchless accuracy.

Joe judged but did not analyze. She said Miss Schenectady was always right, but that the way she was right was "horrid." Consequently she did not look to her aunt for sympathy or assistance, and though they had more than once talked of Ronald Surbiton since receiving his cable from England, Joe had not said anything of her intentions regarding him. When the second telegram arrived from New York, saying that he would be in Boston on the following morning, Joe begged that Miss Schenectady would be at home to receive him when he came.

"Well, if you insist upon it, I expect I shall have to," said Miss Schenectady. She did not see why her niece should require her presence at the interview; young men may call on young ladies in Boston without encountering the inevitable chaperon, or being obliged to do their talking in the hearing of a police of papas, mammas, and aunts. But as Joe "insisted upon it," as the old lady said, she "expected there were no two ways about it." Her expectations were correct, for Joe would have refused absolutely to receive Ronald alone.

"I know the value of a stern aunt, my dear," she had said to Sybil the day previous. When matters were arranged, therefore, they went to bed, and in the morning Miss Schenectady sat in state in the front drawing-room, reading the life of Mr. Ticknor until Ronald should arrive. Joe was up-stairs writing a note to Sybil Brandon, wherein the latter was asked to lunch and to drive in the afternoon. Ronald could not come before ten o'clock with any kind of propriety, and they could have luncheon early and then go out; after which the bitterness of death would be past.

It was not quite ten o'clock when Ronald Surbiton rang the bell, and was turned into the drawing-room to face an American aunt for the first time in his life.

"Miss Schenectady?" said he, taking the proffered hand of the old lady and then bowing slightly. He pronounced her name Schenectady, with a strong accent on the penultimate syllable.

"Schenectady," corrected his hostess. "I expect you are Mr. Surbiton."

"A—exactly so," said Ronald, in some embarrassment.

"Well, we are glad to see you in Boston, Mr. Surbiton." Miss Schenectady resumed her seat, and Ronald sat down beside her, holding his hat in his hand.

"Put your hat down," said the old lady. "What sort of a journey did you have?"

"Very fair, thanks," said Ronald, depositing his hat on the floor beside him, "in fact I believe we came over uncommonly quick for the time of year. How is"—

"What steamer did you come by?" interrupted Miss Schenectady.

"The Gallia. She is one of the Cunarders. But as I was going to ask"—

"Yes, an old boat, I expect. So you came on right away from New York without stopping?"

"Exactly," answered Ronald. "I took the first train. The fact is, I was so anxious—so very anxious to"—

"What hotel are you at here?" inquired Miss Schenectady, without letting him finish.

"Brunswick. How is Miss Thorn?" Ronald succeeded at last in putting the question he so greatly longed to ask—the only one, he supposed, which would cause a message to be sent to Joe announcing his arrival.

"Joe? She is pretty well. I expect she will be down in a minute. Are you going to stay some while, Mr. Surbiton?"

Ronald thought Miss Schenectady the most pitiless old woman he had ever met. In reality she had not the most remote intention of being anything but hospitable. But her idea of hospitality at a first meeting seemed to consist chiefly in exhibiting a great and inquisitive interest in the individual she wished to welcome. Besides, Joe would probably come down when she was ready, and so it was necessary to talk in the mean time. At last Ronald succeeded in asking another question.

"Excuse the anxiety I show," he said simply, "but may I ask whether Miss Thorn is at home?"

"Perhaps if you rang the bell I could send for her," remarked the old lady in problematic answer.

"Oh, certainly!" exclaimed Ronald, springing to his feet, and searching madly round the room for the bell. Miss Schenectady watched him calmly.

"I think if you went to the further side of the fire-place you would find it—back of the screen," she suggested.

"Thanks; here it is," cried Ronald, discovering the handle in the wall.

"Yes, you have found it now," said Miss Schenectady with much indifference. "Perhaps you find it cold here?" she continued, observing that Ronald lingered near the fire-place.

"Oh dear, no, thanks, quite the contrary," he answered.

"Because if it is you might—Sarah, I think you could tell Miss Josephine that Mr. Surbiton is in the parlor, could not you?"

"Oh, if it is any inconvenience"—Ronald began, misunderstanding the form of address Miss Schenectady used to her handmaiden.

"Why?" asked Miss Schenectady, in some astonishment.

"Nothing," said Ronald, looking rather confused; "I did not quite catch what you said."

There was a silence, and the old lady and the young man looked at each other.

Ronald was a very handsome man, as Joe knew. He was tall and straight and deep-chested. His complexion was like a child's, and his fine moustache like silk. His thick fair hair was parted accurately in the middle, and his smooth, white forehead betrayed no sign of care or thought. His eyes were blue and very bright, and looked fearlessly at every one and everything, and his hands were broad and clean-looking. He was perfectly well dressed, but in a fashion far less extreme than that affected by Mr. Topeka and young John C. Hannibal. There was less collar and more shoulder to him, and his legs were longer and straighter than theirs. Nevertheless, had he stood beside John Harrington, no one would have hesitated an instant in deciding which was the stronger man. With all his beauty and grace, Ronald Surbiton was but one of a class of handsome and graceful men. John Harrington bore on his square brow and in the singular compactness of his active frame the peculiar sign-manual of an especial purpose. He would have been an exception in any class and in any age. It was no wonder Joe had wished to compare the two.

In a few moments the door opened, and Joe entered the drawing-room. She was pale, and her great brown eyes had a serious expression in them that was unusual. There was something prim in the close dark dress she wore, and the military collar of most modern cut met severely about her throat. If Ronald had expected a very affectionate welcome he was destined to disappointment; Joe had determined not to be affectionate until all was over. To prepare him in some measure for what was in store, she had planned that he should be left alone for a time with Miss Schenectady, who, she thought, would chill any suitor to the bone.

"My dear Ronald," said Joe, holding out her hand, "I am so glad to see you." Her voice was even and gentle, but there was no gladness in it.

"Not half so glad as I am to see you," said Ronald, holding her hand in his, his face beaming with delight. "It seems such an age since you left!"

"It is only two months, though," said Joe, with a faint smile. "I ought to apologize, but I suppose you have introduced yourself to Aunt Zoë." She could not call her Aunt Zoruiah, even for the sake of frightening Ronald.

"What did you think when you got my telegram?" asked the latter.

"I thought it was very foolish of you to run away just when the hunting was so good," answered Joe with decision.

"But you are glad, are you not?" he asked, lowering his voice, and looking affectionately at her. Miss Schenectady was again absorbed in the life of Mr. Ticknor.

"Yes," said Joe, gravely. "It is as well that you have come, because I have something to say to you, and I should have had to write it. Let us go out. Would you like to go for a walk?"

Ronald was delighted to do anything that would give him a chance of escaping from Aunt Zoruiah and being alone with Joe.

"I think you had best be back to lunch," remarked Miss Schenectady as they left the room.

"Of course, Aunt Zoë," answered Joe. "Besides, Sybil is coming, you know." So they sallied forth.

It was a warm day; the snow had melted from the brick pavement, and the great icicles on the gutters and on the trees were running water in the mid-day sun. Joe thought a scene would be better to get over in the publicity of the street than in private. Ronald, all unsuspecting of her intention, walked calmly by her side, looking at her occasionally with a certain pride, mixed with a good deal of sentimental benevolence.

"Do you know," Joe began presently, "when your cable came I felt very guilty at having written to you that you might come?"

"Why?" asked Ronald, innocently. "You know I would come from the end of the world to see you. I have, in fact."

"Yes, I know," said Joe wearily, wishing she knew exactly how to say what she was so thoroughly determined should be said.

"What is the matter, Joe?" asked Ronald, suddenly. He smiled rather nervously, but his smooth brow was a little contracted. He anticipated mischief.

"There is something the matter, Ronald," she said at last, resolved to make short work of the revelation of her feelings. "There is something very much the matter."

"Well?" said Surbiton, beginning to be alarmed.

"You know, Ronald dear, somehow I think you have thought—honestly, I know you have thought for a long time that you were to marry me."

"Yes," said Ronald with a forced laugh, for he was frightened. "I have always thought so; I think so now."

"It is of no use to think it, Ronald dear," said Joe, turning very pale. "I have thought of it too—thought it all over. I cannot possibly marry you, dear boy. Honestly, I cannot." Her voice trembled violently. However firmly she had decided within herself, it was a very bitter thing to say; she was so fond of him.

"What?" asked Ronald hoarsely. But he turned red instead of pale. It was rather disappointment and anger that he felt at the first shock than sorrow or deep pain.

"Do not make me say it again," said Joe, entreatingly. She was not used to entreating so much as to commanding, and her voice quavered uncertainly.

"Do you mean to say," said Ronald, speaking loudly in his anger, and then dropping his voice as he remembered the passers-by,—"do you mean to tell me, Joe, after all this, when I have come to America just because you told me to, that you will not marry me? I do not believe it. You are making fun of me."

"No, Ronald," Joe answered sorrowfully, but regaining her equanimity in the face of Surbiton's wrath, "I am in earnest. I am very, very fond of you, but I do not love you at all, and I never can marry you."

Ronald was red in the face, and he trod fast and angrily, tapping the pavement with his stick. He was very angry, but he said nothing.

"It is much better to be honest about it," said Joe, still very pale; and when she had spoken, her little mouth closed tightly.

"Oh, yes," said Ronald, who was serious by this time; "it is much better to be honest, now that you have brought me three thousand miles to hear what you have to say—much better. By all means."

"I am very sorry, Ronald," Joe answered. "I really did not mean you to come, and I am very sorry,—oh, more sorry than I can tell you,—but I cannot do it, you know."

"If you won't, of course you can't," he said. "Will you please tell me who he is?"

"Who?—what?" asked Joe, coldly. She was offended at the tone.

"The fellow you have pitched upon in my place," he said roughly.

Joe looked up into his face with an expression that frightened him. Her dark eyes flashed with an honest fire, He stared angrily at her as they walked slowly along.

"I made a mistake," she said slowly. "I am not sorry. I am glad. I would be ashamed to marry a man who could speak like that to any woman. I am sorry for you, but I am glad for myself." She looked straight into his eyes, until he turned away. For some minutes they went on in silence.

"I beg your pardon, Joe," said Ronald presently, in a subdued tone.

"Never mind, Ronald dear, I was angry," Joe answered. But her eyes were full of tears, and her lips quivered.

Again they went on in silence, but for a longer time than before. Joe felt that the blow was struck, and there was nothing to be done but to wait the result. It had been much harder than she had expected, because Ronald was so angry; she had expected he would be pained. He, poor fellow, was really startled out of all self-control. The idea that Joe could ever ultimately hesitate about marrying him had never seemed to exist, even among the remotest possibilities. But he was a gentleman in his way, and so he begged her pardon, and chewed the cud of his wrath in silence for some time.

"Joe," he said at last, with something of his usual calm, though he was still red, "of course you are really perfectly serious? I mean, you have thought about it?"

"Yes," said Joe; "I am quite sure."

"Then perhaps it is better we should go home," he continued.

"Perhaps so," said Joe. "Indeed, it would be better."

"I would like to see you again, Joe," he said in a somewhat broken fashion. "I mean, by and by, when I am not angry, you know."

Joe smiled at the simple honesty of the proposition.

"Yes, Ronald dear, whenever you like. You are very good, Ronald," she added.

"No, I am not good at all," said Ronald sharply, and they did not speak again until he left her at Miss Schenectady's door. Then she gave him her hand.

"I shall be at home until three o'clock," said she.

"Thanks," he answered; so they parted.

Joe had accomplished her object, but she was very far from happy. The consciousness of having done right did not outweigh the pain she felt for Ronald, who was, after all, her very dear friend. They had grown up together from earliest childhood, and so it had been settled; for Ronald was left an orphan when almost a baby, and had been brought up with his cousin as a matter of expediency. Therefore, as Joe said, it had always seemed so very natural. They had plighted vows when still in pinafores with a ring of grass, and later they had spoken more serious things, which it hurt Joe to remember, and now they were suffering the consequence of it all, and the putting off childish illusions was bitter.

It was not long before Sybil Brandon came in answer to Joe's invitation. She knew what trouble her friend was likely to be in, and was ready to do anything in the world to make matters easier for her. Besides, though Sybil was so white and fair, and seemingly cold, she had a warm heart, and had conceived a very real affection for the impulsive English girl. Miss Schenectady had retired to put on another green ribbon, leaving the life of Mr. Ticknor open on the table, and the two girls met in the drawing-room. Joe was still pale, and the tears seemed ready to start from her eyes.

"Dear Sybil—it is so good of you to come," said she.

Sybil kissed her affectionately and put her arm round her waist. They stood thus for a moment before the fire.

"You have seen him?" Sybil asked presently. Joe had let her head rest wearily against her friend's shoulder, and nodded silently in answer. Sybil bent down and kissed her soft hair, and whispered gently in her ear,—"Was it very hard, dear?"

"Oh, yes—indeed it was!" cried Joe, hiding her face on Sybil's breast. Then, as though ashamed of seeming weak, she stood up boldly, turning slightly away as she spoke. "It was dreadfully hard," she continued; "but it is all over, and it is very much better—very, very much, you know."

"I am so glad," said Sybil, looking thoughtfully at the fire. "And now we will go out into the country and forget all about it—all about the disagreeable part of it."

"Perhaps," said Joe, who had recovered her equanimity, "Ronald may come too. You see he is so used to me that after a while it will not seem to make so very much difference after all."

"Of course, if he would," said Sybil, "it would be very nice. He will have to get used to the idea, and if he does not begin at once, perhaps he never may."

"He will be just the same as ever when he gets over his wrath," answered Joe confidently.

"Was he very angry?"

"Oh, dreadfully! I never saw him so angry."

"It is better when men are angry than when they are sorry," said Sybil. "Something like this once happened to me, and he got over it very well. I think it was much more my fault, too," she added thoughtfully.

"Oh, I am sure you never did anything bad in your life," said Joe affectionately. "Nothing half so bad as this—my dear Snow Angel!" And so they kissed again and went to lunch.

"I suppose you went to walk," remarked Miss Schenectady, when they met at table.

"Yes," said Joe, "we walked a little."

"Well, all Englishmen walk, of course," continued her aunt.

"Most of them can," said Joe, smiling.

"I mean, it is a great deal the right thing there. Perhaps you might pass me the pepper."

Before they had finished their meal the door opened, and Ronald Surbiton entered the room.

"Oh—excuse me," he began, "I did not know"—

"Oh, I am so glad you have come, Ronald," cried Joe, rising to greet him, and taking his hand. "Sybil, let me introduce Mr. Surbiton—Miss Brandon."

Sybil smiled and bent her head slightly. Ronald bowed and sat down between Sybil and Miss Schenectady.

Chapter IX

Josephine Thorn never read newspapers, partly because she did not care for the style of literature known as journalistic, and partly, too, because the papers always came at such exceedingly inconvenient hours. If she had possessed and practiced the estimable habit of "keeping up with the times," she would have observed an article which appeared on the morning after the skating party, and which dealt with the speech John Harrington had made in the Music Hall two days previous. Miss Schenectady had read it, but she did not mention it to Joe, because she believed in John Harrington, and wished Joe to do likewise, wherefore she avoided the subject; for the article treated him roughly. Nevertheless, some unknown person sent Joe a copy of the paper through the post some days later, with a bright red pencil mark at the place, and Joe, seeing what the subject was, read it with avidity. As she read, her cheek flushed, her small mouth closed like a vise, and she stamped her little foot upon the floor.

It was evident that the writer was greatly incensed at the views expressed by John, and he wrote with an ease and a virulence which proclaimed a practiced hand. "The spectacle of an accomplished Democrat," said the paper, "is always sufficiently unusual to attract attention: but to find so rare a bird among ourselves is indeed a novel delight. The orator who alternately enthralled and insulted a considerable audience at the Music Hall, two nights ago, laid a decided claim both to accomplishment and to democracy. He himself informed his hearers that he was a Democrat; and, indeed, it was necessary that he should state his position, for it would have been impossible to decide from the tone and quality of his opinions whether he were a socialist, a reformer, a conservative, or an Irishman. Perchance he has discovered the talisman by which it is possible for a man to be all four, and yet to be a man, Furthermore, he claims to be an orator. No one could listen to the manifold intonations of his voice, or witness the declamatory evolutions of his body, without feeling an inward conviction that the gentleman on the platform intended to present himself to us as an orator.

"Lest we be accused of partiality and prejudice, we will at once state that we believe it possible for a man to be singular in his manner and quaint in his mode of phrasing, and yet to utter an opinion in some one direction which, if neither novel nor interesting, nor even tenable, shall yet have the one redeeming merit of representing a conceivable point of view. But when a man begins by stating that he belongs to the Democrats and then claims as his own the views of his political opponents, winding up by demanding the sympathy and support of a third party, the obvious conclusion is that he is either a lunatic, a charlatan, or both. A man cannot serve God and Mammon, neither can any man serve both the Irish and Chinese.

"Mr. John Harrington has made a great discovery. He has discovered that we require a Civil Service. This is apparently the ground on which he states himself to be a Democrat. If we remember rightly, the Civil Service Convention, which sat in discussion of the subject in the summer of 1881, was presided over by a prominent member of the Republican party. As some time has elapsed since then, and the gentlemen connected with the movement are as active and as much interested in it as ever, our orator will pardon us for questioning his right of discovery on the one hand, and his claim to be considered a Democrat on the strength of it, on the other. A Civil Service is doubtless a good thing, even a very good thing, and in due time we shall certainly have it; but that the Constitution of the United States is on the verge of dissolution at the hands of our corrupt public officers, that our finance is only another name for imminent bankruptcy, or that the new millennium of Washington morals will be organized by Mr. John Harrington—these things we deny in toto, from beginning to end. So wide and deep is our skepticism, that we even doubt whether 'war, famine, revolution, or all three together' would have instantly ensued if Mr. John Harrington had not delivered his speech on Wednesday evening.

"In illustration—or rather, in the futile attempt to illustrate—Mr. Harrington put forth a series of similes that should make any dead orator turn in his grave. The nation was successively held up to our admiration in the guise of a sick man, a cripple, a banker, a theatrical company, and a peddler of tape and buttons. We were bankrupt, diseased; and our bones, like those of the Psalmist, were all out of joint; and if our hearts did not become like melting wax in the midst of our bodies, it was not the fault of Mr. John Harrington, but rather was it due to the hardening of those organs against the voice of the charmer.

"The Navigation Act called down the choicest of the orator's vessels of wrath. Fools had made it, worse than fools submitted to it, and the reason why the Salem docks were no longer crowded with the shipping of the Peabody family was that there were ferry-boats in Boston harbor, a train of reasoning that must be clear to the mind of the merest schoolboy. Mr. Harrington further stated that these same ferry-boats—not to mention certain articles he terms 'mudscows,' with which we have no acquaintance— are built of old timber, copper, and nails, obtained by breaking tip the fleets of the Peabody family, which is manifestly a fraud on the nation. As far as the ferry-boats are concerned, we believe we are in a position to state that they are not built of old material; as regards the aforesaid 'mudscows' we can give no opinion, not having before heard of the article, which we presume is not common in commerce, and may therefore be regarded as an exception to the universal rule that things in general should not be made of old timber, copper, and rusty nails.

"We will not weary our readers with any further attempt at unraveling the opinions, illustrations, and rhetoric of Mr. John Harrington, Democrat and orator. The possession of an abundant vocabulary without any especial use for it in the shape of an idea will not revolutionize modern government, whatever may be the opinion of the individual so richly gifted; nor will any accomplished Democrat find a true key to success in following a course of politics which consists in one half of the world trying to drive paradoxes down the throat of the other half. It will not do, and Mr. Harrington will find it out. He will find out also that the differences which exist between the Republican and the Democratic parties are far deeper and wider than he suspects, and do not consist in such things as the existence or non-existence of a Civil Service, free trade, or mudscows; and when these things are forever crushed out of his imagination it will be time enough to give him a name, seeing he is neither Republican nor Democrat, nor Tammany, nor even a Stalwart, nor a three-hundred-and-sixer—seeing, in fact, that he is not an astronomical point in any political heaven with which the world is acquainted, but only the most nebulous of nebulae which have yet come within our observation."

Joe read the article rapidly, and then read the last paragraph again and threw the paper aside. She sat by the fire after breakfast, and Miss Schenectady had come into the room several times and had gone out again, busied with much housekeeping. For Miss Schenectady belonged to the elder school of Boston women, who "see to things" themselves in the intervals of literature, gossip, and transcendental philosophy. But Joe sat still for nearly half an hour after she had done reading and nursed her wrath, while she toasted her little feet at the fire. At last she made up her mind and rose.

"I am going to see Sybil, Aunt Zoë," she said, meeting the old lady at the door.

"Well, if she is up at this time of day," answered Miss Schenectady.

"Oh, I fancy so," said Joe.

Mrs. Sam Wyndham's establishment was of the modern kind, and nobody was expected to attend an early breakfast of fish, beefsteaks, buckwheat cakes, hot rolls, tea, coffee, and chocolate at eight o'clock in the morning. Visitors did as they pleased, and so did Mrs. Sam, and they met at luncheon, a meal which Sam Wyndham himself was of course unable to attend. Joe knew this, and knew she was certain to find Sybil alone. It was Sybil she wanted to see, and not Mrs. Wyndham. But as she walked down Beacon Street the aspect of affairs changed in her mind.

Joe had not exaggerated when she said to Vancouver that she had a very good memory, and it would have been better for him if he had remembered the fact. Joe had not forgotten the conversation with him in the evening after Harrington's speech, and in reading the article that had been sent to her she instantly recognized a phrase, word for word as Vancouver had uttered it. In speaking to her he had said that politics "consisted in one half of the world trying to drive paradoxes down the throat of the other half." It was true that in the article John Harrington was warned that he would discover the fallacy of this proposition, but in Joe's judgment this did not constitute an objection. Vancouver had written the article, and none other; Vancouver, who professed a boundless respect for John, and who constantly asserted that he took no active part whatever in politics. It was inconceivable that the coincidence of language should be an accident. Vancouver had made the phrase when making conversation, and had used it in his article; Joe was absolutely certain of that, and being full of her discovery and of wrath, she was determined to consult with her dearest friend as to the best way of revenging the offense on its author.

But as she walked down Beacon Street she reflected on the situation. She was sure Sybil would not understand why she cared so much, and Sybil would form hasty ideas as to the interest Joe took in Harrington. That would never do. It would be better to speak to Mrs. Sam Wyndham, who was herself so fond of John that she would seize with avidity on the information, from whatever source it came. But then Mrs. Wyndham was fond of Vancouver also. No, she was not. When Joe thought of it she was sure that though Vancouver was devoted to Mrs. Sam, Mrs. Sam did not care for him excepting as an agreeable person of even temper, who was useful in society. But for Harrington she had a real friendship. If it came to the doing of a service, Mrs. Wyndham would do it. Joe's perceptions were wonderfully clear and just.

But when she reached the house she was still uncertain, and she passed on, intending to turn back and go in as soon as she had made up her mind. In spite of all that she could argue to herself it seemed unsafe—unwise, at least. Sybil might laugh at her, after all; Mrs. Wyndham might possibly tell Vancouver instead of telling John. It would be better to tell John herself; she remembered having once spoken to him about Vancouver, and she could easily remind him of the conversation. She would probably see him that evening at a party she was going to; and yet it was so hard to have to keep it all to herself for so many hours, instead of telling. Nevertheless she would go and see Sybil, taking care, of course, to say nothing about the article.

At the time Joe was walking up and down Beacon Street in the effort to come to a decision, John Harrington found himself face to face with a very much more formidable problem. He stood before the fire-place in his rooms in Charles Street, with an extinguished cigar between his teeth, his face paler than usual, and a look of uncertainty on his features that was oddly out of keeping with his usual mood. He wore an ancient shooting coat, and his feet were trust into a pair of dingy leather slippers; his hands were in his pockets, and he was staring vacantly at the clock.

On the oak writing-table that filled the middle of the room lay an open telegram. It was dated from Washington, and conveyed the simple information that Senator Caleb Jenkins had died at five o'clock that morning. It was signed by an abbreviation that meant nothing except to John himself. The name of the senator was itself fictitious, and stood for another which John knew.

The table was covered with Government reports, for when the message came John was busy studying a financial point of importance to him. The telegram had lain on the table for half an hour, and John still stood before the fire-place, staring at the clock.

The senator had not been expected to live, in fact it was remarkable that he should have lived so long. But when a man has been preparing for a struggle during many months, he is apt to feel that the actual moment of the battle is indefinitely far off. But now the senator was dead, and John meant to stand in his place. The battle was begun. No one who has not seen some of the inside workings of political life can have any idea of what a man feels who is about to stand as a candidate in an election for the first time in his life. For months, perhaps for years, he has been engaged with political matters; his opinions have been formed by himself or by others into a very definite shape; it may be that, like Harrington, he has frequently spoken to large audiences with more or less success; he may have written pamphlets and volumes upon questions of the day, and his writings may have roused the fiercest criticism and the most loyal support. All this he may have done, and done it well, but when the actual moment arrives for him to stand upon his feet and address his constituents, no longer for the purpose of making them believe in his opinions, but in order to make them believe in himself, he is more than mortal if he does not feel something very unpleasantly resembling fear.

It is one thing to express a truth, it is another to set one's self upon a pedestal and declare that one represents it, and is in one's own person the living truth itself. John was too honest and true a man not to feel a positive reluctance to singing his own praises, and yet that is what most electioneering consists in.

But to be elected a senator in Massachusetts is a complicated affair. A man who intends to succeed in such an enterprise must not let the grass grow under his feet. In a few hours the whole machinery of election must be at work, and before night he would have to receive all sorts and conditions of men and electioneering agents. The morning papers did not contain any notice of the senator's death, as they had already gone to press when the news reached them, if indeed it was as yet public property. But other papers appeared at mid-day, and by that time the circumstances would undoubtedly be known. John struck a match and relit his cigar. The moment of hesitation was over, the last breathing-space before the fight, and all his activity returned. Half an hour later he went out with a number of written telegrams in his hand, and proceeded to the central telegraph office.

The case was urgent. In the first place the governor of the state would, according to law and custom, immediately appoint a senator pro tempore to act until the legislature should elect the new senator in place of the one deceased. Secondly, the legislature, which meets once a year, was already in session, and the election would therefore take place immediately, unless some unusual delay were created, and this was improbable.

In spite of the article which had so outraged Josephine Thorn's sense of justice, there were many who believed in John Harrington as the prophet of the new faith, as the senator of reform and the orator of the future, and his friends were numerous and powerful, both in the electing body and among the non-official mass of prominent persons who make up the aggregate of public opinion. It had long been known that John Harrington would be brought forward at the next vacancy, which, in the ordinary course of things, would have occurred in about a year's time, at the expiration of the senior senator's term of office, but which had now been suddenly caused by the death of his colleague. John was therefore aware that his success must depend almost immediately upon the present existing opinion of him that prevailed, and as he made his way through the crowded streets to the telegraph office, he realized that no effort of his own would be likely to make a change in that opinion at such short notice. At first it had seemed to him as though he were on a sudden brought face to face with a body of men whom he must persuade to elect him as their representative, and in spite of his great familiarity with political proceedings, the idea was extremely disagreeable to him. But on more mature reflection it was clear to him that he was in the hands of his friends, that he had said his say and had done all he would now be able to do in the way of public speaking or public writing, and that his only possible sphere of present action lay in exerting such personal influence as he possessed.

John Harrington was ambitious, or, to speak more accurately, he was wholly ruled by a dominant aspiration. He was convinced by his own study and observation, as well as by a considerable amount of personal experience, that great reforms were becoming necessary in the government of the country, and he was equally sure that a man was needed who should be willing to make any sacrifice for the sake of creating a party to inaugurate such changes. In his opinion the surest step towards obtaining influence in the affairs of the country was a seat in the senate, and with an unhesitating belief in the truth and honesty of the principles he desired to make known, he devoted every energy he possessed to the attainment of his object.

To him government seemed the most important function of society, the largest, the broadest, and the noblest; to help, if possible, to be a leader in the establishment of what was good for the country, and to be the very foremost in destroying that which was bad, were in his view the best objects and aims for a strong man to follow. And John Harrington knew himself to be strong, and believed himself to be right, and thus armed he was prepared for any struggle.

The quality of vanity exists in all men, not least in those whose chief profession is modesty; and seeing that it is a universal element, created and inherent in every one, it is impossible to say it is bad in itself. For it is impossible to conceive any human creature without it. A recent philosopher of reputation has taught that by vanity, by the desire to appear attractive to the other sex, man has changed his own person from the form of a beast to the image of God. Vanity is a mighty power and incentive, as great as hunger and thirst, and much more generally active in the affairs of civilized humanity. And yet its very name means hollowness. "The hollowness of hollowness, all things are hollowness," said the preacher, and his translators have put the word vanity in his mouth, because it means the same thing. But in itself, being hollow, it is neither bad nor good; its badness or goodness lies in those things whereof a man makes choice to fill the void, the inexpressible and indefinable craving within his soul; as also hunger is only bad when it is satisfied by bad things, or not satisfied at all, so that in the one case it leads to disease, and in the other to the committing of crimes in the desire for satisfaction. Many a poor fellow was hung by the neck in old times for stealing a loaf to stop his hunger, and many a man of wit goes to the mad-house nowadays because the void of his vanity is unfilled.

But vanity is called by yet another name when its disagreeable side is hidden, and when its emptiness has come to crave for great things. It is pride, then honorable pride, then ambition, and perhaps at the last it is called heroic sacrifice. Vanity is an unsatisfied desire, hollow in itself, but capable of holding both bad and good. It is not identical with self-complacency, nor yet with conceit.

Probably John Harrington had originally possessed as much of this mysterious quality as most men who are conscious of strength and talent. It had never manifested itself in small things, and its very extent had made many things seem small which were of the highest importance to other men. He had worked as a boy at all manner of studies like other boys, but the idea of laboring in distasteful matters for the sake of being first among his companions seemed utterly absurd to him. From the time he had begun to think for himself—and he was young when he reached that stage— he had formed a rooted determination to be first in his country, to be a great reformer or a great patriot, and he cared to study nothing that was not connected with this idea. When his name was first heard in public life, it was as the author of a pamphlet advocating certain sweeping measures of which no one else had ventured to dream as yet. He would have smiled now had he taken the trouble to read again some of those earlier productions of his. It had seemed so easy to move the world then, and it seemed so hard now. But nevertheless he meant to move it, and as each year brought him increased strength and wider experience, it brought with it also the conviction of ultimate success. He had long forgotten to hope for the sudden and immediate power to stir the world, for he had discovered that it was a labor of years, the work of a lifetime; but if he had ever had any doubts as to the result of that work, he had forgotten them also.

And now his strength, his aspirations, his vanity, and his intellect were roused together to the highest activity of which they were capable, the hour having come for which he had longed through half his lifetime, and though it was but the first trial, in which he might fail, it had for him all the importance of the supreme crisis of his existence. No wonder that his face was pale and his lips set as he walked back to his lodgings from the telegraph office. As he walked down the hill by the railings of the Common he came upon Josephine Thorn, standing at the entrance of one of the boarded walks, as though hesitating whether to go in. He was close to her as he bowed, and something in her face made him stop.

"Good morning, Miss Thorn," he said. She nodded gravely and hesitated. He was about to go on, thinking she was in one of those moods which he called capricious. But she stopped him.

"Mr. Harrington, I want to speak to you," she said quickly, seeing that her opportunity was on the point of slipping away.

"Yes?" said John, smiling faintly.

"Mr. Harrington—did you read that article about you, the day after the skating party?"

"Yes," said John. "It was not complimentary, if I remember."

"It was vile," said Joe, the angry color rising to her temples again. "It was abominable. It was written by Mr. Vancouver."

John started slightly.

"I think you must be mistaken," he said.

"No, I am not mistaken. There were things in it, word for word as he said them to me just after the speech. I am perfectly sure."

John looked very gravely at Joe, as though to be sure of her honesty. There was no mistaking the look in her eyes.

"Miss Thorn," John said, "Vancouver may have said those very things to some one else, who wrote them and printed them. But in any case, I am exceedingly obliged to you for the information"—

"You are not angry?" Joe began, already repenting.

"No—how could I be? It may be important. The junior senator for Massachusetts died this morning, and there may be an election at any moment. I have not told any one else, but it will be known everywhere in an hour's time. Good-by, and many thanks."

"You will be senator, of course?" said Joe, in great excitement.

"I cannot tell," John answered. "Are you going down the hill?"

"No—thanks—I am going home," said Joe. "Good-by."

Chapter X

Joe had been mistaken in thinking that Ronald would be less well received than herself. There was of course the usual amount of gossip concerning him, but as he refrained from eccentricities of dress when asked to dinner, and did not bet that he would ride his horse into the smoking-room of the Somerset Club, the gossip soon lost ground against the list of his good qualities. Moreover, he was extremely good-looking, and his manner was modesty itself. He admired everything he saw, partly because it was new to him, and partly because there was a good deal to admire.

For a day or two after the final scene with Joe he had avoided seeing her. He had not been able to resist the temptation to go back on the same day, and he had spent some hours in considering that human affairs are extremely mutable. But the scenes about him were too new, and very many of the faces he saw were too attractive, to allow of his brooding for long over his misfortune. His first impulse had been to go away again on the very evening of his arrival. He had gone to see Joe, arriving during luncheon, in the expectation of seeing her alone again. There would be a scene of solemn farewell, in which he would bid her be happy in her own way, in a tone of semi-paternal benevolence, after which he would give her his blessing, and bid farewell to the pomps and vanities of society. He would naturally retire gloomily from the gay world, and end his miserable existence in the approved Guy Livingstone fashion of life, between cavendish tobacco, deep drinking, and high play. Joe would then repent of the ruin she had caused, and that would be a great satisfaction. There was once a little boy in Boston whose hands were very cold as he went to school. But he blew on them savagely, saying, "I am glad of it! It serves my father right for not buying me my gloves." That was Ronald's state of mind. He had led the most sober of lives, and the wildest dissipation he remembered was the Lord Mayor's supper to the Oxford and Cambridge crews, when he himself had been one of the winners. But surely, for a disappointed lover there could be no course so proper as a speedy death by dissipation—which would serve Joe right. Therefore, on his return to his hotel, he ordered whiskey, in a sepulchral tone of voice. He tasted it, and thought it detestable.

On reflection, he would put off the commencement of his wild career until the evening after he had seen Joe again. The ravages of drink would not be perceptible so soon, after all. He changed his tie for one of a darker hue, ate sparingly of a beefsteak, and went back to bid Joe a last farewell.

Sybil Brandon and Miss Schenectady were elements in the solemn leave-taking which Ronald had not anticipated. Sybil, moreover, made a great effort, for she was anxious to help Joe as much as possible in her difficulties. She talked to Ronald with a vivacity that was unusual, and Joe herself was astonished at the brilliance of her conversation. She had always thought Sybil very reserved, if not somewhat shy.

Perhaps Sybil pitied Ronald a little. He was very quiet in his manner, though after the first few minutes he found himself talking much as usual. True, he often looked at Joe, and then was silent; but then again he looked at Sybil, and his tongue was unloosed. He was grateful after a time, and he was also flattered. Besides, he could not help noticing that his new acquaintance was extremely beautiful. His conscience smote him as he realized that he was thinking of her appearance, and he immediately quieted the qualm by saying that it was but natural admiration for an artistic object. Ronald did not know much about artists and that sort of people, but the expression formed itself conveniently in his mind.

The consequence was that he accepted an invitation to drive with the two girls after luncheon, and when they left him at his hotel, a proceeding against which he vehemently protested on the score of propriety, he reluctantly acknowledged to himself that he had enjoyed the afternoon very much.

"Come and see us after five o'clock," said Sybil. "I will present you to Mrs. Wyndham. Nine hundred and thirty-six, Beacon Street," she added, laughing.

"With great pleasure—thanks," said Ronald.

"Good-by, Ronald dear," said Joe pleasantly.

"Good-by," he answered in a doubtful tone of voice, as he raised his hat; and the two girls drove away.

Sybil was apparently in very good spirits.

"Do not be frightened, Joe dearest," she said. "We will manage it very well. He is not hurt in the least."

"Really, I do not believe he is—so very much, you know," Joe answered. But she was thoughtful, and did not speak again for some time.

It was on the morning after this that Joe read the article on John's speech, and met him by the Common. Ronald did not call during the day, and in the evening Joe went to her party as she had intended; but neither Sybil nor John Harrington were there. Sybil did not go to parties, and John probably had too much to do. But at supper Joe chanced to be standing near Mrs. Sam Wyndham.

"Oh, I so much wanted to see you, Miss Thorn," said the latter. "I wanted to tell you how much we like your cousin, Mr. Surbiton. He came today, and I have asked him to dinner to-morrow."

"Yes?" said Joe, turning a shade paler. "I am so glad you like him. He is a very nice boy."

"He is perfectly lovely," said Mrs. Sam, enthusiastically. "And he is so natural, you would not know he was English at all."

"Really?" said Joe, raising her eyebrows a little, but laughing at the same time.

"Oh my dear," said Mrs. Wyndham, "I always forget you are not one of us. Besides, you are, you see."

Mrs. Wyndham rarely said a tactless thing, but this evening she was in such good spirits that she said what came uppermost in her thoughts. Joe was not offended; she was only bored.

"Will you not come and dine too, to-morrow night?" asked Mrs. Wyndham, who was anxious to atone.

"Thanks, awfully," said Joe, "but I have to dine with the Aitchisons."

Pocock Vancouver, pale and exquisite as ever, came up to the two ladies.

"Can I get you anything, Mrs. Wyndham?" he inquired, after a double bow.

"No, thank you. Johnny Hannibal is taking care of me," answered Mrs. Sam, coldly.

"Miss Thorn, what can I get you?" he asked, turning to Joe.

"Nothing, thanks," said Joe, "Mr. Biggielow is getting me something." She did not look at Vancouver as she answered, and the angry color began to rise to her temples. Vancouver, who was not used to repulses such as these, and was too old a soldier to give up a situation so easily, stood a moment playing with his coat tails. A sudden thought passed through Joe's mind. It struck her that, considering the situation of affairs, it would be unwise to break off her acquaintance with Vancouver at the present time. Her first honest impulse was to cut him and never speak to him again. But it was better to act with more deliberation. In the first place, there might be more to be learnt which might be of service to John; secondly, people would talk about it if she cut him, and would invent some story to the effect that he had proposed to marry her, or that she had proposed to marry him. It was contrary to her nature to pretend anything she did not feel, but it would nevertheless be a mistake to quarrel openly with Vancouver.

"On second thoughts—if you would get me a glass of water"—she said, speaking to him. He instantly disappeared; but even in the moment before he departed to execute her command he had time to express by his look a sense of injury forgiven, which did not escape Joe.

"What a hypocrite the man is!" she thought.

Vancouver on his part could form no conception of the cause of the coldness the two ladies had shown him. He could not know that Joe had discovered in him the writer of the article, still less could he have guessed that Joe had told John, and that John had told Mrs. Sam. He could only suppose that the two had been talking of something, and were annoyed at being interrupted.

When he came back with the glass of water Mr. Biggielow had just brought Joe some salad. The usual struggle began between the two men. Mr. Bonamy Biggielow was a little poet.

"I ought to thank you, Miss Thorn, instead of you thanking me," said Vancouver, in a seductive voice, on one side of Joe.

"Is it not the most crowded supper you ever saw?" remarked Mr. Biggielow on the other side.

"Why?" said Joe, eating her salad and looking straight before her.

"I thought you were going to send me away. I was so glad when you condescended to make use of me," answered Vancouver.

Mr. Biggielow also answered Joe's interrogation.

"Well," he said, "I mean it is thronged with people. There is a decided 'sound of revelry by night'."

"Youth and beauty? That sort of thing?" said Joe to Biggielow. Then turning to Vancouver, she added, "Why should I send you away?"

"I hope there is no reason," he said gravely. "In fact, I am sure there is none, except that you would of course always do exactly as you pleased about that and everything else."

"Yes, indeed," Joe answered, and her lip curled a little proudly, "you are quite right about that. But then, you know, I did not send you away."

"Thanks, again," said Vancouver.

"Do let me get you something more, Miss Thorn," suggested Mr. Biggielow. "No? There is any amount of pâtés. You always like"—

"Of course you have heard about Harrington?" said Vancouver in a low voice close to Josephine's ear.

"No, really," she answered. "Will you take my plate? And the glass— thanks." Mr. Bonamy Biggielow was obliged to retire. "You mean about the senatorship?" asked Joe.

"Yes. The senator died this morning. Harrington will make a fight for it. He has many friends."

"Among whom you count yourself, doubtless," remarked Joe.

"Not politically, of course. I take no active part"—

"Yes, I know." Joe knew the remainder of the sentence by heart. "Then you will have a glorious opportunity for maintaining an armed neutrality."

"Oh, if it comes to that," said Vancouver mildly, "I would rather see Harrington senator than some of our own men. At all events, he is honest."

"At all events!" Joe repeated. "You think, perhaps, that some man of your own party may be elected who will not turn out to be honest?"

"Well, the thing is possible. You see, politics are such a dirty business —all kinds of men get in."

Joe laughed in a way that made Vancouver nervous. He was beginning to know her, and he could tell when some sharp thrust was coming by the way she laughed. Nevertheless, he was fascinated by her.

"It is not long since you told me that Mr. Harrington's very mild remark about extinguishing bribery and corruption was a piece of gross exaggeration," said Joe. "Why do you say politics are dirty work?"

"There is a great difference," answered Vancouver.

"What difference? Between what?"

"Between saying that the business of politics is not clean, and saying that all public officers are liars, like the Cretans."

"Who is exaggerating now?" asked Joe scornfully.

"Of course it is I," answered Vancouver, submissively. "If it is not a rude question, did not that dress come from Egypt?"

"Yes." The garment in question was made of a kind of soft white, fluted material over a rose-colored silk ground. The raised flutings followed the exquisite lines of Joe's figure, and had the double merit of accentuating its symmetry, and of so leading the eye as to make her height seem greater than it really was. Cut square at the neck, it showed her dazzling throat at its best advantage, and a knot of pink lilies at the waist harmonized delicately with the color of the whole.

"It is just like you," said Vancouver, "to have something different from everybody else. I admire Eastern things so much, and one gets so tired of the everlasting round of French dresses."

"I am glad you like it," said Joe, indifferently.

"I am so anxious to meet your cousin, Miss Thorn," said Vancouver, trying a new subject. "I hear there is to be a dinner for him to-morrow night at Mrs. Sam Wyndham's. But of course I am not asked."

"Why 'of course'?" inquired Joe quickly.

"I believe Mrs. Wyndham thinks I dislike Englishmen," said Vancouver at random. "But she is really very much mistaken."

"Really?"

"Yes—I should be willing to like any number of Englishmen for the sake of being liked by one Englishwoman." He looked at Joe expressively as he spoke.

"Really?"

"Indeed, yes. Do you not believe me?"

"Oh, yes," said Joe. "Why should I not believe you?" Her voice was calm, but that same angry flush that had of late so often shown itself began to rise slowly at her temples. Vancouver saw it, and thought she was blushing at what he said.

"I trust you will," said Vancouver. "I trust that some day you will let me tell you who that Englishwoman is."

It was horrible; he was making love to her, this wretch, whom she despised. She turned her head away to hide the angry look in her eyes.

"Thanks—no, if you do not mind," said she. "I do not care to receive confidences,—I always forget to forget them." It was not in order that Pocock Vancouver might make love to her that she had sent away Bonamy Biggielow, the harmless little poet. She wished him back again, but he was embarked in an enterprise to dispute with Johnny Hannibal a place near Miss St. Joseph. Mrs. Wyndham had long since disappeared.

"Will you please take me back to my aunt?" said Joe. As they passed from the supper-room they suddenly came upon John Harrington, who was wandering about in an unattached fashion, apparently looking for some one. He bowed and stared a little at seeing Joe on Vancouver's arm, but she gave him a look of such earnest entreaty that he turned and followed her at a distance to see what would happen. Seeing her sit down by her aunt, he came up and spoke to her, almost thrusting Vancouver aside with his broad shoulders. Vancouver, however, did not dispute the position, but turned on his heel and went away.

"Oh, I am so glad," said Joe, with a sigh of relief. "I thought I should never get away from him!"

It is amazing what a difference the common knowledge of a secret will make in the intimacy of two people.

"I was rather taken aback at seeing you with him," said John. "Not that it can make any difference to you," he added quickly, "only you seemed so angry at him this morning."

"But it does"—Joe began, impulsively. "That is, I began by meaning to cut him, and then I thought it would be a mistake to make a scandal."

"Yes," said John, "it would be a great mistake. Besides, I would not for all the world have you take a part in this thing. It would do no good, and it might do harm."

"I think I have taken a part already," said Joe, somewhat hurt.

"Yes, I know. I am very grateful, but I hope you will not think any more about it, nor allow it to influence you in any way."

"But what is the use of friends if they do not take a part in one's quarrels?" asked Joe.

John looked at her earnestly for a few seconds, and saw that she was perfectly sincere. He had grown to like Josephine of late, and he was grateful to her for her friendship. Her manner that morning, when she told him of her discovery, had made a deep impression on him.

"My dear Miss Thorn," he said earnestly, in a low voice, "you are too good and kind, and I thank you very heartily for your friendship. But I think you were very wise not to cut Vancouver, and I hope you will not quarrel with anybody for any matter so trivial." The color came to Joe's face, but not for anger this time.

"Trivial!" she exclaimed.

"Yes, trivial," John repeated. "Remember that it is the policy of that paper to abuse me, and that if Vancouver had not written the article, the editor could have found some one else easily enough who would have done it."

"But it is such a dastardly thing!" said Joe. "He always says to every one that he has the greatest respect for you, and then he does a thing like this. If I were you I would kill him—I am sure I would."

"That would not be the way to win an election nowadays," said John, laughing.

"Oh, I would not care about that," said Joe, hotly. "But I dare say it is very silly of me," she added. "You do not seem to mind it at all."

"It is not worth while to lose one's temper or one's soul for the iniquities of Mr. Pocock Vancouver," said John. "The man may do me harm, but as I never expected his friendship or help, he neither falls nor rises in my estimation on that account. Blessed are they who expect nothing!"

"Blessed indeed," said Joe. "But one cannot help expecting men who have the reputation of being gentlemen to behave decently."

"Vancouver has a right to his political opinions, and a perfect right to express them in any way he sees fit," said John.

"Oh, of course," said Joe, impatiently. "This is a free country, and that sort of thing. But if he means to express political opinions he should not cry aloud at every tea-party in town that he is neutral and takes no active part in politics. I think that writing violent articles in a newspaper is a very active part indeed. And he should not go about saying that he has the highest reverence for a man, and then call him a lunatic and a charlatan in print, unless he is willing to sign his name to it, and take the consequences. Should he? I think it is vile, and horrid, and abominable, and nasty, and I hate him."

"With the exception of the peroration to that speech," said John, who was very much amused, "I am afraid I must agree with you. A man certainly ought not to do any of those things."

"Then why do you defend him?" asked Joe, with flashing eyes.

"Because, on general principles, I do not think a man is so much worse than his fellows because he does things they would very likely do in his place. There are things done every day, all over the world, quite as bad as that, and no one takes much notice of them. Almost every businessman is trying to get the better of some other business man by fair means or foul."

"You do not seem to have a very exalted idea of humanity," said Joe.

"A large part of humanity is sick," said John, "and it is as well to be prepared for the worst in any illness."

"I wish you were not so tremendously calm, you know," said Joe, looking thoughtfully into John's face. "I am afraid it will injure you."

"Why in the world should it injure me?" asked John, much astonished at the remark.

"I have a presentiment"—she checked herself suddenly. "I do not like to tell you," she added.

"I would like to hear what you think, if you will tell me," said John, gravely.

"Well, do not be angry. I have a presentiment that you will not be made senator. Are you angry?"

"No indeed. But why?"

"Just for that very reason; you are too calm. You are not enough of a partisan. Every one is a partisan here."

John was silent, and his face was grave and thoughtful. The remark was profound in its way, and showed a far deeper insight into political matters than he imagined Joe possessed. He had long regarded Mrs. Wyndham as a woman of fine sense and judgment, and had often asked her opinion on important questions. But in all his experience she had never said anything that seemed to strike so deeply at the root of things as this simple remark of Josephine's.

"I am afraid you are angry," said Joe, seeing that he was grave and silent.

"You have set me thinking, Miss Thorn," he answered.

"You think I may be right?" she said.

"The idea is quite new to me, I think it is perhaps the best definition of the fact that I ever heard. But it is not what ought to be."

"Of course not," Joe answered. "Nothing is just what it ought to be. But one has to take things as they are."

"And make them what they should be," added John, and the look of strong determination came into his face.

"Ah, yes," said Joe, softly. "Make things what they should be. That is the best thing a man can live for."

"Perhaps we might go home, Joe," said Miss Schenectady, who had been conversing for a couple of hours with another old lady of literary tastes.

"Yes, Aunt Zoë," said Joe, rousing herself, "I think we might."

"Shall I see you to-morrow night at Mrs. Wyndham's dinner?" asked John, as they parted.

"No, I refused. Good-night."

As Joe sat by her aunt's side in the deep dark carriage on the way home, her hands were cold and she trembled from head to foot. And when at last she laid her head upon her pillow there were tears in her eyes and on her cheeks.

"Is it possible that I can be so heartless?" she murmured to herself.

Chapter XI

Ronald went to see Sybil Brandon at five o'clock, and as it chanced he found her alone. Mrs. Wyndham, she said, had gone out, or rather she had not yet come home; but if Ronald would wait, she would certainly be in.

Ronald waited, and talked to Miss Brandon in the mean while. He had a bereaved air when he arrived, which was calculated to excite sympathy, and his conversation was subdued in tone, and grave in subject. But Sybil did her best to cheer him, and in the fullness of her sympathy did perhaps more than was absolutely necessary. Ronald's wound was not deep, but he had a firm conviction that it ought to be.

Any man would have thought the same in his place. Certainly, few people would have understood what they felt in such a position. He had grown up believing he was to marry a young and charming woman of whom he was really exceedingly fond, and now he was suddenly told that the whole thing was a mistake. It was enough to break a man's heart, and yet Ronald's heart was not broken, and to his great surprise beat nearly as regularly the day after his disaster as it had done during the whole two-and-twenty years of his life. He could not understand his own calmness, and he was sure that he ought to be profoundly grieved over the whole affair, so that his face was drawn into an expression of solemnity somewhat out of keeping with its singular youthful freshness of color and outline.

The idea of devoting himself to the infernal gods as a sacrifice to the blighted passion had passed away in the course of the drive on the previous afternoon. He had felt no inclination to drown his cares in drink during the evening, but on the contrary he had gone for a brisk walk in Beacon Street, and had ascertained by actual observation, and the assistance of a box of matches, the precise position of No. 936. This had occupied some time, as it is a peculiarity of Boston to put the number of the houses on the back instead of the front, so that the only certain course to follow in searching for a friend, is to reach the rear of his house by a circuitous route through side streets and back alleys, and then, having fixed the exact position of his residence by astronomical observation, to return to the front and inquire for him. It is true that even then one is frequently mistaken, but there is nothing else to be done.

It was perhaps not extraordinary that Ronald should be at some pains to find out where Mrs. Wyndham lived, for Sybil was the only person besides Joe and Miss Schenectady whom he had yet met, and he wanted company, for he hated and dreaded solitude with his whole heart. Having traveled all the night previous, he went home and slept a sounder sleep than falls to the lot of most jilted lovers.

The next day he rose early and "did" Boston. It did not take him long, and he said to himself that half of it was very jolly, and half of it was too utterly beastly for anything. The Common, and the Gardens, and Commonwealth Avenue, you know, were rather pretty, and must have cost a deuce of a lot of money in this country; but as for the State House, and Paul Revere's Church, and the Old South, and the city generally, why, it was simply disgusting, all that, you know. And in the afternoon he went to see Sybil Brandon, and began talking about what he had seen.

She was, if anything, more beautiful than ever, and as she looked at him, and held out her hand with a friendly greeting, Ronald felt himself actually blushing, and Sybil saw it and blushed too, a very little. Then they sat down by the window where there were plants, and they looked out at the snow and the people passing. Sybil asked Ronald what he had been doing.

"I have been doing Boston," he said. "Of course it was the proper thing. But I am afraid I do not know much about it."

"But do you like it?" she asked. "It is much more important, I think, to know whether you like things or dislike them, than to know everything about them. Do not you think so?"

"Oh, of course," said Ronald. "But I like Boston very much; I mean the part where you live. All this, you know—Commonwealth Place, and the Public Park, you know, and Beacon Avenue, of course, very much. But the city "—

"You do not like the city?" suggested Sybil, seeing he hesitated, and smiling at his strange confusion of names.

"No," said Ronald. "I think it is so cramped and ugly, and all little narrow streets. But then, of course, it is such a little place. You get into the country the moment you walk anywhere."

"It seems very big to the Bostonians," said Sybil, laughing.

"Oh, of course. You have lived here all your life, and so it is quite different."

"I? Dear me no! I am not a Bostonian at all."

"Oh," said Ronald, "I thought you were. That was the reason I was not sure of abusing the city to you. But it is not a bad place, I should think, when you know lots of people, and that was such a pretty drive we went yesterday."

"Yes, it must seem very new to you. Everything must, I should think, most of all this casual way we have of receiving people. But there really is a Mrs. Wyndham, with whom I am staying, and she will be in before long."

"Oh—don't—don't mention her," said Ronald, hastily, "I mean it—it is of no importance whatever, you know." He blushed violently.

Sybil laughed, and Ronald blushed again, but in all his embarrassment lie could not help thinking what a silvery ring there was in her voice.

"I am afraid Mrs. Wyndham would not like it, if she heard you telling me she was not to be mentioned, and was not of any importance whatever. But she is a very charming woman, and I am very fond of her."

"She is your aunt, I presume, Miss Brandon?" said Ronald.

"My aunt?" repeated Sybil. "Oh no, not at all—only a friend."

"Oh, I thought all unattached young ladies lived with aunts here, like Miss Schenectady." Ronald smiled grimly at the recollections of the previous day.

"Not quite that," said Sybil, laughing. "Mrs. Wyndham is not the least like Miss Schenectady. She is less clever and more human."

"Really, I am so glad," said Ronald. "And she talks so oddly—Joe's—Miss Thorn's aunt. Could you tell me, if it is not a rude question, why so many people here are never certain of anything? It strikes me as so absurdly ridiculous, you know. She said yesterday that 'perhaps, if I rang the bell, she could send a message.' And the man at the hotel this morning had no postage stamps, and said that perhaps if I went to the General Post Office I might be able to get some there."

"Yes," said Sybil, "it is absurd, and one catches it so easily."

"But would it not be ridiculous if the guard called out at a station, 'Perhaps this is Boston!' or 'Perhaps this is New York?' It would be too utterly funny."

"I am afraid that if you begin to make a list of our peculiarities yon will find funnier things than that," said Sybil, laughing. "But then we always laugh at you in England, so that it is quite fair."

"Oh, we are very absurd, I know," said Ronald, "but I think we are much more comfortable. For instance, we do not have niggers about who call us 'Mister.'"

"You must not use such words in Boston, Mr. Surbiton," said Sybil. "Seriously, there are people who would be very much offended. You must speak of 'waiters of color,' or 'the colored help;' you must be very careful."

"I will," said Ronald. "Thanks. Is everything rechristened in that way? I am afraid I shall always be in hot water."

"Oh yes, there are no men and women here. They are all ladies and gentlemen, or 'the gurls,' and 'the fellows.' But it is very soon learnt."

"Yes, I can imagine," said Ronald, very much amused. "But—by the bye, this is the season here, is not it?"

So they chattered together for nearly an hour about the merest nothings, not saying anything particularly witty, but never seeming to each other in the least dull. Ronald had gone to Sybil for consolation, and he was so well consoled that he was annoyed when Mrs. Wyndham came in and interrupted his tête-à-tête. Sybil introduced Ronald, and when he rose to go, after a quarter of an hour, Mrs. Wyndham asked him to dinner on the following day.

That night, when Ronald was alone in his room at the hotel, he took Josephine's photograph from a case in his bag and set it before him on the table. He would think about her for a while, and reflect on his situation; and he sat down for that purpose, his chin resting on his folded hands. Dear Joe—he loved her so dearly, and she was so cruel not to marry him! But, somehow, as he looked, he seemed to see through the photograph, and another face came and smiled on him. Again and again he called his attention back, and tried to realize that the future would be very blank and dreary without Joe; but do what he would, it did not seem so blank and dreary after all; there was somebody else there.

"Joe is quite right," he said aloud. "I am a brute." And he went to bed, trying hard to be disgusted with himself. But his dreams were sweet, for he dreamed he was sitting among the ferns at Mrs. Wyndham's house, talking to Sybil Brandon.

"Why, my dear," said Mrs. Wyndham, when Ronald was gone, "he is perfectly charming. We have positively found a new man."

"Yes," said Sybil. "I am so glad you asked him to dinner. I do not think he is very clever, but he talks easily, and says funny things."

"I suppose he has come over to marry his cousin—has not he?" inquired Mrs. Wyndham.

"No," replied Sybil, "he is not going to marry Joe Thorn," she answered absently; for she was thinking of something, and her tone indicated such absolute certainty in the matter that Mrs. Wyndham looked quickly at her.

"Well, you seem quite certain about it, any way," she said.

"I? Oh—well, yes. I think it is extremely unlikely that he will marry her."

"I almost wish I had offered to take him to the party to-night," said Mrs. Wyndham, evidently unsatisfied. "However, as he is coming to-morrow, that will do quite as well. Sybil, dear, you look tired. Why don't you go and lie down before dinner?"

"Oh, because—I am not tired, really. I am always pale, you know."

"Well, I am tired to death myself, my dear, and as there is no one here I will say I am not at home, and rest till dinner."

Mrs. Wyndham had been as much startled as any one by news of the senator's death that morning, and though she always professed to agree with her husband she was delighted at the prospect of John Harrington's election. She had been a good friend to him, and he to her, for years, and she cared much more for his success than for the turn of events. She had met him in the street that afternoon, and they had perambulated the pavement of Beacon Street for more than an hour in the discussion of the future. John had also told her that he was now certain that Vancouver was the writer of the offensive articles that had so long puzzled him; at all events that the especial one which had appeared the morning after the skating-party was undoubtedly from his pen. Mrs. Wyndham, who had long suspected as much, was very angry when she found that her suspicions had been so just, and she proposed to deal summarily with Vancouver. John, however, begged her to temporize, and she promised to be prudent.

"By the way," she said to Sybil, as she was about to leave the room, "it was a special providence that you did not marry Vancouver. He has turned out badly."

Sybil started slightly and looked up. Her experience with Pocock Vancouver was a thing she rarely referred to. She had undoubtedly given him great encouragement, and had then mercilessly refused him, to the great surprise of every one. But as that had occurred a year and a half ago, it was quite natural that she should treat him like any one else, now, just as though nothing had happened. She looked up at Mrs. Wyndham in some surprise.

"What has he done?" she asked.

"You know how he always talks about John Harrington?"

"He always says he respects him immensely."

"Very well. It is he who has been writing those scurrilous articles that we have talked about so much."

"How disgraceful!" exclaimed Sybil. "How perfectly detestable! Are you quite sure?"

"There is not the least doubt about it. John Harrington told me himself."

"Oh, then of course it is true," said Sybil. "How dreadful!"

"Harrington takes it in the calmest way, as though he had expected it all his life. He says they were never friends, and that Vancouver has a perfect right to his political opinions. I never saw anybody so cool in my life."

"What a splendid fellow he is!" exclaimed Sybil. "There is something lion-like about him. He would forgive an enemy a thousand times a day, and say the man who injured him had a perfect right to his opinions."

"Why gracious goodness, Sybil, how you talk!" cried Mrs. Wyndham; "you are not in love with the man yourself, are you, my dear?"

"I?" asked Sybil. Then she laughed. "No, indeed! I would not marry him if he asked me."

"Why not?"

"Oh, I would never marry a celebrity like that. He is splendid, and noble, and honest; but everything in him is devoted to his career. There is no room for a woman at all."

"I think the amount of solid knowledge about men that you dear, sweet, lovely, beautiful, innocent little girls possess is something just too perfectly amazing!" said Mrs. Wyndham, slowly, and with great emphasis.

"If we do," said Sybil, "it is not surprising. I am sure I do not wonder at girls knowing a great deal about the world. Everything is discussed before them, and marriage and men are the usual topics of conversation. The wonder is that girls still make so many mistakes in their choice, after listening to the combined experience of all the married women of their acquaintance for several years. It shows that no one is infallible."

"What a funny girl you are, Sybil!" exclaimed Mrs. Wyndham. "I think you turn the tables on me altogether."

"Yes? Well, I have experiences of my own now," said Sybil, leaning back against an enormous cushion.

Mrs. Wyndham came and sat upon the arm of the easy-chair, and put one arm round Sybil's neck and kissed her.

"Sybil, dear," she said affectionately, and then stopped.

They sat in silence for some time, looking at the great logs burning in the deep fire-place.

"Sybil, dear," Mrs. Wyndham began again, presently, "why did you refuse Vancouver? You do not mind telling me, do you?"

"Why do you ask?" said Sybil. "It makes no difference now."

"No, perhaps not. Only I always thought it strange. He must have done something you did not like, of course."

"Yes, that was it. He did something I did not like. Mr. Harrington would have said he had a perfect right to do as he pleased. But I could not marry him after that."

"Was it anything so very bad?" asked Mrs. Wyndham, affectionately, smoothing Sybil's thick fair hair.

"It was not as deep as a well, nor as broad as a house," said Sybil, with a faint, scornful laugh; "but it was enough. It would do."

"I wish you would tell me, dear," persisted Mrs. Wyndham. "I have a particular reason for wanting to know."

"Well, I would not have told before this other affair came out," said Sybil. "I would not marry him because he tried to find out from poor mamma's man of business whether we were rich. And the day after he got the information that I was rich enough to suit him, he proposed. But mamma knew all about what had gone on and told me, and so I refused him. She said I was wrong, and would not have told me if she had known it would make any difference. And now you say I was right. I am sure I was; it was only a fancy I had for him, because he was so clever and well-bred. Besides, he is much too old."

"He is old enough to be your father, my dear," said Mrs. Wyndham; "but I think you were a little hard on him. Almost any man would do the same. We here in Boston, of course, always know about each other. It was a little mean of him, no doubt, but it was not a mortal crime."

"I think it was low," said Sybil, decisively. "To think of a man as rich as that caring for a paltry twenty or thirty thousand a year."

"I know, my dear," said Mrs. Wyndham, "it is mean; but they all do it, and life is uncertain, and so is business I suppose, and twenty or thirty thousand a year does make a difference to most people, I expect."

Mrs. Wyndham looked at the fire reflectively, as though not absolutely certain of the truth of the proposition. Sam Wyndham was commonly reputed to be worth a dozen millions or so. He would have been very well off even in New York, and in Boston he was rich.

"It would make a great difference to me," said Sybil, laughing, "for it is all I have in the world. But I am glad I refused Vancouver on that ground, all the same. If it had not been for that I should have married him—just imagine!"

"Yes, just imagine!" exclaimed Mrs. Wyndham. "And to have had him turn out such an abominable blackguard!"

"There is no mistaking what you think of him now, at all events," said Sybil.

"No, my dear. And now we have talked so long that it is time to dress for dinner."

How Mrs. Wyndham went to the party and met Joe Thorn has already been told. It was no wonder that Mrs. Sam treated Vancouver so coldly, and she repulsed him again more than once during the evening. When Joe was gone, John Harrington went up to her.

"I came very late," he said, "and at first I could not find you, and then I had to say something to Miss Thorn. But I wanted to see you especially."

"Give me your arm," said Mrs. Wyndham, "and we will go into the conservatory. I have something especial to say to you, too." Once out of the thick of the party, they sat down. "I have discovered something more about our amiable friend," she continued. "It is a side-light on his character—something he did a year and a half ago. Do you remember his flirtation with Sybil Brandon at Saratoga and then at Newport?"

"Yes, I was in Newport most of the summer."

"You don't know why she refused him, though. It's perfectly rich!" Mrs. Sam laughed dryly.

"No; I only know she did, and every one seemed very much astonished," answered John. "She refused him because he had been trying to find out how much she was worth. It speaks volumes for the characters of both of them, does it not?"

"Yes, indeed," said John. "What a Jew that man is! He is as rich as Croesus."

"Oh, well, as I told her, most men would do it."

"I suppose so," John answered, laughing a little. "A man the other night told me he was going to make inquiries concerning the fortunes of his beloved one. He said he had no idea of buying a pig in a poke. That was graceful, was it not?"

Mrs. Wyndham laughed aloud. "He was honest, at all events. By the bye, do you know you have a fanatic admirer in Sybil Brandon?"

"No, really? I like her very much, too: and I am very glad if she likes me."

"She said she would not marry you if you asked her, though," said Mrs. Sam, laughing again. "You see you must not flatter yourself too much."

"I do not. I should not think of asking her to marry me. Did she give any especial reason why she would inevitably refuse me?"

"Yes, indeed; she said you were lion-like, and, oh, the most delightful things! But she said she would not marry you if you asked her, because you are a celebrity and devoted to your career, so that there is no room for a woman in your life. Is that true?"

"I am not so sure," said John, thoughtfully. "Perhaps she is right in the way she means. I never thought much about it."

Chapter XII

The idea Joe had formed about Vancouver was just, in the main, and she was not far wrong in disliking him and thinking him dangerous. Nevertheless John Harrington understood the man better. Vancouver was so constituted that his fine intellect and quick perception were unsupported by any strong principle of individuality. He was not capable of hatred—he could only be spiteful; he could not love, he could only give a woman what he could spare of himself. He would at all times rather avoid an open encounter, but he rarely neglected an opportunity of dealing a thrust at any one he disliked, when he could do so safely. He was the very opposite of John, who never said of any one what he would not say to themselves, and granted to every man the broadest right of judgment and freedom of opinion. Nevertheless there was not enough real strength in anything Vancouver felt to make him very dangerous as an opponent, nor valuable as a friend. Had it not been for the important position he had attained by his clever subtlety in affairs, and by the assistance of great railroad magnates who found in him a character and intelligence precisely suited to their ends, Pocock Vancouver would have been a neutral figure in the world, lacking both the enterprise to create an idea and the courage to follow it out. It was most characteristic of his inherent smallness, that in spite of his wealth and the very large operations that must be constantly occupying his thoughts, he could demean himself to write anonymous articles in a daily paper, in the hope of injuring a man he disliked.

It is true that his feeling against Harrington was as strong as anything in his nature. He detested John's strength because he had once made him a confidence and John had done him a favor. He disliked him also because he knew that wherever they chanced to be together John received an amount of consideration and even of respect which he himself could not obtain with all his money and all his cleverness. His mind, too, delighted in detail and revolted against John's sweeping generalities. For these several reasons Vancouver had taken great delight in writing and printing sundry vicious criticisms upon John in the absolute certainty of not being found out. The editor of the paper did not know Vancouver's name, for the articles came through the post with a modest request that they might be inserted if they were of any use; and they were generally so pungent and to the point that the editor was glad to get them, especially as no remuneration was demanded.

As for the confidence Vancouver had once made to John, it was another instance of his littleness. At the time when Vancouver was anxious to marry Sybil Brandon, John Harrington was very intimate at the house, and was, in Vancouver's opinion, a dangerous rival; at all events he felt that the contest was not an agreeable one, nor altogether to his own advantage. Accordingly he tried every means to clear the coast, as he expressed it; but although John probably had no intention of marrying Sybil, and Sybil certainly had never thought of marrying John, the latter was fond of her society, and of her mother's, and came to the cottage on the Newport cliff with a regularity that drove Vancouver to the verge of despair. Pocock at last could bear it no longer and asked John to dinner. Over a bottle of Pommery Sec he confided his passion, and hinted that John was the obstacle to his wooing. Harrington raised his eyebrows, smiled, wished Vancouver all success, and left Newport the next day. If Vancouver had not disgusted Sybil by his inquiries concerning her fortune, he would have married her, and his feelings towards John would have been different. But to know that Harrington had done him the favor of going away, knowing that he was about to offer himself to Miss Brandon, and then to have failed in his suit was more than the vanity of Mr. Pocock Vancouver could bear with any sort of calmness, and the consequence was that he disliked John as much as he disliked anybody or anything in the world. There is no resentment like the resentment of wounded vanity, nor any self-reproach like that of a man who has shown his weakness.

When Mrs. Wyndham told John the story of Vancouver's failure he could have told her the rest, had he chosen, and she would certainly have been very much amused. But John was not a man to betray a confidence, even that of a man who had injured him, and so he merely laughed and kept his own counsel. He would have scorned to speak to Vancouver about the articles, or to make any change in his manner towards him. As he had said to Josephine, he had expected nothing from the man, and now he was not disappointed.

Meanwhile Vancouver, who was weakly but frequently susceptible to the charms of woman, had made up his mind that if Josephine had enough pin-money she would make him an admirable wife, and he accordingly began to make love to her in his own fashion, as has been seen. A day or two earlier Joe would have laughed at him, and it would perhaps have amused her to hear what he had to say, as it amuses most young women to listen to pretty speeches. But Joe was between two fires, so to speak; she was under the two influences that were strongest with her. She loved John Harrington with all her heart, and she hated Vancouver with all her strength. It is true that her hatred was the only acknowledged passion, for her maidenly nature was not able yet to comprehend her love; and the mere thought that she cared for a man who did not care for her brought the hot blush to her cheek. But the love was in her heart all the same, strong and enduring, so that Vancouver found the fortress doubly guarded.

He could not entirely explain to himself her conduct at the party. She had always seemed rather willing to accept his attentions and to listen to his conversation, but on this particular evening, just when he wished to make a most favorable impression, she had treated him with surprising coldness. There was a supreme superiority in the way she had at first declined his services, and had then told him he might be permitted to get her a glass of water. The subsequent satisfaction of having ousted Mr. Bonamy Biggielow, the little poet, from his position at her side was small enough, and was more than counterbalanced and destroyed by her returning to her chaperon at the first soft-tongued insinuation of a desire to flirt, which Vancouver ventured to speak. Moreover, when Harrington almost pushed him aside and sat down by Josephine, Vancouver could bear it no longer, but turned on his heel and went away, with black thoughts in his heart. It seemed as though John was to be always in his way.

It would be hard to say what he would have felt had he known that Josephine Thorn, John Harrington, and Mrs. Sam Wyndham all knew of his journalistic doings. And yet it was nearly certain that no one of the three would ever speak to him on the subject. Joe would not, because she knew John would not like it; John himself despised the whole business too much to condescend to reproach Vancouver; and, finally, Mrs. Wyndham was too much a woman of the world to be willing to cause a scandal when it could possibly be avoided. She liked Vancouver too, and regretted what he had done. Her liking only extended to his conversation and agreeable manners, for she was beginning to despise his character; but he had so long been an habitué about the house that she could not make up her mind to turn him out. But for all that, she could not help being cold to him at first.

John himself was too busy with important matters to bestow much thought on Vancouver or his doings. His day had been spent in interviews and letter-writing; fifty people had been to see him at his rooms, and he had dispatched more than that number of letters. At five o'clock he had slipped out with the intention of dining at his club before any one else was there, but he had met Mrs. Wyndham in the street, and had spent his dinner-hour with her. At half-past six he had another appointment in his rooms, and it was not till nearly eleven that he was able to get away and look in upon the party, when he met Joe. For a week this kind of life would probably last, and then all would be over, in one way or another, but meanwhile the excitement was intense.

On the next day Ronald came to see Joe before ten o'clock. The time hung heavily on his hands, and he found it impossible to occupy himself with his troubles. There were moments when the first impression of disappointment returned upon him very strongly, but he was conscious of a curious duplicity about his feelings, and he knew well enough in his inmost heart that he was only evoking a fictitious regret out of respect for what he thought he ought to feel.

"Tell me all about the people here, Joe," said he, sitting down beside her almost as though nothing had happened. "Who is Mrs. Wyndham, to begin with?"

"Mrs. Wyndham—she is Sam Wyndham's wife. Just that," said Joe.

"And Sam Wyndham?"

"Oh—he is one of the prevalent profession. He is a millionaire. In fact he is one of the real ones."

"When do they get to be real?" asked Ronald.

"Oh, when they have more than ten millions. The other ones do not count much. It is much more the thing to be poor, unless you have ten millions."

"That is something in my favor, at all events," said Ronald.

"Very much. You have been to see Mrs. Wyndham, then?"

"Oh yes, I went yesterday, and she has asked me to dinner to-night. It is awfully good of her, I must say."

"You will like her very much, and Sybil Brandon too," said Joe. "Sybil is an adorable creature."

"She is most decidedly good-looking, certainly. There is no doubt about it." Ronald pulled his delicate moustache a little. "Though she is quite different style from you, Joe," he added presently, as though he had discovered a curious fact in natural history.

"Of course. Sybil is a great beauty, and I am only pretty," answered Joe in perfectly good faith.

"I think you are a great beauty too," said Ronald critically. "I am sure most people think so, and I have heard lots of men say so. Besides, you are much more striking-looking than she is."

"Oh, nonsense, Ronald!"

"Joe—who is Mr. Vancouver?"

"Vancouver! Why do you ask especially?"

"It is very natural, I am sure," said Ronald in a somewhat injured tone. "You wrote about him. He was the only person you mentioned in your letter-that is, he and a man called Harrington."

"Mr. Vancouver—Mr. Pocock Vancouver—is a middle-aged man of various accomplishments," said Joe, "more especially distinguished by the fact that Sybil Brandon refused to marry him some time ago. He is an enemy of Mr. Harrington's, and they are both friends of Mrs. Wyndham's."

"Ah!" ejaculated Ronald, "and who is Harrington?"

"Mr. John Harrington is a very clever person who has to do with politics," said Joe, without hesitation, but as she continued she blushed a little. "He is always being talked about because he wants to reform everything. He is a great friend of ours."

"Oh—I thought so," said Ronald. "What sort of a fellow is he?"

"I suppose he is five-and-thirty years old; he is neither tall nor short, and he has red hair," said Joe.

"What a beauty!" laughed Ronald.

"He is not at all ugly, you know," said Joe, still blushing.

"Shall I ever see him?"

"You will see him to-night at Mrs. Wyndham's; he told me he was going."

"Oh—are you going too, Joe?"

"No. I have another dinner-party. You will have to do without me."

"I suppose I shall always have to do without you, now." said Ronald disconsolately.

"Don't be silly, Ronald!"

"Silly!" repeated Surbiton in injured tones. "You call it silly to be cut up when one is treated as you have treated me! It is too bad, Joe!"

"You are a dear, silly old thing," said his cousin affectionately, "and I will say it as much as I please. It is ever so much better, because we can always be like brother and sister now, and we shall not marry and quarrel over everything till we hate each other."

"I think you are very heartless, all the same," said Ronald.

"Listen to me, Ronald"--

"You will go and marry one of these middle-aged people with red hair"—

"Be quiet," said Joe, stamping her little foot. "Listen to me. I will not marry you because I like you and I do not love you, and I never mean to marry any middle-aged person. I shall not marry at all, most probably. Will you please to imagine what life would have been like if we had married first, and found out afterwards that we had made a mistake."

"Of course that would have been awful," said Ronald. "But then it would not be a mistake, because I love you—like anything, Joe!"

"Oh, nonsense! You are quite mistaken, my dear boy, because some day you will fall desperately in love with some one else, and you will like me just as much as ever"—

"Of course I should," said Ronald indignantly. "Nothing would ever make any difference at all!"

"But, Ronald," retorted Joe laughing, "if you were desperately in love with some one else, how could you still be just as fond of me?"

"I don't know, but I should," said Ronald. "Besides, it is absurd, for I shall never love any one else."

"We shall see; but of course if you never do, we shall always be just the same as we are now."

"Well—that would not be so bad, you know," said Ronald with a certain air of resignation.

After this conversation Ronald became reconciled to the situation. Joe's remark that he would be able to love some one else very much without being—any the less fond of herself made him reflect, and he came to the conclusion that the case was conceivable after all. He therefore agreed within himself that he would think no more about the matter for the present, but would take what came in his way, and trust that Joe would ultimately change her mind. But he went to Mrs. Wyndham's that evening with a firm determination to dislike John Harrington to the best of his ability.

A middle-aged man with red hair! Five-and-thirty was undoubtedly middle-age. Short, too. But Joe had blushed, and there was no doubt about it; this was the man who had won her affections. Ronald would hate him cordially.

But John refused to be hated. His manner was easy and courteous, but not gentle. He was evidently no lady's man. He talked to the men more than to the women, and he was utterly without affectation. Indeed, he was not in the least like what Ronald had expected.

Moreover, Ronald was seated next to Sybil Brandon at dinner, and drove every one away who tried to disturb the tête-à-tête he succeeded in procuring with her afterwards. He was surprised at his own conduct, but he somehow connected it in his mind with his desire to hate Harrington. It was not very clear to himself, and it certainly would have been incomprehensible to any one else, but the presence of Harrington stimulated him in his efforts to amuse Miss Brandon.

Sybil, too, in her quiet way, was very willing to be amused, and she found in Ronald Surbiton an absolute freshness of ideas that gave her a new sense of pleasure. Her affair with Vancouver had made a deep impression on her mind, and her mother's death soon afterwards had had the effect of withdrawing her entirely from the world. It was no wonder, therefore, that she liked this young Englishman, so different from most of the men she knew best. It was natural, too, that he should want to talk to her, for she was the only young girl present. At last, as Ronald began to feel that intimacy which sometimes grows out of a simple conversation between two sympathetic people, he turned to the subject he had most in mind, if not most in his heart.

"You and my cousin are very intimate, Miss Brandon, I believe?" he said.

"Yes—I have grown very fond of her in a few weeks." Sybil wondered whether Ronald was going to make confidences. It seemed to her rather early in the acquaintance.

"Yes, she told me," said Ronald. "She is very fond of you, too; I went to see her this morning."

"I suppose you go every day," said Sybil, smiling.

"No—not every day," answered Ronald. "But this morning I was asking her about some of the people here. She seems to know every one."

"Yes indeed, she is immensely popular. Whom did she tell you about?"

"Oh—Mrs. Wyndham, and Mr. Wyndham, and Mr. Vancouver, and Mr. Harrington. He is immensely clever, she says," added Ronald, with a touch of irony in his voice. "What do you think about him, Miss Brandon?"

"I cannot judge very well," said Sybil. "He is a great friend of mine, and I do not care in the least whether my friends are clever or not."

"Joe does," said Ronald. "She hates stupid people. She is very clever too, you know, and so I suppose she is right about Harrington."

"Oh yes; I was only speaking of myself," answered Sybil. "He is probably the strongest man in this part of the world."

"He looks strong," said Ronald, who was a judge of athletes.

"I mean in the way of brains," said Sybil. "But he is more than that, for he is so splendidly honest."

"But lots of people are honest," said Ronald, who did not want to concede too much to the man he meant to dislike.

"Perhaps, but not so much as he is. I do not believe John Harrington ever in his life said anything that could possibly convey a false impression, or ever betrayed a confidence." Sybil looked calmly across the room at John, who was talking earnestly to Sam Wyndham.

"But has he no defects at all? What a model of faultlessness!" exclaimed Ronald.

"People say he is self-centred, whatever that may mean. He is certainly a very ambitious man, but his ambitions are large, and he makes no secret of them. He will make a great stir in the world some day."

Ronald would have liked to ask about Vancouver also, but he fortunately remembered what Joe had told him that morning, and did not ask his questions of Sybil. But he went home that night wondering what manner of man this Harrington might be, concerning whom such great things were said. He was conscious also that he had not been very wise in what he had asked of Sybil, and he was dissatisfied at not having heard anything about the friendship that existed between Harrington and Joe. But on the whole he had enjoyed the evening very much—almost too much, when he remembered the things Joe had said to him in the morning. It ought not to be possible, he thought, for a jilted lover to look so pleasantly on life.

"Well," said Sam Wyndham to his wife when everybody was gone, and he had lit a big cigar; "well, it was a pleasant kind of an evening, was not it?"

"Yes," said Mrs. Sam, sitting down in a low easy-chair for a chat with her husband. "What a nice boy that young Englishman is."

"I was just going to say so," said Sam. "He made himself pretty comfortable with Sybil, did he not? I could not help thinking they looked a very pretty pair as they sat in that corner. What is he?"

"He is Miss Thorn's cousin. Sam, you really must not drop your ashes on the carpet. There are no end of saucers and things about."

"Oh, bother the carpet, my dear," said Sam good-naturedly; "tell me about that young fellow—what is his name?—Surbiton, is not it?"

"Yes—well, there is not very much to tell. He is here traveling for amusement, just like any other young Englishman. For my part I expected he had come here to marry his cousin, because Englishmen always marry their cousins. But Sybil says it is not true."

"How does she come to know?" inquired Sam, rolling his cigar in his mouth and looking at the ceiling.

"I suppose Miss Thorn told her. She ought to know, any way."

"Well, one would think so. By the way, this election is going to turn out a queer sort of a business, I expect. John says the only thing that is doubtful is that fellow Patrick Ballymolloy and his men. Now is not that just about the queerest thing you ever heard of? A set of Irishmen in the Legislature who are not sure they can manage to vote for a Democratic senator?"

"Yes, that is something altogether new," said Mrs. Wyndham. "But it seems so funny that John should come telling you all about his election, when you are such a Republican, and would go straight against him if you had anything to say about it."

"Oh, he knows I don't vote or anything," said Sam.

"Of course you don't vote, because you are not in the Legislature. But if you did, you would go against him, would not you?"

"Well, I am not sure," answered Sam in a drawl of uncertainty. "I tell you what it is, my dear, John Harrington is not such a bad Republican after all, though he is a Democrat. And it is my belief he could call himself a Republican, and could profess to believe just the same things as he does now, if he only took a little care."

Chapter XIII

A council of three men sat in certain rooms, in Conduit Street, London. There was nothing whatever about the bachelor's front room overlooking the thoroughfare to suggest secrecy, nor did any one of the three gentlemen who sat in easy-chairs, with cigars in their mouths, in any way resemble a conspirator. They were neither masked nor wrapped in cloaks, but wore the ordinary garb of fashionably civilized life. For the sake of clearness and convenience, they can be designated as X, Y, and Z. X was the president on the present occasion, but the office was not held permanently, devolving upon each of the three in succession at each successive meeting.

X was a man sixty years of age, clean-shaved, with smooth iron-gray hair and bushy eyebrows, from beneath which shone a pair of preternaturally bright blue eyes. His face was of a strong, even, healthy red; he was stout, but rather thick and massive than corpulent; his hands were of the square type, with thick straight fingers and large nails, the great blue veins showing strongly through the white skin. He was dressed in black, as though in mourning, and his clothes fitted smoothly over his short heavy figure.

Y was very tall and slight, and it was not easy to make a guess at his age, for his hair was sandy and thick, and his military moustache concealed the lines about his mouth. His forehead was high and broad, and the extreme prominence between his brows made his profile look as though the facial angles were reversed, as in certain busts of Greek philosophers. His fingers were well shaped, but extremely long and thin. He wore the high collar of the period, with a white tie fastened by a pin consisting of a single large pearl, and it was evident that the remainder of his dress was with him a subject of great attention. Y might be anywhere from forty to fifty years of age.

Z was the eldest of the three, and in some respects the most remarkable in appearance. He was well proportioned, except that his head seemed large for his body. His face was perfectly colorless, and his thin hair was white and long and disorderly. A fringe of snowy beard encircled his throat like a scarf, but his lips and cheeks were clean-shaved. The dead waxen whiteness of his face was thrown into startling relief by his great black eyes, in which there was a depth and a fire when he was roused that contrasted strongly with his aged appearance. His dress was simple in the extreme, and of the darkest colors.

The three sat in their easy-chairs round the coal fire. It was high noon in London, and the weather was moderately fine; that is to say, it was possible to read in the room without lighting the gas. X held a telegram in his hand.

"This is a perfectly clear case against us," he remarked in a quiet, business-like manner.

"It has occurred at such an unfortunate time," said Y, who spoke very slowly and distinctly, with an English accent.

"We shall do it yet," said Z, confidently.

"Gentlemen," said the president, "it will not do to hesitate. There is an individual in this case who will not let the grass grow under his feet. His name is Mr. Patrick Ballymolloy. We all know about him, I expect?"

"I know him very well indeed," said old Z. "It was I who put him in the book." He rose quickly and took a large volume from a shelf near by. It was a sort of ledger, with the letters of the alphabet printed on the cut edges of the leaves.

"I don't believe Y knows him," said the president. "Please read him to us." Z turned over the leaves quickly.

"B—Bally—Ballymolloy-Patrick—Yes," he said, finding the place. "Patrick Ballymolloy. Irish iron man. Boston, Mass. Drinks. Takes money from both sides. Voted generally Democratic ticket. P.S. 1882, opposed B. in election for Governor. Iron interest increased. P.S. 1883, owns twenty votes in House. Costs more than he did. That is all," said Z, shutting up the book.

"Quite enough," said the president. "Mr. Patrick Ballymolloy and his twenty votes will bother us. What a pity J.H. made that speech!"

"It appears that as Patrick has grown rich, Patrick has grown fond of protection, then," remarked Y, crossing one long leg over the other.

"Exactly," said Z. "That is it. Now the question is, who owns Patrick? Anybody know?"

"Whoever can pay for him, I expect," said the president.

"Now I have an idea," said the old man suddenly, and again he dived into the book. "Did either of you ever know a man called Vancouver?"

"Yes—I know all about him," said Y, and a contemptuous smile hinted beforehand what he thought of the man.

"I made an entry about him the other day," said the president. "You will find a good deal against his name."

"Here he is," said Z again. "Pocock Vancouver. Railways. Rep. Boston, Mass. Was taxed in 1870 for nearly a million dollars. Weak character, very astute. Takes no money. Believed to be dissipated, but he cleverly conceals it. Never votes. Has extensive financial interests. 1880, taxed for nearly three millions. 1881, paid ten thousand dollars to Patrick Ballymolloy (D) for carrying a motion for the Monadminck Railroad (see Railroads). 1882, voted for Butler"—

"Hollo!" exclaimed the president.

"Wait," said Z, "there is more. 1883, thought to be writer of articles against J.H. in Boston 'Daily Standard.' Subsequently confirmed by J.H. That is all."

"Yes," said the president, "that last note is mine. Harrington wired it yesterday with other things. But I was hurried and did not read his old record. Things could not be much worse. You see Harrington has no book with him, or he would know all this, and be on the lookout."

"Has he figured it out?" inquired Y.

"Yes, he has figured it out. He is a first-rate man, and he has the whole thing down cold. Ballymolloy and his twenty votes will carry the election, and if Vancouver cares he can buy Mr. Ballymolloy as he has done before. He does care, if he is going to take the trouble to write articles against J.H., depend upon it."

"Well, there is nothing for it," said Z, who, in spite of his age, was the most impulsive of the three. "We must buy Ballymolloy ourselves, with his twenty men."

"I think that would be a mistake," said the president.

"Do you?" said Z. "What do you say?" he asked, turning to Y.

"Nothing," replied Y.

"Then we will argue it, I suppose," said Z.

"Certainly," said the president. "I will begin." He settled himself in his chair and knocked the ashes from his cigar.

"I will begin by stating the exact position," he said. "In the first place this whole affair is accidental, resulting from the death of the junior senator. No one could foresee this event. We had arranged to put in John Harrington at the regular vacancy next year, and we are now very busy with a most important business here in London. If we were on the spot, as one of us could have been had we known that the senator would die, it would have been another matter. This thing will be settled by next Saturday at the latest, but probably earlier. I am opposed to buying Ballymolloy, because it is an uncertain purchase. He has taken money from both sides, and if he has the chance he will do it again. If we were present it would be different, for we could hold him to his bargain.

"We do not like buying, and we only do it in very urgent cases, and when we are certain of the result. To buy without certainty is simply to begin a system of reckless bribery, which is exactly what we want to put down. Moreover, it is a bad plan to bribe a man who is interested in iron. The man in that business ought to be with us any way, without anything but a little talking to. When you have stated any reasons to the contrary I will tell you what I propose instead. That is all."

During the president's little speech, Y and Z had listened attentively. When he had finished, Z turned in his chair and took his cigar from his lips.

"I think," said Z, "that the case is urgent. The question is just about coming to a head, and we want all the men we can get at any price. It will not do to let a chance slip. If we can put J.H. in the senate now, we may put another man in at the vacancy. That makes two men instead of one. I am aware that it would be an improbable thing to get two of our men in for Massachusetts; but I believe it can be done, and for that reason I think we ought to make an effort to get J.H. in now. It may cost something, but I do not believe it is uncertain. I expect Vancouver is not the sort of man to spend much just for the sake of spite. The question of buying as a rule is another matter. None of us want that; but if the case is urgent I think there is no question about its being right. Of course it is a great pity J.H. said anything about protection in that speech. He did not mean to, but he could not help it, and at all events he had no idea his election was so near. If we are not certain of the result, J.H. ought to withdraw, because it will injure his chance at the vacancy to have him defeated now. That is all I have to say."

"I am of opinion," said the president, "that our best plan is to let John Harrington take his chance. You know who his opponent is, I suppose?"

"Ira C. Calvin," said Y and Z together.

"Calvin refused last night," said the president, "and they have put Jobbins in his place. Here is the telegram. It is code three," he remarked, handing it to Z.

Z read it, and his face expressed the greatest surprise.

"But Jobbins belongs to us," he cried. "He will not move hand or foot unless we advise him!"

"Of course," said the president. "But Mr. Ballymolloy does not know that, nor any other member of the Legislature. Harrington himself does not know it. Verdict, please."

"Verdict against buying," said Y.

"Naturally," said Z. "What a set of fools they are! How about withdrawing Harrington?"

"I object," said the president. "Proceed."

"I think it will injure his chance at the vacancy to have him defeated now, as I said before. That is all," said Z.

"I think it would be dangerous to withdraw him before so weak a man as Jobbins. It would hurt his reputation. Besides, our second man is in Washington arguing a case; and, after all, there is a bare chance that J.H. may win. If he does not, we win all the same, for Jobbins is in chains. Verdict, please."

Y was silent, and smoked thoughtfully. For five minutes no one spoke, and the president occupied the time in arranging some papers.

"Let him stand his chance," said Y, at last. In spite of the apparent informality of the meetings of the three, there was an unchangeable rule in their proceedings. Whenever a question arose, the member who first objected to the proposition argued the case briefly, or at length, with the proposer, and the third gave the verdict, against which there was no appeal.

These three strong men possessed between them an enormous power. It rarely happened that they could all meet together and settle upon their course of action by word of month, but constant correspondence and the use of an extensive set of telegraphic codes kept them in unbroken communication. No oaths or ceremonies bound them together, for they belonged to a small community of men which has existed from the earliest days of American independence, and which took its rise before that period.

Into this council of three, men of remarkable ability and spotless character were elected without much respect of age whenever a vacancy occurred. They worked quietly, with one immutable political purpose, with which they allowed no prejudiced party view to interfere. Always having under their immediate control some of the best talent in the country, and frequently commanding vast financial resources, these men and their predecessors had more than once turned the scale of the country's future. They had committed great mistakes, but they had also brought about noble results. It had frequently occurred that all the three members of the council simultaneously held seats in the senate, or that one or more were high in office. More than one President since Washington had sat at one time or another in the triumvirate; secretaries of state, orators, lawyers, financiers, and philanthropists had given the best years of their lives to the duties of the council; and yet, so perfect was the organization, the tests were so careful, and so marvelously profound was the insight of the leaders into human character, that of all these men, not one had ever betrayed the confidence placed in him. In the truest sense they and their immediate supporters formed an order; an order of true men, with whom the love of justice, honor, and freedom took the place of oath and ceremonial, binding them by stronger obligations than ever bound a ring of conspirators or a community of religious zealots.

The great element of secrecy as regards the outer world lay in the fact that only two men at any one time knew of the existence of the council of three, and these were those who were considered fit to sit in the council themselves. Even these two did not know more than one of the three leaders as such, though probably personally and even intimately acquainted with all three. The body of men whom the council controlled was ignorant of its existence therefore, and was composed of the personal adherents of each of the three. Manifestly one member of the council could, with the consent and cooperation of the other two, command the influence of the whole body of political adherents in favor of one of his friends, at any time, leaving the individual in entire ignorance of the power employed for his advancement. When a vacancy occurred in the council, by death or old age of any member, one of the two already designated took the place, while the other remained ignorant of the fact that any change had occurred, unless the vacancy was caused by the withdrawal of the member he had known, in which case he was put in communication with that member with whom he was most intimately acquainted. By this system of management no one man knew more than one of the actual leaders until he was himself one of the three. At the present time Z had been in the council nearly thirty years, and X for upwards of twenty, while Y, who was in reality fifty years old, had received his seat fifteen years before, at the age of thirty-five. A year ago one of the men selected to fill a possible vacancy had died, and John Harrington was chosen in his place.

It has been seen that the three kept a sort of political ledger, which was always in the hands of the president for the time being, whose duty it was to make the insertions necessary from time to time. Some conception of the extent and value of the book may be formed from the fact that it contained upwards of ten thousand names, including those of almost every prominent man, and of not a few remarkable women in the principal centres of the country. The details given were invariably brief and to the point, written down in a simple but safe form of cipher which was perfectly familiar to every one of the three. This vast mass of information was simply the outcome of the personal experience of the leaders, and of their trusted friends, but no detail which could by any possibility be of use escaped being committed to paper, and the result was in many cases a positive knowledge of future events, which, to any one unacquainted with the system, must have appeared little short of miraculous.

"What time is it in Boston?" inquired the president, rising and going to the writing-table.

"Twenty-eight minutes past seven," said Y, producing an enormous three-dial time-piece, set to indicate simultaneously the time of day in London, Boston, and Washington.

"All right, there is plenty of time," answered X, writing out a dispatch on a broad white sheet of cable office paper. "See here—is this all right?" he asked, when he had done.

The message ran as follows: "Do not withdraw. If possible gain Ballymolloy and men, but on no account pay for them. If asked, say iron protection necessary at present, and probably for many years."

Y and Z read the telegram, and said it would do. In ten minutes it was taken to the telegraph office by X's servant.

"And now," said X, lighting a fresh cigar, "we have disposed of this accident, and we can turn to our regular business. The question is broadly, what effect will be produced by suddenly throwing eight or ten millions of English money into an American enterprise?"

"When Englishmen are not making money, they are a particularly disagreeable set of people to deal with," remarked Y, who would have been taken for an Englishman himself in any part of the world.

And so the council left John Harrington, and turned to other matters which do not in any way concern this tale.

John received the dispatch at half-past ten o'clock in the morning after the dinner at Mrs. Wyndham's, and he read it without comprehending precisely the position taken by his instructor. Nevertheless, the order coincided with what he would have done if left to himself. He of course could not know that even if his opponent were elected it would be a gain to his own party, for the outward life of Mr. Jobbins gave no cause for believing that he was in anybody's power. Harrington was left to suppose that, if he failed to get the votes of Patrick Ballymolloy and his party, the election would be a dead loss. Nevertheless, he rejoiced that the said Patrick was not to be bought. An honorable failure, wherein he might honestly say that he had bribed no one, nor used any undue pressure, would in his opinion be better than to be elected ten times over by money and promises of political jobbery.

The end rarely justifies the means, and there are means so foul that they would blot any result into their own filthiness. All that the world can write; or think, or say, will never make it honorable or noble to bribe and tell lies. Men who lie are not brave because they are willing to be shot at, in some instances, by the men their falsehoods have injured. Men who pay others to agree with them are doing a wrong upon the dignity of human nature, and they very generally end by saying that human nature has no dignity at all, and very possibly by being themselves corrupted.

Nevertheless, so great is the interest which men, even upright and honorable men, take in the aims they follow, that they believe it possible to wade knee-deep through mud, and then ascend to the temple of fame without dragging the mud with them, and befouling the white marble steps.

"Political necessity!" What deeds are done in thy name! What a merciful and polite goddess was the necessity of the ancients, compared with the necessity of the moderns. Political necessity has been hard at work in our times from Robespierre to Sedan, from St. Helena to the Vatican, from the Tea-chests of Boston Harbor to the Great Rebellion. Political necessity has done more lying, more bribery, more murdering, and more stealing in a century, than could have been invented by all the Roman emperors together, with the assistance of the devil himself.

Chapter XIV

In all the endless folk-lore of proverbs, there is perhaps no adage more true than that which warns young people to beware of a new love until they have done with the old, and as Ronald Surbiton reflected on his position, the old rhyme ran through his head. Ho was strongly attracted by Sybil Brandon, but, at the same time, he still felt that he ought to make an effort to win Joe back. It seemed so unmanly to relinquish her without a struggle, just because she said she did not love him. It could not be true, for they had loved each other so long.

When Ronald looked out of the window of his room in the hotel, on the morning after Mrs. Wyndham's dinner, the snow was falling as it can only fall in Boston. The great houses opposite were almost hidden from view by the soft, fluttering flakes, and below, in the broad street, the horse-cars moved slowly along like immense white turtles ploughing their way through deep white sand. The sound of the bells was muffled as it came up, and the scraping of the Irishmen's heavy spades on the pavement before the hotel followed by the regular fall of the great shovels full on the heap, as they stacked the snow, sounded like the digging of a gigantic grave.

Ronald felt that his spirits were depressed. He watched the drifting storm for a few minutes, and then turned away and looked for a novel in his bag, and filled a pipe with some English tobacco he had jealously guarded from the lynx-eyed custom-house men in New York, and then sat down with a sigh before his small coal fire, and prepared to pass the morning, in solitude.

But Ronald was not fond of reading, and at the end of half an hour he threw his book and his pipe aside, and stretched his long limbs. Then he rose and went to the window again with an expression of utter weariness such as only an Englishman can put on when he is thoroughly bored. The snow was falling as thickly as ever, and the turtle-backed horse-cars crawled by through the drifts, more and more slowly. Ronald turned away with an impatient ejaculation, and made up his mind that he would go and see Joe at once. He wrapped himself carefully in a huge ulster overcoat and went out.

Joe was sitting alone in the drawing-room, curled up in an old-fashioned arm-chair by the fire, with a book in her lap which she was not reading. She had asked her aunt for something about politics, and Miss Schenectady had given her the "Life of Rufus Choate," in two large black volumes. The book was interesting, but in Joe's mind it was but a step from the speeches and doings of the great and brilliant lawyer-senator to the speeches and doings of John Harrington. And so after a while the book dropped upon her knee and she leaned far back in the chair, her great brown eyes staring dreamily at the glowing coals.

"I was so awfully lonely," said Ronald, sitting down beside her, "that I came here. You do not mind, Joe, do you?"

"Mind? No! I am very glad. It must be dreadfully lonely for you at the hotel. What have you been doing with yourself?"

"Oh—trying to read. And then, I was thinking about you."

"That is not much of an occupation. See how industrious I am. I have been reading the 'Life and Writings of Rufus Choate.' I am getting to be a complete Bostonian."

"Have you read it all? I never heard of him. Who was he?"

"He was an extremely clever man. He must have been very nice, and his speeches are splendid. You ought to read them."

"Joe, you are going to be a regular blue-stocking! The idea of spending your time in reading such stuff. Why, it would be almost better to read the parliamentary reports in the 'Times!' Just fancy!" Ronald laughed at the idea of any human being descending to such drudgery.

"Don't be silly, Ronald. You do not know anything about it," said Joe.

"Oh, it is of no use discussing the question," answered Ronald. "You young women are growing altogether too clever, with your politics, and your philosophy, and your culture. I hate America!"

"If you really knew anything about it, you would like it very much. Besides, you have no right to say you hate it. The people here have been very good to you already. You ought not to abuse them."

"No—not the people. But just look at that snow-storm, Joe, and tell me whether America is a place for human beings to live in."

"It is much prettier than a Scotch mist, and ever so much clearer than a fog in London," retorted Joe.

"But there is nothing for a fellow to do on a day like this," said Ronald sulkily.

"Nothing, but to come and see his cousin, and abuse everything to her, and try to make her as discontented as himself," said Joe, mimicking his tone.

"If I thought you liked me to come and see you"—began Ronald.

"Well?"

"It would be different, you know."

"I like you when you are nice and good-tempered," said Joe. "But when you are bored you are simply—well, you are dreadful." Joe raised her eyebrows and tapped with her fingers on the arm of the chair.

"Do you think I can ever be bored when I come to see you, Joe?" asked Ronald, changing his tone.

"You act as if you were, precisely. You know people who are bored are generally bores themselves."

"Thanks," said Ronald. "How kind you are!"

"Do say something nice, Ronald. You have done nothing but find fault since you came. Have you heard from home?"

"No. There has not been time yet. Why do you ask?"

"Because I thought you might say something less disagreeable about home than you seem able to say about things here," said Joe tartly.

"You do not want me this morning. I will go away again," said Ronald with a gloomy frown. He rose to his feet, as though about to take his leave.

"Oh, don't go, Ronald." He paused. "Besides," added Joe, "Sybil will be here in a little while."

"You need not offer me Miss Brandon as an inducement to stay with you, Joe, if you really want me. Twenty Miss Brandons would not make any difference!"

"Really?" said Joe smiling. "You are a dear good boy, Ronald, when you are nice," she added presently. "Sit down again."

Ronald went back to his seat beside her, and they were both silent for a while. Joe repented a little, for she thought she had been teasing him, and she reflected that she ought to be doing her best to make him happy.

"Joe—do not you think it would be very pleasant to be always like this?" said Ronald after a time.

"How—like this?"

"Together," said Ronald softly, and a gentle look came into his handsome face, as he looked up at his cousin. "Together—only in our own home."

Joe did not answer, but the color came to her cheeks, and she looked annoyed. She had hoped that the matter was settled forever, for it seemed so easy for her. Ronald misinterpreted the blush. For the moment the old conviction came back to him that she was to be his wife, and if it was not exactly love that he felt, it was a satisfaction almost great enough to take its place.

"Would it not?" said he presently.

"Please do not talk about it, Ronald. What is the use? I have said all there is to say, I am sure."

"But I have not," he answered, insisting. "Please, Joe dearest, think about it seriously. Think what a cruel thing it is you are doing." His voice was very tender, but he was perfectly calm; there was not the slightest vibration of passion in the tones. Joe did not wholly understand; she only knew that he was not satisfied with the first explanation she had given him, and that she felt sorry for him, but was incapable of changing her decision.

"Must I go over it all again?" she asked piteously. "Did I not make it clear to you, Ronald? Oh—don't talk about it!"

"You have no heart, Joe," said Ronald hotly. "You don't know what you make me suffer. You don't know that this sort of thing is enough to wreck a man's existence altogether. You don't know what you are doing, because you have no heart—not the least bit of one."

"Do not say that—please do not," Joe entreated, looking at him with imploring eyes, for his words hurt her. Then suddenly the tears came in a quick hot gush, and she hid her face in her hands. "Oh, Ronald, Ronald—it is you who do not know," she sobbed.

Ronald did not quite know what to do; he never did when Joe cried, but fortunately that disaster had not occurred often since he was very small. He was angry with himself for having disturbed and hurt her, but he did not know what to do, most probably because he did not really love her.

"Joe," he said, looking at her in some embarrassment, "don't!" Then he rose and rather timidly laid a hand on her shoulder. But she shrank from him with a petulant motion, and the tears trickled through her small white hands and fell upon her dark dress and on the "Life of Rufus Choate."

"Joe, dear"—Ronald began again. And then, in great uncertainty of mind, he went and looked out of the window. Presently he came back and stood before her once more.

"I am awfully sorry I said it, Joe. Please forgive me. You don't often cry, you know, and so"—He hesitated.

Joe looked up at him with a smile through her tears, beautiful as a rose just wet with a summer shower.

"And so—you did not think I could," she said. She dried her eyes quickly and rose to her feet. "It is very silly of me, I know, but I cannot help it in the least," said she, turning from him in pretense of arranging the knickknacks on the mantel.

"Of course you cannot help it, Joe, dear; as if you had not a perfect right to cry, if you like! I am such a brute—I know."

"Come and look at the snow," said Joe, taking his hand and leading him to the window. Enormous Irishmen in pilot coats, comforters, and india-rubber boots, armed with broad wooden spades, were struggling to keep the drifts from the pavement. Joe and Ronald stood and watched them idly, absorbed in their own thoughts.

Presently a booby sleigh drawn by a pair of strong black horses floundered up the hill and stopped at the door.

"Oh, Ronald, there is Sybil, and she will see I have been crying. You must amuse her, and I will come back in a few minutes." She turned and fled, leaving Ronald at the window.

A footman sprang to the ground, and nearly lost his footing in the snow as he opened a large umbrella and rang the bell. In a moment Sybil was out of the sleigh and at the door of the house; she could not sit still till it was opened, although the flakes were falling as thickly as ever.

"Oh"—she exclaimed, as she entered the room and was met by Ronald, "I thought Joe was here." There was color in her face, and she took Ronald's hand cordially. He blushed to the eyes, and stammered.

"Miss Thorn is—she—indeed, she will be back in a moment. How do you do? Dreadful weather, is not it?"

"Oh, it is only a snowstorm," said Sybil, brushing a few flakes from her furs as she came near the fire. "We do not mind it at all here. But of course you never have snow in England."

"Not like this, certainly," said Ronald. "Let me help you," he added, as Sybil began to remove her cloak.

It was a very sudden change of company for Ronald; five minutes ago he was trying, very clumsily and hopelessly, to console Joe Thorn in her tears, feeling angry enough with himself all the while for having caused them. Now he was face to face with Sybil Brandon, the most beautiful woman he remembered to have seen, and she smiled at him as he took her heavy cloak from her shoulders, and the touch of the fur sent a thrill to his heart, and the blood to his cheeks.

"I must say," he remarked, depositing the things on a sofa, "you are very courageous to come out, even though you are used to it."

"You have come yourself," said Sybil, laughing a little. "You told me last night that you did not come here every day."

"Oh—I told my cousin I had come because I was so lonely at the hotel. It is amazingly dull to sit all day in a close room, reading stupid novels."

"I should think it would be. Have you nothing else to do?"

"Nothing in the wide world," said Ronald with a smile. "What should I do here, in a strange place, where I know so few people?"

"I suppose there is not much for a man to do, unless he is in business. Every one here is in some kind of business, you know, so they are never bored."

Ronald wished he could say the right thing to reestablish the half-intimacy he had felt when talking to Sybil the night before. But it was not easy to get back to the same point. There was an interval of hours between yesterday and to-day—and there was Joe.

"I read novels to pass the time," he said, "and because they are sometimes so like one's own life. But when they are not, they bore me."

Sybil was fond of reading, and she was especially fond of fiction, not because she cared for sensational interests, but because she was naturally contemplative, and it interested her to read about the human nature of the present, rather than to learn what any individual historian thought of the human nature of the past.

"What kind of novels do you like best?" she asked, sitting down to pass the time with Ronald until Josephine should make her appearance.

"I like love stories best," said Ronald.

"Oh, of course," said Sybil gravely, "so do I. But what kind do you like best? The sad ones, or those that end well?"

"I like them to end well," said Ronald, "because the best ones never do, you know."

"Never?" There was something in Sybil's tone that made Ronald look quickly at her. She said the word as though she, too, had something to regret.

"Not in my experience," answered Surbiton, with the decision of a man past loving or being loved.

"How dreadfully gloomy! One would think you had done with life, Mr. Surbiton," said Sybil, laughing.

"Sometimes I think so, Miss Brandon," answered Ronald in solemn tones.

"I suppose we all think it would be nice to die, sometimes. But then the next morning things look so much brighter."

"I think they often look much brighter in the evening," said Ronald, thinking of the night before.

"I am sure something disagreeable has happened to you to-day, Mr. Surbiton," said Sybil, looking at him. Ronald looked into her eyes as though to see if there were any sympathy there.

"Yes, something disagreeable has happened to me," he answered slowly. "Something very disagreeable and painful."

"I am sorry," said Sybil simply. But her voice sounded very kind and comforting.

"That is why I say that love stories always end badly in real life," said Ronald. "But I suppose I ought not to complain." It was not until he had thought over this speech, some minutes later, that he realized that in a few words he had told Sybil the main part of his troubles. He never guessed that she was so far in Joe's confidence as to have heard the whole story before. But Sybil was silent and thoughtful.

"Love is such an uncertain thing," she began, after a pause; and it chanced that at that very moment Joe opened the door and entered the room. She caught the sentence.

"So you are instructing my cousin," she said to Sybil, laughing. "I approve of the way you spend your time, my children!" No one would have believed that, twenty minutes earlier, Joe had been in tears. She was as fresh and as gay as ever, and Ronald said to himself that she most certainly had no heart, but that Sybil had a great deal,—he was sure of it from the tone of her voice.

"What is the news about the election, Sybil?" she asked. "Of course you know all about it at the Wyndhams'."

"My dear, the family politics are in a state of confusion that is simply too delightful," said Sybil.

"You know it is said that Ira C. Calvin has refused to be a candidate, and the Republicans mean to put in Mr. Jobbins in his place, who is such a popular man, and so good and benevolent-quite a philanthropist."

"Does it make very much difference?" asked Joe anxiously. "I wish I understood all about it, but the local names are so hard to learn."

"I thought you had been learning them all the morning in Choate," put in Ronald, who perceived that the conversation was to be about Harrington.

"It does make a difference," said Sybil, not noticing Ronald's remark, "because Jobbins is much more popular than Calvin, and they say he is a friend of Patrick Ballymolloy, who will win the election for either side he favors."

"Who is this Irishman?" inquired Ronald.

"He is the chief Irishman," said Sybil laughing, "and I cannot describe him any better. He has twenty votes with him, and as things stand he always carries whichever point he favors. But Mr. Wyndham says he is glad he is not in the Legislature, because it would drive him out of his mind to decide on which side to vote—though he is a good Republican, you know."

"Of course he could vote for Mr. Harrington in spite of that," said Joe, confidently. "Anybody would, who knows him, I am sure. But when is the election to come off?"

"They say it is to begin to-day," said Sybil.

"We shall never hear anything unless we go to Mrs. Wyndham's," said Joe. "Aunt Zoë is awfully clever, and that, but she never knows in the least what is going on. She says she does not understand politics."

"If you were a Bostonian, Mr. Surbiton," said Sybil, "you would get into the State House and hear the earliest news."

"I will do anything in the world to oblige you," said Ronald gravely, "if you will only explain a little"—

"Oh no! It is quite impossible. Come with me, both of you, and we will get some lunch at the Wyndhams' and hear all about it by telephone."

"Very well," said Joe. "One moment, while I get my things." She left the room. Ronald and Sybil were again alone together.

"You were saying when my cousin came in, that love was a very uncertain thing," suggested Ronald, rather timidly.

"Was I?" said Sybil, standing before the mirror above the mantelpiece, and touching her hat first on one side and then on the other.

"Yes," answered Ronald, watching her. "Do you know, I have often thought so too."

"Yes?"

"I think it would be something different if it were quite certain. Perhaps it would be something much less interesting, but much better."

"I think you are a little confused, Mr. Surbiton," said Sybil, and as she smiled, Ronald could see her face reflected in the mirror.

"I—yes—that is—I dare say I am," said he, hesitatingly. "But I know exactly what I mean."

"But do you know exactly what you want?" she asked with a laugh.

"Yes indeed," said he confidently. "But I do not believe I shall ever get it."

"Then that is the 'disagreeable and painful thing' you referred to, as having happened this morning, I suppose," remarked Sybil, calmly, as she turned to take up her cloak which lay on the sofa. Ronald blushed scarlet.

"Well—yes," he said, forgetting in his embarrassment to help her.

"It is so heavy," said Sybil. "Thanks. Do you know that you have been making confidences to me, Mr. Surbiton?" she asked, turning and facing him, with a half-amused, half-serious look in her blue eyes.

"I am afraid I have," he answered, after a short pause. "You must think I am very foolish."

"Never mind," she said gravely. "They are safe with me."

"Thanks," said Ronald in a low voice.

Josephine entered the room, clad in many furs, and a few minutes later all three were on their way to Mrs. Wyndham's, the big booby sleigh rocking and leaping and ploughing in the heavy dry snow.

Chapter XV

Pocock Vancouver was also abroad in the snowstorm. He would not in any case have stayed at home on account of the weather, but on this particular morning he had very urgent business with a gentleman who, like Lamb, rose with the lark, though he did not go to bed with the chickens. There are no larks in Boston, but the scream of the locomotives answers nearly as well.

Vancouver accordingly had himself driven at an early hour to a certain house not situated in the West End, but of stone quite as brown, and having a bay window as prominent as any sixteen-foot-front on Beacon Street; those advantages, however, did not prevent Mr. Vancouver from wearing an expression of fastidious scorn as he mounted the steps and pulled the polished German silver handle of the door-bell. The curl on his lip gave way to a smile of joyous cordiality as he was ushered into the presence of the owner of the house.

"Indeed, I'm glad to see you, Mr. Vancouver," said his host, whose extremely Celtic appearance was not belied by unctuous modulation of his voice, and the pleasant roll of his softly aspirated consonants.

This great man was no other than Mr. Patrick Ballymolloy. He received Vancouver in his study, which was handsomely furnished with bright green wall-paper, a sideboard on which stood a number of decanters and glasses, several leather easy-chairs, and a green china spittoon.

In personal appearance, Mr. Patrick Ballymolloy was vastly more striking than attractive. He was both corpulent and truculent, and his hands and feet were of a size and thickness calculated to crush a paving-stone at a step, or to fell an ox at a blow. The nails of his fingers were of a hue which is made artificially fashionable in eastern countries, but which excites prejudice in western civilization from an undue display of real estate. A neck which the Minotaur might have justly envied surmounted the thickness and roundness of Mr. Ballymolloy's shoulders, and supported a head more remarkable for the immense cavity of the mouth, and for a quantity of highly pomaded sandy hair, than for any intellectuality of the brows or high-bred fineness of the nose. Mr. Ballymolloy's nose was nevertheless an astonishing feature, and at a distance called vividly to mind the effect of one of those great glass bottles of reddened water, behind which apothecaries of all degrees put a lamp at dusk in order that their light may the better shine in the darkness. It was one of the most surprising feats of nature's alchemy that a liquid so brown as that contained in the decanters on Patrick's sideboard should be able to produce and maintain anything so supernaturally red as Patrick's nose.

Mr. Ballymolloy was clad in a beautiful suit of shiny black broadcloth, and the front of his coat was irregularly but richly adorned with a profusion of grease-spots of all sizes. A delicate suggestive mezzotint shaded the edges of his collar and cuffs, and from his heavy gold watch-chain depended a malachite seal of unusual greenness and brilliancy.

Vancouver took the gigantic outstretched hand of his host in his delicate fingers, with an air of cordiality which, if not genuine, was very well assumed.

"I'm glad to see you, sir," said the Irishman again.

"Thanks," said Vancouver, "and I am fortunate in finding you at home."

Mr. Ballymolloy smiled, and pushed one of his leather easy-chairs towards the fire. Both men sat down.

"I suppose you are pretty busy over this election, Mr. Ballymolloy," said Vancouver; blandly.

"Now, that's just it, Mr. Vancouver," replied the Irishman. "That's just exactly what's the matter with me, for indeed I am very busy, and that's the truth."

"Just so, Mr. Ballymolloy. Especially since the change last night. I remember what a good friend you have always been to Mr. Jobbins."

"Well, as you say, Mr. Vancouver, I have been thinking that I and Mr. Jobbins are pretty good friends, and that's just about what it is, I think."

"Yes, I remember that on more than one occasion you and he have acted together in the affairs of the state," said Vancouver, thoughtfully.

"'Ah, but it's the soul of him that I like," answered Mr. Ballymolloy very sweetly. "He has such a beautiful soul, Mr. Jobbins; it does me good, and indeed it does, Mr. Vancouver."

"As you say, sir, a man full of broad human sympathies. Nevertheless I feel sure that on the present occasion your political interests will lead you to follow the promptings of duty, and to vote in favor of the Democratic candidate. I wish you and I did not differ in politics, Mr. Ballymolloy."

"And, indeed, there is not so very much difference, if it comes to that, Mr. Vancouver," replied Patrick in conciliating tones. "But it's just what I have been thinking, that I will vote for Mr. Harrington. It's a matter of principle with me, Mr. Vancouver, and that's it exactly."

"And where should we all be without principles, Mr. Ballymolloy? Indeed I may say that the importance of principles in political matters is very great."

"And it's just the greatest pity in the world that every one has not principles like you, Mr. Vancouver. I'm speaking the truth now." According to Mr. Patrick Ballymolloy's view of destiny, it was the truth and nothing but the truth. He knew Vancouver of old, and Vancouver knew him.

"You flatter me, sir," said Pocock, affecting a pleased smile. "To tell the truth, there is a little matter I wanted to speak to you about, if you can spare me half an hour.".

"Indeed, I'm most entirely delighted to be at your service, Mr. Vancouver, and I'm glad you came so early in the morning."

"The fact is, Mr. Ballymolloy, we are thinking of making an extension on one of our lines; a small matter, but of importance to us."

"I guess it must be the branch of the Pocahontas and Dead Man's Valley you'll be speaking of, Mr. Vancouver," said the Irishman, with sudden and cheerful interest.

"Really, Mr. Ballymolloy, you are a man of the most surprising quickness. It is a real pleasure to talk with you on such matters. I have no doubt you understand the whole question thoroughly."

"Well, it's of no use at all to say I know nothing about it, because I have heard it mentioned, and that's the plain truth, Mr. Vancouver. And it will take a deal of rail, too, and that's another thing. And where do you think of getting the iron from, Mr. Vancouver?"

"Well, I had hoped, Mr. Ballmolly," said Vancouver, with some affected hesitation, "that as an old friend, we might be able to manage matters with you. But, of course, this is entirely unofficial, and between ourselves."

Mr. Ballymolloy nodded with something very like a wink of one bloodshot eye. He knew what he was about.

"And when will you be thinking of beginning the work, Mr. Vancouver?" he inquired, after a short pause.

"That is just the question, or rather, perhaps, I should say the difficulty. We do not expect to begin work for a year or so."

"And surely that makes no difference, then, at all," returned Patrick. "For the longer the time, the easier it will be for me to accommodate you."

"Ah—but you see, Mr. Ballymolloy, it may be that in a year's time these new-fangled ideas about free trade may be law, and it may be much cheaper for us to get our rails from England, as Mr. Vanderbilt did three or four years ago, when he was in such a hurry, you remember."

"And, indeed, I remember it very well, Mr. Vancouver."

"Just so. Now you see, Mr. Ballymolloy, I am speaking to you entirely as a friend, though I hope I may before long bring about an official agreement. But you see the difficulty of making a contract a year ahead, when a party of Democratic senators and Congressmen may by that time have upset the duty on steel rails, don't you?"

"And indeed, I see it as plain as day, Mr. Vancouver. And that's why I was saying I wished every one had such principles as yourself, and I'm telling you no lie when I say it again." Verily Mr. Ballymolloy was a truthful person!

"Very well. Now, do not you think, Mr. Ballymolloy, that all this talk about free trade is great nonsense?"

"And, surely, it will be the ruin of the whole country, Mr. Vancouver."

"Besides, free trade has nothing to do with Democratic principles, has it? You see here am I, the best Republican in Massachusetts, and here are you, the best Democrat in the country, and we both agree in saying that it is great nonsense to leave iron unprotected."

"Ah, it's the principle of you I like, Mr. Vancouver!" exclaimed Ballymolloy in great admiration. "It's your principles are beautiful, just!"

"Very good, sir. Now of course you are going to vote for Mr. Harrington to-day, or to-morrow, or whenever the election is to be. Don't you think yon might say something to him that would be of some use? I believe he is very uncertain about protection, you see. I think you could persuade him, somehow."

"Well, now, Mr. Vancouver, it's the truth when I tell you I was just thinking of speaking to him about it, just a little, before I went up to the State House. And indeed I'll be going to him immediately."

"I think it is the wisest plan," said Vancouver, rising to go, "and we will speak about the contract next week, when all this election business is over."

"Ah, and indeed, I hope it will be soon, sir," said Ballymolloy. "But you'll not think of going out again in the snow without taking a drop of something, will you, Mr. Vancouver?" He went to the sideboard and poured out two stiff doses of the amber liquid.

"Since you are so kind," said Vancouver, graciously taking the proffered glass. He knew better than to refuse to drink over a bargain.

"Well, here goes," he said.

"And luck to yourself, Mr. Vancouver," said Ballymolloy.

"I think you can persuade him, somehow," said Vancouver, as his host opened the street-door for him to go out.

"And, indeed, I think so too," said Ballymolloy. Then he went back to his study and poured out a second glass of whiskey. "And if I cannot persuade him," he continued in soliloquy, "why, then, it will just be old Jobbins who will be senator, and that's the plain truth."

Vancouver went away with a light heart, and the frank smile on his delicate features was most pleasant to see. He knew John Harrington well, and he was certain that Mr. Ballymolloy's proposal would rouse the honest wrath of the man he detested.

Half an hour later Mr. Ballymolloy entered Harrington's room in Charles Street. John was seated at the table, fully dressed, and writing letters. He offered his visitor a seat.

"So the election is coming on right away, Mr. Harrington," began Patrick, making himself comfortable, and lighting one of John's cigars.

"So I hear, Mr. Ballymolloy," answered John with a pleasant smile. "I hope I may count on you, in spite of what you said yesterday. These are the times when men must keep together."

"Now Mr. Harrington, you'll not believe that I could go to the House and vote against my own party, surely, will you now?" said Patrick. But there was a tinge of irony in his soft tones. He knew that Vancouver could make him great and advantageous business transactions, and he treated him accordingly. John Harrington was, on the other hand, a mere candidate for his twenty votes; he could make John senator if he chose, or defeat him, if he preferred it, and he accordingly behaved to John with an air of benevolent superiority. "I trust you would do no such thing, Mr. Ballymolloy," said John gravely. "Without advocating myself as in any way fit for the honors of the Senate, I can say that it is of the utmost importance that we should have as many Democrats in Congress as possible, in the Senate as well as in the House."

"Surely you don't think I doubt that, Mr. Harrington? And indeed the Senate is pretty well Democratic as it is."

"Yes," said John, smiling, "but the more the better, I should think. It is a very different matter from the local legislature, where changes may often do good."

"Indeed and it is, Mr. Harrington. And will you please to tell me what you will do about free trade, when you're in the Senate, sir?"

"I am afraid I cannot tell you anything that I did not tell you yesterday, Mr. Ballymolloy. I am a tariff reform man. It is a great Democratic movement, and I should be bound to support it, even if I were not myself so thorough a believer in it as I am."

"Now see here, Mr. Harrington, it's the gospel truth I'm telling you, when I say you're mistaken. Here are plenty of us Democrats who don't want the least little bit of free trade. I'm in the iron business, Mr. Harrington, and you won't be after thinking me such an all-powerful galoot as to cut my own nose off, will you?"

"Well, not exactly," said John, who was used to many peculiarities of language in his visitors. "But, of course, iron will be the thing last on the tariff. I am of opinion that it is necessary to put enough tax on iron to protect home-producers at the time of greatest depression. That is fair, is not it?"

"I dare say you may think so, Mr. Harrington," said Ballymolloy, knocking the ashes from his cigar. "But you are not an iron man, now, are you?"

"Certainly not," said John. "But I have studied the question, and I know its importance. In a reformation of the tariff, iron would be one of the things most carefully provided for."

"Oh, I know all that," said Ballymolloy, somewhat roughly, "and there's not much you can tell me about tariff reform that I don't know, neither. And when you have reformed other things, you'll be for reforming iron, too, just to keep your hands in. And, indeed, I've no objection whatever to your reforming everything you like, so long as you don't interfere with me and mine. But I don't trust the principles of the thing, sir; I don't trust them the least little bit, and for me I would rather there were not to be any reforming at all, except for the Chinamen, and I don't care much for them, neither, and that's a fact."

"Very good, Mr. Ballymolloy. Every man has a right to his free opinion. But we stand on the reform platform, for there is no country in the world where reform is more needed than it is here. I can only repeat that the interests of the iron trade stand high with the Democratic party, and that it is highly improbable that any law will interfere with iron for many years. I cannot say more than that and yet stick to facts."

"Always stick to facts, Mr. Harrington. You will find the truth a very important thing indeed, and good principles too, in dealing with plain-spoken men like myself, sir. Stick to the truth, Mr. Harrington, forever and ever."

"I propose to, Mr. Ballymolloy," answered John, internally amused at the solemn manner of his interlocutor.

"And then I will put the matter to you, Mr. Harrington, and indeed it's a plain matter, too, and not the least taste of dishonesty in it, at all. I've been thinking I'd make you senator if you'll agree to go against free trade, and that's just what I'll do, and no more."

"It is impossible for me to make such a bargain, Mr. Ballymolloy. After your exposition of the importance of truth I am surprised that you should expect me to belie my whole political life. As I have told you, I am prepared to support laws to protect iron as much as is necessary. Free trade nowadays does not mean cutting away all duties; it means a proper adjustment of them to the requirements of our commerce. A proper adjustment of duties could not possibly be interpreted to mean any injury to the iron trade. You may rely upon that, at all events."

"Oh, and I'm sure I can," said Ballymolloy incredulously, and he grew, if possible, redder in the face than nature and the action of alcohol had made him. "And I'm not only sure of it, but I'll swear it's gospel truth. But then, you know, I'm of opinion that by the time you've done reforming the other things, the reformed gentlemen won't like it, and then they'll just turn round and eat you up unless you reform us too, and that just means the ruin of us."

"Come now, Mr. Ballymolloy, that is exaggeration," said John. "If you will listen to me for a moment"—

"I haven't got the time, sir, and that's all about it. If you'll protect our interests and promise to do it, you'll be senator. The election is coming on, Mr. Harrington, and I'd be sorry to see you thrown out."

"Mr. Ballymolloy, I had sincerely hoped that you would support me in this matter, but I must tell you once more that I think you are unreasonable. I vouch for the sufficient protection of your interests, because it is the belief of our party that they need protection. But it is not necessary for you to have an anti-reform senator for that purpose, in the first place; and secondly, the offer of a seat in the Senate would never induce me to change my mind, nor to turn round and deny everything that I have said and written on the subject."

"Then that is your last word of all, Mr. Harrington?" said Ballymolloy, heaving his heavy body out of the easy-chair. But his voice, which had sounded somewhat irate during the discussion, again rolled out in mellifluous tones.

"Yes, Mr. Ballymolloy, that is all I have to say."

"And indeed it's not so very bad at all," said Patrick. "You see I just wanted to see how far you were likely to go, because, though I'm a good Democrat, sir, I'm against free trade in the main points, and that's just the truth. But if you say you will stand up for iron right through, and use your best judgment, why, I guess you'll have to be senator after all. It's a great position, Mr. Harrington, and I hope you'll do honor to it."

"I hope so, indeed," said John. "Can I offer you a glass of wine, or anything else, Mr. Ballymolloy?"

"Indeed, and it's dirty weather, too," said Patrick. "Thank you, I'll take a little whiskey."

John poured out a glass.

"You won't let me drink alone, Mr. Harrington?" inquired Patrick, holding his tumbler in his hand. To oblige him, after the manner of the country, John poured out a small glass of sherry, and put his lips to it. Ballymolloy drained the whiskey to the last drop.

"You were not really thinking I would vote for Mr. Jobbins, were you now, Mr. Harrington?" he asked, with a sly look on his red face.

"I always hope that the men of my party are to be relied upon, Mr. Ballymolloy," said John, smiling politely.

"Very well, they are to be relied upon, sir. We are, every man of us, to the last drop of Christian blood in our blessed bodies," said Patrick, with a gush of patriotic enthusiasm, at the same time holding out his heavy hand. Then he took his leave.

"You had better have said 'to the last drop of Bourbon whiskey in the blessed bottle!'" said John to himself when his visitor was gone. Then he sat down for a while to think over the situation.

"That man will vote against me yet," he thought.

He was astonished to find himself nervous and excited for the first time in his life. With characteristic determination he went back to his desk, and continued the letter which the visit of the Irish elector had interrupted.

Meanwhile Mr. Patrick Ballymolloy was driven to the house of the Republican candidate, Mr. Jobbing.

Chapter XVI

Sybil was right when she said the family politics at the Wyndhams' were disturbed. Indeed the disturbance was so great that Mrs. Wyndham was dressed and down-stairs before twelve o'clock, which had never before occurred in the memory of the oldest servant.

"It is too perfectly exciting, my dears," she exclaimed as Joe and Sybil entered the room, followed—at a respectful distance by Ronald. "I can't stand it one minute longer! How do you do, Mr. Surbiton?"

"What is the latest news?" asked Sybil.

"I have not heard anything for ever so long. Sam has gone round to see— perhaps he will be back soon. I do wish we had 'tickers' here in the house, as they do in New York; it is such fun watching when anything is going on."

She walked about the room as she talked, touching a book on one table and a photograph on another, in a state of great excitement. Ronald watched her in some surprise; it seemed odd to him that any one should take so much interest in a mere election. Joe and Sybil, who knew her better, made themselves at home.

It appeared that although Sam had gone to make inquiries, it was very improbable that anything would be known until late in the afternoon. There was to be a contest of some sort, but whether it would end in a single day, or whether Ballymolloy and his men intended to prolong the struggle for their own ends, remained to be seen.

Meanwhile Mrs. Wyndham walked about her drawing-room descanting upon the iniquities of political life, with an animation that delighted Joe and amused Ronald.

"Well, there is nothing for it, you see," she said at last. "Sam evidently does not mean to come home, and you must just stay here and have some lunch until he does."

The three agreed, nothing loath to enjoying one another's company. There is nothing like a day spent together in waiting for an event, to bring out the characteristics of individuals. Mrs. Wyndham fretted and talked, and fretted again. Joe grew silent, pale, and anxious as the morning passed, while Sybil and Ronald seemed to enjoy themselves extremely, and talked without ceasing. Outside the snow fell thick and fast as ever, and the drifts rose higher and higher.

"I do wish Sam would come back," exclaimed Mrs. Wyndham at last, as she threw herself into an easy-chair, and looked at the clock.

But Sam did not come, nevertheless, and Joe sat quietly by the fire, wishing she were alone, and yet unwilling to leave the house where she hoped to have the earliest information.

The two who seemed rapidly growing indifferent to the issue of the election were Sybil and Ronald, who sat together with a huge portfolio of photographs and sketches between them, laughing and talking pleasantly enough. Joe did not hear a word of their conversation, and Mrs. Wyndham paid little attention to it, though her practiced ears could have heard it all if need be, while she herself was profoundly occupied with some one else.

The four had a somewhat dreary meal together, and Ronald was told to go into Sam's study and smoke if he liked, while Mrs. Wyndham led Joe and Sybil away to look at a quantity of new things that had just come from Paris. Ronald did as he was bid and settled himself for an hour, with a plentiful supply of newspapers and railroad literature.

It was past three o'clock when Sam Wyndham entered the room, his face wet with the snowflakes and red with excitement.

"Hollo!" he exclaimed, seeing Ronald comfortably ensconced in his favorite easy-chair. "How are you?"

"Excuse me," said Ronald, rising quickly. "They told me to come in here after lunch, and so I was waiting until I was sent for, or told to come out."

"Very glad to see you, any way," said Sam cordially. "Well, I have been to hear about an election—a friend of ours got put up for senator. But I don't expect that interests you much?"

"On the contrary," said Ronald, "I have heard it so much talked of that I am as much interested as anybody. Is it all over?"

"Oh yes, and a pretty queer business it was. Well, our friend is not elected, anyway"—

"Has Mr. Harrington been defeated?" asked Ronald quickly.

"It's my belief he has been sold," said Sam. "But as I am a Republican myself and a friend of Jobbins, more or less, I don't suppose I feel so very bad about it, after all. But I don't know how my wife will take it, I'm sure," said Sam presently. "I expect we had better go and tell her, right off."

"Then he has really lost the election?" inquired Ronald, who was not altogether sorry to hear it.

"Why, yes—as I say, Jobbins is senator now. I should not wonder if Harrington were a good deal cut up. Come along with me, now, and we will tell the ladies."

The three ladies were in the drawing-room. Mrs. Wyndham and Joe sprang to their feet as Sam and Ronald entered, but Sybil remained seated and merely looked up inquiringly.

"Oh now, Sam," cried Mrs. Wyndham, in great excitement, "tell us all about it right away. We are dying to know!"

Joe came close to Mrs. Wyndham, her face very pale and her teeth clenched in her great anxiety. Sam threw back the lapels of his coat, put his thumbs in the armholes of his broad waistcoat, and turned his head slightly on one side.

"Well," he said slowly, "John's wiped out."

"Do you mean to say he has lost the election?" cried Mrs. Wyndham.

"Yes—he's lost it. Jobbins is senator."

"Sam, you are perfectly horrid!" exclaimed his spouse, in deepest vexation.

Josephine Thorn spoke no word, but turned away and went alone to the window. She was deathly pale, and she trembled from head to foot as she clutched the heavy curtain with her small white fingers.

"Poor Mr. Harrington!" said Sybil thoughtfully. "I am dreadfully sorry."

Mr. and Mrs. Wyndham and Ronald moved toward the fire where Sybil was sitting. No one spoke for a few seconds. At last Mrs. Wyndham broke out:

"Sam, it's a perfect shame!" she said. "I think all those people ought to be locked up for bribery. I am certain it was all done by some horrid stealing, or something, now, was not it?"

"I don't know about that, my dear," said Sam reflectively. "You see they generally vote fair enough in these things. Well, may be that fellow Ballymolloy has made something out of it. He's a pretty bad sort of a scamp, any way, I expect. Sorry you are so put out about it, but Jobbins is not so very bad, after all."

Sybil suddenly missed Joe from the group, and looked across to where she stood by the window. A glance told her that something was wrong, and she rose from her seat and went to her friend. The sight of Josephine's pale face frightened her.

"Joe, dear," she said affectionately, "you are ill—come to my room." Sybil put one arm round her waist and quietly led her away. Ronald had watched the little scene from a distance, but Mr. and Mrs. Wyndham continued to discuss the result of the election.

"It is exactly like you, Sam, to be talking in that way, instead of telling me just how it happened," said Mrs. Wyndham. "And then to say it is not so very bad after all!"

"Oh, I will tell you all about it right away, my dear, if you'll only give me a little time. You're always in such an immense fever about everything that it's perfectly impossible to get along."

"Are you going to begin?" said Mrs. Wyndham, half vexed with her husband's deliberate indifference.

"Well, as near as I can make out it was generally thought at the start that John had a pretty good show. The Senate elected him right away by a majority of four, which was so much to the good, for of course his friends reckoned on getting him in, if the Senate hadn't elected him, by the bigger majority of the House swamping the Senate in the General Court. But it's gone just the other way."

"Whatever is the General Court?" asked Ronald, much puzzled.

"Oh, the General Court is when the House and the Senate meet together next day to formally declare a senator elected, if they have both chosen the same man, or to elect one by a general majority if they haven't."

"Yes, that is it," added Mrs. Wyndham to Ronald, and then addressing her husband, "Do go on, Sam; you've not told us anything yet."

"Well, as I said, the Senate elected John Harrington by a majority of four. The House took a long time getting to work, and then there was some mistake about the first vote, so they had to take a second. And when that was done Jobbins actually had a majority of eighteen. So John's beaten, and Jobbins will be senator anyhow, and you must just make the best you can out of it."

"But I thought you said when the House and the Senate did not agree, the General Court met next day and elected a senator?" asked Ronald again; "and in that case Mr. Harrington is not really beaten yet."

"Well, theoretically he's not," said Sam, "because of course Jobbins is not actually senator until he has been elected by the General Court, but the majority for him in the House was so surprisingly large, and the majority for John so small in the Senate, and the House is so much larger than the Senate, that the vote to-morrow is a dead sure thing, and Jobbins is just as much senator as if he were sitting in Washington."

"I suppose you will expect me to have Mr. Jobbins to dinner, now. I think the whole business is perfectly mean!"

"Don't blame me, my dear," said Sam calmly. "I did not create the Massachusetts Legislature, and I did not found the State House, nor discover America, nor any of these things. And after all, Jobbins is a very respectable man and belongs to our own party, while Harrington does not. When I set up creating I'll make a note of one or two points, and I'll see that John is properly attended to."

"You need not be silly, Sam," said Mrs. Wyndham. "What has become of those girls?"

"They went out of the room some time ago," said Ronald, who had been listening with much amusement to the description of the election. He was never quite sure whether people could be serious when they talked such peculiar language, and he observed with surprise that Mr. and Mrs. Wyndham talked to each other in phrases very different from those they used in addressing himself.

Sybil had led Joe away to her room. She did not guess the cause of Joe's faintness, but supposed it to be a momentary indisposition, amenable to the effects of eau-de-cologne. She made her lie upon the great cretonne sofa, moistening her forehead, and giving her a bottle of salts to smell.

But Joe, who had never been ill in her life, recovered her strength in a few minutes, and regaining her feet began to walk about the room.

"What do you think it was, Joe, dear?" asked Sybil, watching her.

"Oh, it was nothing. Perhaps the room was hot, and I was tired."

"I thought you looked tired all the morning," said Sybil, "and just when I looked at you I thought you were going to faint. You were as pale as death, and you seemed holding yourself up by the curtains."

"Did I?" said Joe, trying to laugh. "How silly of me! I felt faint for a moment—that was all. I think I will go home."

"Yes, dear—but stay a few minutes longer and rest yourself. I will order a carriage—it is still snowing hard." Sybil left the room.

Once alone, Joe threw herself upon the sofa again. She would rather have died than have told any one, even Sybil Brandon, that it was no sickness she felt, but only a great and overwhelming disappointment for the man she loved.

Her love was doubly hers—her very own—in that it was fast locked in her own heart, beyond the reach of any human being to know. Of all that came and went about her, and flattered her, and strove for her graces, not one suspected that she loved a man in their very midst, passionately, fervently, with all the strength she had. Ronald's suspicions were too vague, and too much the result of a preconceived idea, to represent anything like a certainty to himself, and he had not mentioned them to her.

If anything can determine the passion of love in a woman, it is the great flood of sympathy that overflows her heart when the man she loves is hurt, or overcome in a great cause. When, for a little moment, that which she thinks strongest and bravest and most manly is struck down and wounded and brought low, her love rises up and is strong within her, and makes her more noble in the devotion of perfect gentleness than a man can ever be.

"Oh, if only he could have won!" Joe said again and again to herself. "If only he could have won, I would have given anything!"

Sybil came back in a few moments, and saw Joe lying down, still white and apparently far from well. She knelt upon the floor by her side and taking her hands, looked affectionately into her face.

"There is something the matter," she said. "I know—you cannot deceive me —there is something serious the matter. Will you tell me, Joe? Can I do anything at all to help you?" Joe smiled faintly, grateful for the sympathy and for the gentle words of her friend.

"No, Sybil dear. It is nothing—there is nothing you can do. Thanks, dearest—I shall be very well in a little while. It is nothing, really. Is the carriage there?"

A few minutes later, Joe and Ronald were again at Miss Schenectady's house. Joe recovered her self-control on the way, and asked Ronald to come in, an invitation which he cheerfully accepted.

John Harrington had spent the day in a state of anxiety which was new to him. Enthusiastic by nature, he was calm by habit, and he was surprised to find his hand unsteady and his brain not capable of the intense application he could usually command. Ten minutes after the results of the election were known at the State House, he received a note from a friend informing him with expressions of hearty sympathy how the day had gone.

The strong physical sense of pain which accompanies all great disappointments, took hold of him, and he fell back in his seat and closed his eyes, his teeth set and his face pale with the suffering, while his broad hands convulsively grasped the heavy oaken arms of his chair.

It may be that this same bodily agony, which is of itself but the gross reflection in our material selves of what the soul is bearing, is a wholesome provision that draws our finer senses away from looking at what might blind them altogether. There are times when a man would go mad if his mind were not detached from its sorrow by the quick, sharp beating of his bodily heart, and by the keen torture of the physical body, that is like the thrusting of a red-hot knife between breastbone and midriff.

The expression "self-control" is daily in the blatant mouths of preachers and moralists, the very cant of emptiness and folly. It means nothing, nor can any play of words or cunning twisting of conception ever give it meaning. For the "self" is the divine, imperishable portion of the eternal God which is in man. I may control my limbs and the strength that is in them, and I may force under the appetites and passions of this mortal body, but I cannot myself, for it is myself that controls, being of nature godlike and stronger than all which is material. And although, for an infinitely brief space of time, I myself may inhabit and give life to this handful of most changeable atoms, I have it in my supreme power and choice to make them act according to my pleasure. If I become enamored of the body and its ways, and of the subtleties of a fleeting bodily intelligence, I have forgotten to control those things; and having forgotten that I have free will given me from heaven to rule what is mine, I am no longer a man, but a beast. But while I, who am an immortal soul, command the perishable engine in which I dwell, I am in truth a man. For the soul is of God and forever, whereas the body is a thing of to-day that vanishes into dust to-morrow; but the two together are the living man. And thus it is that God is made man in us every day.

All that which we know by our senses is but an illusion. What is true of its own nature, we can neither see, nor hear, nor feel, nor taste. It is a matter of time, and nothing more, and whatever palpable thing a man can name will inevitably be dissolved into its constituent parts, that these may again agglomerate into a new illusion for future ages. But that which is subject to no change, nor disintegration, nor reconstruction, is the immortal truth, to attain to a knowledge and understanding of which is to be saved from the endless shifting of the material and illusory universe.

John Harrington lay in his chair alone in his rooms, while the snow whirled against the windows outside and made little drifts on the sills. The fire had gone out and the bitter storm beat against the casements and howled in the chimney, and the dusk of the night began to mingle with the thick white flakes, and brought upon the solitary man a great gloom and horror of loneliness. It seemed to him that his life was done, and his strength gone from him. He had labored in vain for years, for this end, and he had failed to attain it. It were better to have died than to suffer the ignominy of this defeat. It were better never to have lived at all than to have lived so utterly in vain. One by one the struggles of the past came up to him; each had seemed a triumph when he was in the glory of strength and hope. The splendid aims of a higher and nobler government, built by sheer truth and nobility of purpose upon the ashes and dust of present corruption, the magnificent purity of the ideal State of which he had loved to dream—all that he had thought of and striven after as most worthy of a true man to follow, dwindled now away into a hollow and mocking image, more false than hollowness itself, poorer and of less substance than a juggler's show.

He clasped his hands over his forehead, and tried to think, but it was of no use. Everything was vague, broken, crushed, and shapeless. Faces seemed to rise to his disturbed sight, and he wondered whether he had ever known these people; a ghastly weariness as of death was upon him, and his arms fell heavily by his sides. He groaned aloud, and if in that bitter sigh he could have breathed away his existence he would have gladly done it.

Some one entered the room, struck a match, and lit the gas. It was his servant, or rather the joint servant of two or three of the bachelors who lived in the house, a huge, smooth-faced colored man.

"Oh, excuthe me, Mister Harrington, I thought you wath out, Thir. There's two o' them notes for you."

John roused himself, and took the letters without a word. They were both addressed in feminine handwriting. The one he knew, for it was from Mrs. Wyndham. The other he did not recognize. He opened Mrs. Wyndham's first.

"DEAR MR. HARRINGTON,—Sam and I are very much put out about it, and sympathize most cordially. We think you might like to come and dine this evening, if you have no other invitation, so I write to say we will be all alone and very glad to see you. Cordially yours,

"JANE WYNDHAM."

"P.S. Don't trouble about the answer."

John read the note through and laid it on the table. Then he turned the other missive over in his fingers, and finally tore open the envelope.

It ran as follows:—

"MY DEAR MR. HARRINGTON,—Please don't be surprised at my writing to you in this way. I was at Mrs. Wyndham's this afternoon and heard all about it, and I must write to tell you that I am very, very sorry. It is too horrible to think how bad and wicked and foolish people are, and how they invariably do the wrong thing. I cannot tell you how sorry we all are, because it is just such men as you who are most needed nowadays, though of course I know nothing about politics here. But I am quite sure that all of them will live to regret it, and that you will win in the end. Don't think it foolish of me to write, because I'm so angry that I can't in the least help it, and I think everybody ought to.

"Yours in sincerity,"

"JOSEPHINE THORN."

Chapter XVII

John read Joe's note many times over before he quite realized what it contained. It seemed at first a singular thing that she should have written to him, and he did not understand it. He knew her as an enthusiastic and capricious girl who had sometimes laughed at him, and sometimes treated him coldly; but who, again, had sometimes talked with him as though he were an old friend. He called to mind the interest she had taken in his doings of late, and how she had denounced Vancouver as his enemy, and he thought of the long conversation he had had with her on the ice under the cold moonlight. He thought of many a sympathetic glance she had given when he spoke of his aims and intentions, of many a gentle word spoken in praise of him, and which at the time he had taken merely as so much small, good-natured flattery, such as agreeable people deal out to each other in society without any thought of evil nor any especial meaning of good. All these things came back to him, and he read the little note again. It was a kindly word, nothing more, penned by a wild, good-hearted girl, in the scorn of consequence or social propriety. It was nothing but that.

And yet, there was something more in it all—something not expressed in the abbreviated words and hurriedly-composed sentences, but something that seemed to struggle for expression. John's experience of womankind was limited, for he was no lady's man, and had led a life singularly lacking in woman's love or sentiment, though singularly dependent on the friendship of some woman. Nevertheless he knew that Joe's note breathed the essence of a sympathy wider than that of mere every-day acquaintance, and deeper, perhaps, than that of any friendship he had known. He could not have explained the feeling, nor reasoned upon it, but he knew well enough that when he next met Joe it would be on new terms. She had declared herself his friend in a way no longer mistakable, for she must have followed her first impulse in writing such a note, and the impulse must have been a strong one.

For a while he debated whether to answer the note or not, almost forgetting his troubles in the tumult of new thoughts it had suggested to him. A note, thought he, required an answer, on general principles—but such a note as this would be better answered in person than by any pen and paper. He would call and see Joe, and thank her for it. But, again, he knew he could not see her until the next day, and that seemed a long time to wait. It would not have been long under ordinary circumstances, but in this case it seemed to him an unreasonable delay. He sat down and took a pen in his fingers.

"Dear Miss Thorn"—he began, and stopped. In America it is more formal to begin without the preliminary "my;" in England the "my" is indispensable, unless people are on familiar terms. John knew this, and reflected that Joe was English. While he was reflecting his eye fell upon a heap of telegraph blanks, and he remembered that he had not given notice of his defeat to the council. He pushed aside the note paper and took a form for a cable dispatch. In a moment Joe was forgotten in the sudden shock that brought his thoughts back to his position. He wrote out a simple message addressed to Z, who was the only one of the three whom he officially knew.

But when he had done that, he fell to thinking about Joe again, and resolved to write the note.

"MY DEAR MISS THORN,—I cannot allow your very friendly words to remain unanswered until tomorrow. It is kind of you to be sorry for the defeat I have suffered, it is kinder still to express your sympathy so directly and so soon. Concerning the circumstances which brought the contest to such a result, I have nothing to say. It is the privilege of elective bodies to choose as they please, and indeed, that is the object of their existence. No one has any right to complain of not being elected, for a man who is a candidate knows from the first what he is undertaking, and what manner of men he has to deal with. Personally, I am a man who has fought a fight and has lost it, and however firmly I still believe in the cause which led me to the struggle, I confess that I am disappointed and disheartened at being vanquished. You are good enough to say you believe I shall win in the end; I can only answer that I thank you very heartily indeed for saying so, though I do not think it is likely that any efforts of mine will be attended with success for a long time.

"Believe me, with great gratitude,

"Very sincerely yours,

"JOHN HARRINGTON."

It was a longer note than he had meant to write, in fact it was almost a letter; but he read it over and was convinced he had said what he meant to say, which was always the principal consideration in such matters. Accordingly the missive was dispatched to its destination. As for Mrs. Wyndham, John determined to accept her invitation, and to answer it in person by appearing at the dinner-hour. He would not let any one think he was so broken-hearted as to be unable to show himself. He was too strong for that, and he had too much pride in his strength.

He was right in going to Mrs. Wyndham's, for she and her husband were his oldest friends, and he understood well enough what true hearts and what honest loyalty lie sometimes concealed in the bosoms of those brisk, peculiar people, who seem unable to speak seriously for long about the most serious subjects, and whose quaint turns of language seem often so unfit to express any deep feeling. But while he talked with his hosts his own thoughts strayed again and again to Joe, and he wondered what kind of woman she really was. He intended to visit her the next day.

The next day came, however, and yet John did not turn his steps up the hill towards Miss Schenectady's house. It was a cloudless morning after the heavy storm, and the great drifts of snow flashed like heaps of diamonds in the sun. All the air was clear and cold, and the red brick pavements were spotted here and there with white patches left from the shovels of the Irishmen. Sleighs of all sizes were ploughing their way hither and thither, breaking out a track in the heavy mass that encumbered the streets. Every one was wrapped in furs, and every one's face was red with the smarting cold.

Joe stayed at home until mid-day, when she went to a luncheon-party of young girls. As usual, they had been sewing for the poor, but Joe thought that she was not depriving the poor people of any very material assistance by staying away from the more industrious part of the entertainment. The sewing they all did together in a morning did not produce results whereby even the very smallest baby could have been clothed, and the part effected by each separate damsel in this whole was consequently somewhat insignificant. Joe would have stayed at home outright had the weather not been so magnificent, and possibly she thought that she might meet John Harrington on her way to the house of her friend in Dartmouth Street.

Fate, however, was against her, for she had not walked thirty yards down the hill before she was overtaken by Pocock Vancouver. He had been standing in one of the semi-circular bay windows of the Somerset Club, and seeing Joe coming down the steep incline, had hurriedly taken his coat and hat and gone out in pursuit of her. Had he suspected in the least how Joe felt toward him, he would have fled to the end of the world rather than meet her.

"Good morning, Miss Thorn," he said, walking rapidly by her side and taking off his hat, "how very early you are to-day."

"It is not early," said Joe, looking at him coldly, "it is nearly one o'clock."

"It would be called early for most people," said Vancouver; "for Mrs. Wyndham, for instance."

"I am not Mrs. Wyndham," said Joe.

"I am going to see Harrington," remarked Vancouver, who perceived that Joe was not in a good humor. "I am afraid he must be dreadfully cut up about this business."

"So you are going to condole with him? I do not believe he is in the least disturbed. He has far too much sense."

"I fancy the most sensible man in the world would be a trifle annoyed at being defeated in an election, Miss Thorn," said Vancouver blandly. "I am afraid you are not very sorry for him. He is an old friend of mine, and though I differ from him in politics, very passively, I cannot do less than go and see him, and tell him how much I regret, personally, that he should be defeated."

Joe's lip curled in scorn, and she flushed angrily. She could have struck Vancouver's pale face with infinite pleasure and satisfaction, but she said nothing in immediate answer.

"Do you not think I am right?" asked Vancouver. "I am sure you do; you have such a good heart." They passed Charles Street as he was speaking, and yet he gave no sign of leaving her.

"I am not sure that I have a good heart, and I am quite sure that you are utterly wrong, Mr. Vancouver," said Joe, in calm tones.

"Really? Why, you quite surprise me, Miss Thorn. Any man in my place ought"—

"Most men in your place would avoid Mr. Harrington," interrupted Joe, turning her clear brown eyes full upon him. Had she been less angry she would have been more cautious. But her blood was up, and she took no thought, but said what she meant, boldly.

"Indeed, Miss Thorn," said Vancouver, stiffly, "I do not understand you in the least. I think what you say is very extraordinary. John Harrington has always been a friend of mine."

"That may be, Mr. Vancouver, but you are certainly no friend of his," said Joe, with a scornful laugh.

"You astonish me beyond measure," rejoined Pocock, maintaining his air of injured virtue, although he inwardly felt that he was in some imminent danger. "How can you possibly say such a thing?"

Joe could bear it no longer. She was very imprudent, but her honest anger boiled over. She stopped in her walk, her back against the iron railings, and she faced Vancouver with a look that frightened him. He was forced to stop also, and he could not do less than return her glance.

"Do you dare to stand there and tell me that you are Mr. Harrington's friend?" she asked in low distinct tones. "You, the writer of articles in the 'Daily Standard,' calling him a fool and a charlatan? You, who have done your very best to defeat him in this election? Indeed, it is too absurd!" She laughed aloud in utter scorn, and then turned to continue her way.

Vancouver turned a shade paler than was natural with him, and looked down. He was very much frightened, for he was a coward.

"Miss Thorn," he said, "I am sorry you should believe such calumnies. I give you my word of honor that I have never either written or spoken against Mr. Harrington. He is one of my best friends."

Joe did not answer; she did not even look at him, but walked on in silence. He did not dare to speak again, and as they reached the corner of the Public Garden he lifted his hat.

"I am quite sure that you will find you have misjudged me, Miss Thorn," he said, with a grieved look. "In the mean while I wish you a very good morning."

"Good-morning," said Joe, without looking at him; and she passed on, full of indignation and wrath.

To tell the truth, she was so much delighted at having spoken her mind for once, that she had not a thought of any possible consequences. The delight of having dealt Vancouver such a buffet was very great, and she felt her heart beat fast with a triumphant pleasure.

But Vancouver turned and went away with a very unpleasant sensation in, him. He wished with all his might that he had not left the comfortable bay window of the Somerset Club that morning, and more than all he wished he could ascertain how Joe had come to know of his journalistic doings. As a matter of fact, what she had said concerning Pocock's efforts against John in the election had been meant in a most general way. But Vancouver thought she was referring to his interview with Ballymolloy, and that she understood the whole matter. Of course, there was nothing to be done but to deny the accusations from beginning to end; but they nevertheless had struck deep, and he was thoroughly alarmed. When he left the club he had had no intention of going to see Harrington; the idea had formed itself while talking with her. But now, again, he felt that he could not go. He had not the courage to face the man he had injured, principally because he strongly suspected that if Joe knew what he had done, John Harrington most likely knew it too.

He was doubly hit. He would have been less completely confused and frightened if the attack had come from Sybil Brandon; but he had had vague ideas of trying to marry Joe, and he guessed that any such plan was now hopelessly out of the question. He turned his steps homeward, uncertain what to do, and hoping to find counsel in solitude.

He took up the letters and papers that lay on his study table, brought by the mid-day post. One letter in particular attracted his attention, and he singled it out and opened it. It was dated from London, and had been twelve days on its way.

"MY DEAR VANCOUVER,

"Enclosed please find Bank of England Post Note for your usual quarterly honorarium, £1250. My firm will address you upon the use to be made of the Proxies lately sent you for the ensuing election of officers of the Pocahontas and Dead Man's Valley R. R., touching your possession of which I beg to reiterate the importance of a more than Masonic discretion. I apprehend that unless the scattered shares should have been quickly absorbed for the purpose of obtaining a majority, these Proxies will enable you to control the election of the proper ticket. If not, and if the Leviathan should decline the overtures that will be made to him during his summer visit to London, I should like your estimate of five thousand shares more, to be picked up in the next three months, which will assure our friends the control. Should the prospective figure be too high, we may elect to sell out, after rigging the market for a boom.

"In either event there will be lots of pickings in the rise and fall of the shares for the old joint account, which has been so profitable because you have so skillfully covered up your tracks.

"Yours faithfully,"

"SAUNDERS GRABBLES."

"P. S. The expectations of the young lady about whom you inquire are involved in such a tangle of conditions as could only have occurred to the excited fancy of an old Anglo-Indian. He left about twenty lacs of rupees in various bonds—G. I. P. and others—to his nephew, Ronald Surbiton, and to his niece jointly, provided that they marry each other. If they do not, one quarter of the estate is to go to the one who marries first, and the remaining three quarters to the other. The estate is in the hands of trustees, who pay an allowance to the heirs. In case they marry each other, the said heirs have power to dispose by will of the inheritance. Otherwise the whole of it reverts to the last survivor, and at his or her death it is to be devoted to founding a home for superannuated governesses."

Vancouver read the letter through with care, and held it a moment in his hand. Then he crushed it angrily together and tossed it into the fire. It seemed as though everything went wrong with him to-day. Not only was no information concerning Joe of any use now. It would be a hard thing to disabuse her of the idea that he had written those articles. After all, though, as he thought the matter over, it could be only guess-work. The manuscripts had always gone through the post, signed with a feigned name, and it was utterly impossible that the editor himself could know who had written them. It would be still more impossible, therefore, for any one else to do more than make a guess. It is easy to deny any statement, however correct, when founded on such a basis. But there was the other thing: Joe had accused him of having opposed John's election to the best of his ability. No one could prove that either. He had even advised Ballymolloy to vote for John, in so many words. On the whole, his conscience was clear enough. Vancouver's conscience was represented by all those things which could by any possibility be found out; the things that no one could ever know gave him no anxiety. In the present case the first thing to be done was plainly to put the whole blame of the articles on the shoulders of some one else, a person of violent political views and very great vanity, who would be greatly flattered at being thought the author of anything so clever. That would not be a difficult task. He would broach the subject to Mrs. Wyndham, telling her that the man, whoever he should be, had told him in strictest confidence that he was the writer. Vancouver would of course tell it to Mrs. Wyndham as a state secret, and she would tell some one else—it would soon be public property, and Joe would hear of it. It would be easy enough to pitch upon some individual who would not deny the imputation, or who would deny it in such a way as to leave the impression on the public mind unchanged, more especially as the articles had accomplished the desired result.

The prime cause of all this, John Harrington himself, sat in his room, unconscious, for the time, of Vancouver's existence. He was in a state of great depression and uncertainty, for he had not yet rallied from the blow of the defeat. Moreover he was thinking of Joe, and her letter lay open on the table beside him. His whole heart went out to her in thanks for her ready sympathy, and he had almost made up his mind to go and see her, as he had at first determined to do.

He would have laughed very heartily at the idea of being in love, for he had never thought of himself in such a position. But he realized that he was fond of Josephine Thorn, that he was thinking of her a great deal, and that the thought was a comfort to him in his distress. He knew very well that he would find a great rest and refreshment in talking to her at present, and yet he could not decide to go to her. John was a man of calm manner and with plenty of hard, practical sense, in spite of the great enthusiasm that burned like a fire within him, and that was the mainspring of his existence. But like all orators and men much accustomed to dealing with the passions of others, he was full of quick intuitions and instincts which rarely betrayed him. Something warned him not to seek her society, and though he said to himself that he was very far from being in love, the thought that he might some day find that he wished to marry her presented itself continually to his mind; and since John had elected to devote himself to celibacy and politics, there was nothing more repugnant to his whole life than the idea of marriage.

At this juncture, while he was revolving in his mind what was best to be done, a telegram was brought to him. It was from Z, and in briefest terms of authority commanded John to hold himself ready to start for London at a moment's notice. It must have been dispatched within a few hours after receiving his own message of the night before, and considering the difference of time, must have been sent from London early in the afternoon. It was clearly an urgent case, and the supreme three had work for John to do, even though he had not been made senator.

The order was a great relief. It solved all his uncertainty and scattered all his doubts to the wind. It gave him new courage and stimulated his curiosity. Z had only sent for him twice before, and then only to call him from Boston or New York to Washington. It was clear that something of very great importance was likely to occur. His energy returned in full, with the anticipation of work to do and of a journey to be made, and before night he was fully prepared to leave on receipt of his orders. His box was packed, and he had drawn the money necessary to take him to London.

As for Joe, he could go and see her now if he pleased. In twenty-four hours he might be gone, never to see her again. But it was too late on that day—he would go on the following morning.

It was still the height of the Boston season, which is short, but merry while it lasts. John had a dinner-party, a musical evening, and a ball on his list for the evening, and he resolved that he would go to all three, and show himself bravely to the world. He was full of new courage and strength since he had received Z's message, and he was determined that no one should know what he had suffered.

The dinner passed pleasantly enough, and by ten o'clock he was at the musical party. There he found the Wyndhams and many other friends, but he looked in vain for Joe; she was not there. Before midnight he was at the dance, pushing his way through crowds of acquaintances, stumbling over loving couples ensconced on the landings of the stairs, and running against forlorn old ladies, whose mouths were full of ice-cream and their hearts of bitterness against the younger generation; and so, at last, he reached the ball-room, where everything that was youngest and most fresh was assembled, swaying and gliding, and backing and turning in the easy, graceful half-walk, half-slide of the Boston step.

As John stood looking on, Joe passed him, leaving the room on Mr. Topeka's arm. There was a little open space before her in the crowd, and Pocock Vancouver darted out with the evident intention of speaking to her. But as she caught sight of him she turned suddenly away, pulling Mr. Topeka round by his arm. It was an extremely "marked thing to do." As she turned she unexpectedly came face to face with John, who had watched the maneuver. The color came quickly to her face, and she was slightly embarrassed; nevertheless she held out her hand and greeted John cordially.

Chapter XVIII

"I am so glad to have found you," said John to Josephine, when the latter had disposed of Mr. Topeka. They had chosen a quiet corner in a dimly-lighted room away from the dancers. "But I suppose it is useless to ask you for a dance?"

"No," said Joe, looking at her card; "I always leave two dances free in the middle of the evening in case I am tired. We will sit them out."

"Thank you," said John, looking at her. She looked pale and a little tired, but wonderfully lovely. "Thank you," he repeated, "and thank you also for your most kind note."

"I wish I could tell you better how very sorry I am," said Joe, impulsively. "It is bad enough to look on and see such things done, but I should think you must be nearly distracted."

"I think I was at first," said John, simply. "But one soon grows used to it. Man is a vain animal, and I suppose no one could lose a fight as I have without being disappointed."

"If you were not disappointed it would be a sign you did not really care," answered Joe. "And of course you must care—a great, great deal. It is a loss to your cause, as well as a loss to yourself. But you cannot possibly give it up; you will win next time."

"Yes," said John, "I hope I shall win some day." But his voice sounded uncertain; it lacked that determined ring that Joe loved so well. She felt as she sat beside him that he was deeply hurt and needed fresh encouragement and strength to restore him to his old self. She longed to help him and to rouse him once more to the consciousness of power and the hope of victory.

"It is my experience," said she with an air of superiority that would have been amusing if she had spoken less earnestly—"it is my experience that one should never think of anything in which one has come to grief. I know, when one is going at a big thing—a double post and rails with a ditch, or anything like that, you know—it would never do to remember that you have come off at the same thing or at something else before. When a man is always remembering his last tumble he has lost his nerve, and had better give up hunting altogether. Thinking that you may get an ugly fall will not help you over anything."

"No," said John, "that is very true."

"You must forget all about it and begin again. You have missed one bird, but you are a good shot, and you will not miss the next."

"You are a most encouraging person, Miss Thorn," said John with a faint smile. "But you know the only test of a good shot is that one hits the mark. I have missed at the first trial, and that is no reason why I should not miss at the second, too."

"You are disappointed and unhappy now," said Joe, gently. "It is very natural indeed. Anybody would feel like that. But you must not believe in yourself any less than your friends believe in you."

"I fancy my friends do not all think alike," answered John. "But I am grateful to you for what you say."

He was indeed grateful, and the soothing sound of her gentle voice was the best refreshment for his troubled spirit. He thought for a moment how brave a man could be with such a woman by his side; and the thought pleased him, the more because he knew that it could not be realized. They sat in silence for a while, contented to be together, and in sympathy. But before long the anxiety for the future and the sense of his peculiar position came over John again.

"Do you know," he said, "there are times when I regret it all very much? I never told any one so before— perhaps I was never so sure of it as I have been since this affair."

"What is it that you regret so much?" asked Joe, softly. "It is a noble life."

"It is, indeed, if only a man knows how to live it," answered John. "But sometimes I think I do not. You once said a very true thing to me about it all. Do you remember?"

"No; what was it?"

"You said I should not succeed because I am not enough of a partisan, and because every one is a partisan here."

"Did I? Yes, I remember saying it," answered Joe, secretly pleased that he should not have forgotten it. "I do not think it is so very true, after all. It is true to-day; but it is for men like you to set things right, to make partisanship a thing of the past. Men ought to make laws because they are just and necessary, not in order that they may profit by them at the expense of the rest of the world. And to have such good laws men ought to choose good men to represent them."

"There is no denying the truth of that," said John. "That is the way to construct the ideal republic. It would be the way to do a great many ideal things. You need only persuade humanity to do right, and humanity will do it. Verily, it is an easy task!" He laughed, a little bitterly.

"It is not like you to laugh in that way," said Joe, gravely.

"No; to tell the truth, I am not overmuch inclined to laugh at anything to-day, excepting myself, and I dare say there are plenty of people who will do that for me without the asking. They will have no chance when I am gone."

Joe started slightly.

"Gone?" she repeated. "Are you going away?"

"It is very likely," said John. "A friend of mine has warned me to be ready to start at a moment's notice on very important business."

"But it is uncertain, then?" asked Joe, quickly. She had turned very white in an instant, and she looked straight across the little room and pulled nervously at her fan. She would not have dared to let her eyes meet John's at that moment.

"Yes, rather uncertain," answered John. "But he would not have sent me such a warning unless it were very likely that he would really want me."

Joe was silent; she could not speak.

"So you see," continued Harrington, "I may leave to-morrow, and I cannot tell when I may come back. That is the reason I was glad to find you here. I would have called to-day, if it had been possible, after I got the message." He spoke calmly, not dreaming of the storm of fear and passion he was rousing in the heart of the fair girl beside him.

"Where—where are you going?" asked Joe in a low voice.

"Probably to England," said John.

Before the words were out of his mouth he turned and looked at her, suddenly realizing the change in her tones. But she had turned away from him. He could see the quiver of her lips and the beating throb of her beautiful throat; and as he watched the outline of her cheek a tear stole slowly over the delicate skin, and trembled, and fell upon her white neck. But still she looked away.

Ah, John Harrington, what have you done? You have taken the most precious and pure thing in this world, the thing men as brave as you have given their heart's best blood to win and have perished for failing, the thing which angels guard and Heaven has in its keeping—the love of a good and noble woman. It has come into your hands and you do not want it. You hardly know it is yours; and if you fully knew it you would not know what to do!

You are innocent, indeed; you have done nothing, spoken no word, given no look that, in your opinion, your cold indifferent opinion, could attract a woman's love. But the harm is done, nevertheless, and a great harm too. When you are old and sensible you will look back to this day as one of sorrow and evil, and you will know then that all greatness and power and glory of realized ambition are nothing unless a man have a woman's love. You will know that a man who cannot love is blind to half the world he seeks to conquer, and that a man who cannot love truly is no true man, for he who is not true to one cannot be true to many. That is the sum and reckoning of what love is worth.

But John knew of nothing beyond friendship, and he could not conceive how friendship could turn into anything else. When he saw the tear on Josephine Thorn's cheek he was greatly disturbed, and vaguely wondered what in the world he should do. The idea that any woman could care enough for him to shed a tear when he left her had never crossed his mind; even now, with the actual fact before his eyes, he doubted whether it were possible. She was ill, perhaps, and suffering pain. Pshaw! it was absurd, it could not be that she cared so much for him.

Seeing she did not move, he sat quite still for a while. His usual tact had deserted him in the extremity of the situation. He revolved in his mind what was best to say. It was safest to suppose that Joe was ill, but he would say something indifferent, in order to see whether she recovered, before he suggested that he might be of assistance.

"It is cold here," he remarked, trying to speak as naturally as possible. "Would you not like to take a turn, Miss Thorn?"

Joe moved a little. She was deadly pale, and in the effort she had made to control her feelings she was unconscious of the tears in her eyes.

"Oh no, thanks," she faltered, "I will not dance just now." She could not say more.

John made up his mind.

"You are ill, Miss Thorn," he said anxiously. "I am sure you are very far from well. Let me get you something, or call your aunt. Shall I?"

"Oh no—don't—that is—please, I think so. I will go home."

John rose quickly, but before he reached the door she called him back.

"Mr. Harrington, it is nothing. Please sit down."

John came back and did as he was bid, more and more surprised and confused.

"I was afraid it was something serious," he said nervously, for he was greatly disturbed.

Joe laughed, a bitter, harsh little laugh, that was bad to hear. She was making a great effort, but she was strong, and bravely forced back her bursting tears.

"Oh no! I was only choking," she said. "I often do. Go on, please, with what you were saying. Why are you going away so suddenly?"

"Indeed," answered John, "I do not know what the business is. I am going if I am required, simply because my friend wants me."

"Do you mean to say," asked Joe, speaking more calmly, "that you will pack up your belongings and go to the end of the world whenever a friend asks you to? It is most tremendously obliging, you know."

"Not for any friend," John replied. "But I would most certainly do it for this particular one."

"You must be very fond of him to do that," said Joe.

"I am under great obligations to him, too. He is certainly the most important man with whom I have any relations. We can trust each other-it would not do to endanger the certainty of good faith that exists between us."

"He must be a very wonderful person," said Joe, who had grown quite calm by this time. "I should like to know him."

"Very possibly you may meet him, some day. He is a very wonderful person indeed, as you say. He has devoted fifty years of his life and strength to the unremitting pursuit of the best aim that any man can set before him."

"In other words," said Joe, "he is your ideal. He is what you hope to be at his age. He must be very old."

"Yes, he is old. As for his representing my ideal, I think he approaches more nearly to it than any man alive. But you would probably not like him."

"Why?"

"He belongs to a class of men whom old-world people especially dislike," answered John. "He does not believe in any monarchy, aristocracy, or distinction of birth. He looks upon titles as a decaying institution of barbarous ages, and he confidently asserts that in two or three generations the republic will be the only form of social contract known amongst the inhabitants of the civilized world."

John was watching Joe while he spoke. He was merely talking because it seemed necessary, and he saw that in spite of her assumed calm she was still greatly agitated. She seemed anxious, however, to continue the conversation.

"It is absurd," said she, "to say that all men are born equal."

"Everything depends on what you mean by the word 'equal.' I mean by it that all men are born with an equal claim to a share in all the essential rights of free citizenship. When a man demands more than that, he is infringing on the rights of others; when he is content with less, he is allowing himself to be robbed."

"But who is to decide just how much belongs to each man?" asked Joe, leaning back wearily against the cushions. She wished now that she had allowed him to call her aunt. It was a fearful strain on her faculties to continue talking upon general subjects and listening to John Harrington's calm, almost indifferent tones.

"The majority decides that," said John.

"But a majority has just decided that you are not to be senator," said Joe. "According to you they were right, were they not?"

"It is necessary that the majority should be free," said John, "and that they should judge of themselves, each man according to his honest belief. Majorities with us are very frequently produced by a handful of dishonest men, who can turn the scale on either side, to suit their private ends. It is the aim we set before us to protect the freedom of majorities. That is the true doctrine of a republic."

"And for that aim," said Joe, slowly, "you would sacrifice everything?"

"Yes, indeed we would," said John, gravely. "For that end we will sacrifice all that we have to give—the care for personal satisfaction, the hope of personal distinction, the peace of a home and the love of a wife. We seek neither distinction nor satisfaction, and we renounce all ties that could hamper our strength or interfere with the persevering and undivided attention we try to give to our work."

"That is a magnificent programme," said Joe, somewhat incredulously. "Do you not think it is possible sometimes to aim too high? You say 'we seek,' 'we try,' as though there were several of you, or at least, some one besides yourself. Do you believe that such ideas as you tell me of are really and seriously held by any body of men?"

Nothing had seemed too high to Josephine an hour earlier, nothing too exalted, nothing so noble but that John Harrington might do it, then and there. But a sudden change had come over her, the deadly cold phase of half melancholy unbelief that often follows close upon an unexpected disappointment, so that she looked with distaste on anything that seemed so full of the enthusiasm she had lost. The tears that bad risen so passionately to her dimmed eyes were suddenly frozen, and seemed to flow back with chilling force to her heart. She coldly asked herself whether she were mad, that she could have suffered thus for such a man, even ever so briefly. He was a man, she said, who loved an unattainable, fanatic idea in the first place, and who dearly loved himself as well for his own fanaticism's sake. He was a man in whom the heart was crushed, even annihilated, by his intellect, which he valued far too highly, and by his vanity, which he dignified into a philosophy of self-sacrifice. He was aiming at what no man can reach, and though he knew his object to be beyond human grasp, he desired all possible credit for having madly dreamed of anything so high. In the sudden revulsion of her strong passion, she almost hated him, she almost felt the power to refute his theories, to destroy his edifice of fantastic morality, and finally to show him that he was a fool among men, and doubly a fool, because he was not even happy in his own folly.

Joe vaguely felt all this, and with it she felt a sense of shame at having so nearly broken down at the news that he was going away. He had thought she was ill; most assuredly he could not have guessed the cause of what he had seen; but nevertheless she had suffered a keen pain, and the tears had come to her eyes. She did not understand it. He might leave her now, if he pleased, and she would not care; indeed, it would be rather a relief if he would go. She no longer asked what she was to him, she simply reflected that, after all was said, he was nothing to her. She felt a quick antagonism to his ideas, to his words, and to himself, and she was willing to show it. She asked him incredulously whether his ideas were really held by others.

"It makes little difference," answered John, "whether they are many or few who think as I do, and I cannot tell how many there may be. The truth is not made truth because many people believe it. The world went round, as Galileo knew, although he alone stood up and said it in the face of mankind, who scoffed at him for his pains."

"In other words, you occupy the position of Galileo," suggested Joe, calmly.

"Not I," said John; "but there are men, and there have been men, in our country who know truths as great as any he discovered, and who have spent their lives in proclaiming them. I know that they are right, and that I am right, and that, however we may fail, others will succeed at last. I know that, come what may, honor and truth and justice will win the day in the end!" His gray eyes glittered as he spoke, and his broad white hands clasped nervously together in his enthusiasm. He was depressed and heartsick at his failure, but it needed only one word of opposition to rouse the strong main thought of his life into the most active expression. But Joe sat coldly by, her whole nature seemingly changed in the few minutes that had passed.

"And all this will be brought about by the measures you advocated the other day," said she with a little laugh. "A civil service, a little tariff reform—that is enough to inaugurate the reign of honor, truth, and justice?"

John turned his keen eyes upon hers. He had begun talking because she had required it of him, and he had been roused by the subject. He remembered the sympathy she had given him, and he was annoyed at her caprice.

"Such things are the mere passing needs of a time," he said. "The truth, justice, and honor, at which you are pleased to be amused, would insure the execution at all times of what is right and needful. Without a foundation composed of the said truth, justice, and honor, to get what is right and needful is often a matter so stupendous that the half of a nation's blood is drained in accomplishing the task, if even it is accomplished after all. I see nothing to laugh at."

Indeed, Joe was only smiling faintly, but John was so deeply impressed and penetrated by the absolute truth of what he was saying, that he had altogether ceased to make any allowances for Joe's caprice of mood or for the disturbance in her manner that he had so lately witnessed. He was beginning to be angry, and she had never seen him in such a mood.

"The world would be a very nice tiresome place to live in," she said, "if every one always did exactly what is absolutely right. I should not like to live among people who would be always so entirely padded and lined with goodness as they must be in your ideal republic."

"It is a favorite and characteristic notion of modern society to associate goodness with dullness, and consequently, I suppose, to connect badness with all that is gay, interesting, and diverting. There is nothing more perverted, absurd, and contemptible than that notion in the whole history of the world."

John was not gentle with an idea when he despised it, and the adjectives fell in his clear utterance like the blows of a sledge-hammer. But as the idea he was abusing had been suggested by Joe, she resented the strong language.

"I am flattered that you should call anything I say by such bad names," she said. "I am not good at arguing and that sort of thing. If I were I think I could answer you very easily. Will you please take me back to my aunt?" She rose in a somewhat stately fashion.

John was suddenly aware that he had talked too much and too strongly, and he was very sorry to have displeased her. She had always let him talk as he pleased, especially of late, and she had almost invariably agreed with him in everything he said, so that he had acquired too much confidence. At all events, that was the way he explained to himself the present difficulty.

"Please forgive me, Miss Thorn," he said humbly, as he gave her his arm to leave the room. "I am a very sanguine person, and I often talk great nonsense. Please do not be angry." Joe paused just as they reached the door.

"Angry? I am not angry," she said with sudden gentleness. "Besides, you know, this is—you are really going away?"

"I think so," said John.

"Then, if you do," she said with some hesitation—"if you do, this is good-by, is it not?"

"Yes, I am afraid it is," said John; "but not for long."

"Not for long, perhaps," she answered; "but I would not like you to think I was angry the very last time I saw you."

"No, indeed. I should be very sorry if you were. But you are not?"

"No. Well then"—she held out her hand—"Good-by, then." She had almost hated him a few minutes ago. Half an hour earlier she had loved him. Now her voice faltered a little, but her face was calm.

John took the proffered hand and grasped it warmly. With all her caprice, and despite the strange changes of her manner toward him, she had been a good friend in a bad time during the last days, and he was more sorry to leave her than he would himself have believed.

"Good-by," he said, "and thank you once more, with all my heart, for your friendship and kindness." Their hands remained clasped for a moment; then she took his arm again, and he led her out of the dimly-lighted sitting-room back among the brilliant dancers and the noise and the music and the whirling crowd.

Chapter XIX

A change has come over Boston in four months, since John Harrington and Josephine Thorn parted. The breath of the spring has been busy everywhere, and the haze of the hot summer is ripening the buds that the spring has brought out. The trees on the Common are thick and heavy with foliage, the Public Garden is a carpet of bright flowers, and on the walls of Beacon Street the great creepers have burst into blossom and are stretching long shoots over the brown stone and the iron balconies. There is a smell of violets and flowers in the warm air, and down on the little pond the swan-shaped boats are paddling about with their cargoes of merry children and calico nursery-maids, while the Irish boys look on from the banks and throw pebbles when the policemen are not looking, wishing they had the spare coin necessary to embark for a ten minutes' voyage on the mimic sea. Unfamiliar figures wander through the streets of the West End, and more than half the houses show by the boarded windows and doors that the owners are out of town.

The migration of the "tax-dodgers" took place on the last day of April; they will return on the second day of December, having spent just six months and one day in their country places, whereby they have shifted the paying of a large proportion of their taxes to more economical regions. It is a very equitable arrangement, for it is only the rich man who can save money in this way, while his poorer neighbor, who has no country-seat to which he may escape, must pay to the uttermost farthing. The system stimulates the impecunious to become wealthy and helps the rich to become richer. It is, therefore, perfectly good and just.

But Boston is more beautiful in the absence of the "tax-dodger" than at any other season. There is a stillness and a peace over the fair city that one may long for in vain during the winter. Business indeed goes on without interruption, but the habitation of the great men of business knows them not. They come up from their cool bowers by the sea, in special trains, in steamers, and in yachts, every morning, and early in the afternoon they go back, so that all day long the broad streets at the west are quiet and deserted, and seem to be basking in the sunshine to recover from the combined strain of the bitter winter and the unceasing gayety that accompanies it.

In the warm June weather Miss Schenectady and Joe still linger in town. The old lady has no new-fangled notions about taxes, and though she is rich and has a pretty place near Newport, she will not go there until she is ready, no, not for all the tax-gatherers in Massachusetts. As for Joe, she does not want to go away. Urgent letters come by every mail entreating her to return to England in time for a taste of the season in London, but they lie unanswered on her table, and often she does not read more than half of what they contain. The books and the letters accumulate in her room, and she takes no thought whether she reads them or not, for the time is weary on her hands and she only wishes it gone, no matter how. Nevertheless she will not go home, and she even begs her aunt not to leave Boston yet.

She is paler than she was and her face looks thin. She says she is well and as strong as ever, but the elasticity is gone from her step, and the light has faded in her brown eyes, so that one might meet her in the street and hardly know her. As she sits by the window, behind the closed blinds, the softened light falls on her face, and it is sad and weary.

It was not until John Harrington was gone that she realized all. He had received the message he expected early on the morning after that memorable parting, and before mid-day he was on his way.

Since then she had heard no word of tidings concerning him, save that she knew he had arrived in England. For anything she knew he might even now be in America again, but she would not believe it. If he had come back he would surely have come to see her, she thought. There were times when she would have given all the world to look on his face again, but for the most part she said to herself it was far better that she should never see him. Where was the use?

Joe was not of the women who have intimate confidants and can get rid of much sorrow by much talking about it. She was too proud and too strong to ask for help or sympathy in any real distress. She had gone to Sybil Brandon when she was about to tell Ronald of her decision, because she thought that Sybil would be kind to him and help him to forget the past; but where she herself was alone concerned, she would rather have died many deaths than confess what was in her heart.

She had gone bravely through the remainder of the season, until all was over, and no one had guessed her disappointment. Such perfect physical strength as hers was not to be broken down by the effort of a few weeks, and still she smiled and talked and danced and kept her secret. But as the long months crawled out their tale of dreary days, the passion in her soul spread out great roots and grew fiercely against the will that strove to break it down. It was a love against which there was no appeal, which had taken possession silently and stealthily, with no outward show of wooing or sweet words; and then, safe within the fortress of her maidenly soul, it had grown up to a towering strength, feeding upon her whole life, and ruthlessly dealing with her as it would. But this love sought no confidence, nor help, nor assistance, being of itself utterly without hope, strong and despairing.

One satisfaction only she had daily. She rejoiced that she had broken away from the old ties, from Ronald and from her English life. To have found herself positively loving one man while she was betrothed to another would have driven her to terrible extremity; the mere idea of going back to her mother and to the old life at home with this wild thought forever gnawing at her heart was intolerable. She might bear it to the end, whatever the end might be, and in silence, so long as none of her former associations made the contrast between past and present too strong. Old Miss Schenectady, with her books and her odd conversation, was as good a companion as any one, since she could not live alone. Sybil Brandon would have wearied her by her sympathy, gentle and loving as it would have been; and besides, Sybil was away from Boston and very happy; it would be unkind, as well as foolish, to disturb her serenity with useless confidences. And so the days went by and the hot summer was come, and yet Joe lingered in Boston, suffering silently and sometimes wondering how it would all end.

Sybil was staying near Newport with her only surviving relation, an uncle of her mother. He was an old man, upward of eighty years of age, and he lived in a strange old place six or seven miles from the town. But Ronald had been there more than once, and he was always enthusiastic in his description of what he had seen, and he seemed particularly anxious that Joe should know how very happy Sybil was in her country surroundings. Ronald had traveled during the spring, making short journeys in every direction, and constantly talking of going out to see the West, a feat which he never accomplished. He would go away for a week at a time and then suddenly appear again, and at last had gravitated to Newport. Thence he came to town occasionally and visited Joe, never remaining more than a day, and sometimes only a few hours. Joe was indifferent to his comings and goings, but always welcomed him in a friendly way. She saw that he was amusing himself, and was more glad than ever that the relations formerly existing between them had been so opportunely broken off. He had never referred to the past since the final interview when Joe had answered him by bursting into tears, and he talked about the present cheerfully enough.

One morning he arrived without warning, as usual, to make one of his short visits. Joe was sitting by the window dressed all in white, and the uniform absence of color in her dress rather exaggerated the pallor of her face than masked it. She was reading, apparently with some interest, in a book of which the dark-lined binding sufficiently declared the sober contents. As she read, her brows bent in the effort of understanding, while the warm breeze that blew through the blinds fanned her tired face and gently stirred the small stray ringlets of her soft brown hair. Ronald opened the door and entered.

"Oh, Ronald!" exclaimed Joe, starting a little nervously, "have you come up? You look like the sunshine. Come in, and shut the door." He did as he was bidden, and came and sat beside her.

"Yes, I nave come up for the day. How are you, Joe dear? You look pale. It is this beastly heat—you ought to come down to Newport for a month. It is utterly idiotic, you know, staying in town in this weather."

"I like it," said Joe. "I like the heat so much that I think I should be cold in Newport. Tell me all about what you have been doing."

"Oh, I hardly know," said Ronald. "Lots of things."

"Tell me what you do in one day—yesterday, for instance. I want to be amused this morning."

"It is not so very amusing, you know, but it is very jolly," answered Ronald. "To begin with, I get up at unholy hours and go and bathe in the surf at the second beach. There are no end of a a lot of people there even at that hour."

"Yes, I dare say. And then?"

"Oh, then I go home and dress: and later, if I do not ride, I go to the club—casino, I beg its pardon!—and play tennis. They play very decently, some of those fellows."

"Are there any nice rides?"

"Just along the roads, you know. But when you get out to Sherwood there are meadows and things—with a brook. That is very fair."

"Do you still go to Sherwood often? How is Sybil?"

"Yes," said Ronald, and a blush rose quickly to his face, "I often go there. It is such a queer old place, you know, full of trees and old summer-houses and graveyards—awfully funny."

"Tell me, Ronald," said Joe, insisting a little, "how is Sybil?"

"She looks very well, so I suppose she is. But she never goes to anything in Newport; she has not been in the town at all yet, since she went to stay with her uncle."

"But of course lots of people go out to see her, do they not?"

"Oh, well, not many. In fact I do not remember to have met any one there," answered Ronald, as though he were trying to recall some face besides Miss Brandon's. "Her uncle is such an odd bird, you have no idea."

"I do not imagine you see very much of him when you go out there," said Joe, with a faint laugh.

"Oh, I always see him, of course," said Ronald, blushing again. "He is about a hundred years old, and wears all kinds of clothes, and wanders about the garden perpetually. But I do not talk to him unless I am driven to it"—

"Which does not occur often," interrupted Joe.

"Oh, well, I suppose not very often. Why should it?"

Ronald was visibly embarrassed. Joe watched him with a look of amusement on her face; but affectionately, too, as though what he said pleased her as well as amused her. There was a short pause, during which Ronald rubbed his hat slowly and gently. Then he looked up suddenly and met Joe's eyes; but he turned away again instantly, blushing redder than ever.

"Ronald," Joe said presently, "I am so glad."

"Glad? Why? About what?"

"I am glad that you like her, and that she likes you. I think you like her very much, Ronald."

"Oh yes, very much," repeated Ronald, trying to seem indifferent.

"Do you not feel as though we were much more like brother and sister now?" asked Joe, after a little while.

"Oh, much!" assented Ronald. "I suppose it is better, too, though I did not think so at first."

"It is far better," said Joe, laying her small, thin hand across her cousin's strong fingers and pressing them a little. "You are free now, and you will probably be very happy before long. Do you not think so?" she asked, looking affectionately into his eyes.

"I hope so," said Ronald, with a last attempt at indifference. Then suddenly his face softened, and he added in a gentler tone, "Indeed, Joe, I think I shall be very happy soon."

"I am so glad," said Joe again, still holding his hand, but leaning her head back wearily in the deep chair. "There is only one thing that troubles me."

"What is that?"

"That horrid will," said Joe. "I am sure we could get it altered in some way."

"We never thought about it before, Joe. Why should we think about it now? It seems to me it is a very good will as things have turned out."

"But, my dear boy," said Joe, "if you are married to Sybil Brandon, you will need ever so much money."

Ronald blushed again.

"I have not asked her to marry me," he said quickly.

"That makes no difference at all," replied Joe. "As I was saying, when you have married her you will need money."

"What an idea!" exclaimed Ronald, indignantly. "As if any one wanted to be rich in order to be happy. Besides, between what I have of my own, and my share of the money, there is nearly four thousand a year; and then there is the place in Lanarkshire for us to live in. As if that were not enough!"

"It is not so very much, though," said Joe, reflecting. "I do not think Sybil has anything at all. You will be as poor as two little church mice; but I will come and stay with you sometimes," Joe added, laughing, "and help you about the bills."

"The bills would take care of themselves," said Ronald, gravely. "They always do. But whatever happens, Joe, my home is always yours. You will always remember that, will you not?"

"Dear Ronald," answered his cousin affectionately, "you are as good as it is possible to be—you really are."

"Ronald," said Joe, after a pause, "I have an idea."

He looked at her inquiringly, but said nothing.

"I might," she continued, smiling at the thought—"I may go and marry first, you know, after all, and spoil it."

"But you will not, will you? Promise me you will not."

"I wish I could," said Joe, "and then you could have the money"—

"But I would not let you," interrupted Ronald. "I would go off and get married by license, and that sort of thing."

"Without asking Miss Brandon?" suggested Joe.

"Nonsense!" ejaculated Ronald, coloring for the twentieth time.

"I think we are talking nonsense altogether," said Joe, seriously. "I do not think, indeed I am quite sure, I shall never marry."

"How absurd!" cried Ronald. "The idea of your not marrying. It is perfectly ridiculous."

The name of John Harrington was on his lips, but he checked himself. John was gone abroad, and with more than usual tact, Ronald reflected that, if Joe had really cared for the man, an allusion to him would be unkind. But Joe only shook her head, and let her cousin's words pass unanswered.

She had long suspected, from Ronald's frequent allusions to Sybil, which were generally accompanied by some change of manner, that he was either already in love with the fair American girl, or that he soon would be, and the acknowledgment she had now received from himself gave her infinite pleasure. In her reflections upon her own conduct she had never blamed herself, but she had more than once thought that he was greatly to be pitied. To have married him six months ago, when she was fully conscious that she did not love him, would have been very wrong; and to have gone back at a later period, when she realized that her whole life was full of her love for John Harrington, would have been a crime. But in spite of that she was often very sorry for Ronald, and feared that she had hurt his happiness past curing. Now, therefore, when she saw how much he loved another, she was exceedingly glad, for she knew that the thing she had done had been wholly good, both for him and for her.

They soon began to talk of other things, but the conversation fell back to the discussion of Newport, and Joe learned with some surprise that Pocock Vancouver assiduously cultivated Ronald's acquaintance, and was always ready to do anything in the world that Ronald desired. It appeared that Vancouver lent Ronald his horses at all times, and was apparently delighted when Ronald would take a mount and stay away all day. The young Englishman, of course, was not loath to accept such offers, having a radical and undisguised contempt for hired horseflesh, and as Sybil lived several miles out of town, it was far the most pleasant plan to ride out to her, and after spending the day there, to ride back in the evening, more especially as it cost him nothing.

Joe was on the point of making some remark upon Vancouver, which would very likely have had the effect of cooling the intimacy between him and Ronald; but she thought better of it, and said nothing. Ronald had had no part in all the questions connected with John's election, and knew nothing of what Vancouver had done in the matter. It was better on many grounds not to stir up fresh trouble, and so long as Vancouver's stables afforded Ronald an easy and economical means of locomotion from Newport to the house of the woman he loved, the friendship that had sprung up was a positive gain. She could not understand the motives that prompted Vancouver in the least. He had made more than one attempt to regain his position with her after the direct cut he had sustained on the evening when she parted with John; but Joe had resolutely set her face against him. Possibly she thought Vancouver might hope to regain her good opinion by a regular system of kindness to Ronald; but it hardly seemed to her as though such a result would reward him for the pains of his diplomacy. Meanwhile it would be foolish of her to interfere with any intimacy which was of real use to Ronald in his suit.

As a matter of fact, Vancouver was carrying out a deliberate plan, and one which was far from ill-conceived. He had not been so blind as not to suspect Joe's secret attachment for John, when she was willing to go to such lengths in her indignation against himself for being John's enemy. But he had disposed of John, as he thought, by assisting, if not actually causing, his defeat. He imagined that Harrington had gone abroad to conceal the mortification he felt at having lost the election, and he rightly argued that for some time Joe would not bestow a glance upon any one else. In the mean time, however, he was in possession of certain details concerning Joe's fortune which could be of use, and he accordingly set about encouraging Ronald's affections in any direction they might take, so long as they were not set upon his cousin. He was not surprised that Ronald should fall in love with Sybil, though he almost wished the choice could have fallen upon some one else, and accordingly he did everything in his power to make life in Newport agreeable for the young Englishman. It was convenient in some respects that the wooing should take place at so central a resort; but had the case been different, Vancouver would not have hesitated to go to Saratoga, Lenox, or Mount Desert, in the prosecution of his immediate purpose, which was to help Ronald to marry any living woman rather than let him return to England a bachelor.

When Ronald should be married, Joe would be in possession of three quarters of her uncle's money—a very considerable fortune. If she was human, thought Vancouver, she would be eternally grateful to him for ridding her of her cousin, whom she evidently did not wish to marry, and for helping her thereby to so much wealth. He reflected that he had been unfortunate in the time when he had decided to be a candidate for her hand; but whatever turn affairs took, no harm was done to his own prospects by removing Ronald from the list of possible rivals. He was delighted at the preference Surbiton showed for Sybil Brandon, and in case Ronald hesitated, he reserved the knowledge he possessed of her private fortune as a final stimulus to his flagging affections. Hitherto it had not seemed necessary to acquaint his friend with the fact that Sybil had an income of some thirty thousand dollars yearly—indeed, no one seemed to know it, and she was supposed to be in rather straitened circumstances.

As for his own chances with Joe, he had carefully hidden the tracks of his journalistic doings in the way he had at once proposed to himself when Joe attacked him on the subject. A gentleman had been found upon whom he had fastened the authorship of the articles in the public estimation, and the gentleman would live and die with the reputation for writing he had thus unexpectedly obtained. He had ascertained beyond a doubt that Joe knew nothing of his interview with Ballymolloy, and he felt himself in a strong position.

Pocock Vancouver had for years taken an infinite amount of pains in planning and furthering his matrimonial schemes. He was fond of money; but in a slightly less degree he was fond of all that is beautiful and intelligent in woman; so that his efforts to obtain for himself what he considered a perfect combination of wit, good looks, and money, although ineffectual, had occupied a great deal of his spare time very agreeably.

Chapter XX

Sherwood was a very old place. It had been built a hundred years at least before the Revolution in the days when the States had English governors, and when its founder had been governor of Rhode Island. His last descendant in the direct line was Sybil Brandon's great-uncle.

The old country-seat was remarkable chiefly for the extent of the gardens attached to the house, and for the singularly advanced state of dilapidation in which everything was allowed to remain. Beyond the gardens the woods stretched down to the sea, unpruned and thick with a heavy undergrowth; from the road the gardens were hidden by thick hedges, and by the forbidding gray front of the building. It was not an attractive place to look at, and once within the precincts there was a heavy sense of loneliness and utter desolation, that seemed to fit it for the very home of melancholy.

The damp sea air had drawn green streaks of mould downwards from each several jointing of the stones; the long-closed shutters of some of the windows were more than half hidden by creepers, bushy and straggling by turns, and the eaves were all green with moss and mould. From the deep-arched porch at the back a weed-grown gravel walk led away through untrimmed hedges of box and myrtle to an ancient summer-house on the edge of a steep slope of grass. To right and left of this path, the rose-trees and box that had once marked the gayest of flower gardens now grew in such exuberance of wild profusion that it would have needed strong arms and a sharp axe to cut a way through. Far away on a wooded knoll above the sea was the old graveyard, where generations of Sherwoods lay dead in their quiet rest, side by side.

But for a space in every year the desolation was touched with the breath of life, and the sweet June air blew away the mould and the smell of death, and the wild flowers and roses sprang up joyfully in the wilderness to greet the song-birds and the butterflies of summer. And in this copious year a double spring had come to Sherwood, for Sybil Brandon had arrived one day, and her soft eyes and golden hair had banished all sadness and shadow from the old place. Even the thin old man, who lived there among the ghosts and shadows of the dead and dying past, smoothed the wrinkles from his forehead, forgetting to long selfishly for his own death, when Sybil came; and with touching thoughtfulness he strove to amuse her, and to be younger for her sake. He found old garments of a gayer time, full thirty years hidden away in the great wardrobes up-stairs, and he put them on and wore them, though they hung loosely about his shaken and withered frame, lest he should be too sad a thing for such young eyes to look upon.

Then Ronald came one day, and the old man took kindly to him, and bade him come often. In the innocence of his old age it seemed good that what youth and life there was in the world should come together; and Ronald treated him with a deference and respect to which he had long been unused. Moreover, Ronald accepted the invitation given him and came as often as he pleased, which, before long, meant every day. When he came in the morning he generally stayed until the evening, and when he came in the afternoon he always stayed as long as Sybil would let him, and rode home late through the misty June moonlight pondering on the happiness the world had suddenly brought forth for him who had supposed, but a few months ago, that all happiness was at an end.

Six months had gone by since Ronald had first seen Sybil, and he had changed in that time from boy to man. Looking back through the past years he knew that he was glad Joe had not married him, for the new purpose of his new life was to love and marry Sybil Brandon. There was no doubt in his mind as to what he would do; the strong nature in him was at last roused, and he was capable of anything in reason or without it to get what he wanted.

Some one has said that an Englishman's idea of happiness is to find something he can kill and to hunt it. That is a metaphor as well as a fact. It may take an Englishman half a lifetime to find out what he wants, but when he is once decided he is very likely to get it, or to die in the attempt. The American is fond of trying everything until he reaches the age at which Americans normally become dyspeptic, and during his comparatively brief career he succeeds in experiencing a surprising variety of sensations. Both Americans and English are tenacious in their different ways, and it is certain that between them they have gotten more things that they have wanted than any other existing nation.

What most surprised Ronald was that, having made up his mind to marry Sybil, he should not have had the opportunity, or perhaps the courage, to tell her so. He remembered how easily he had always been able to speak to Joe about matrimony, and he wondered why it should be so hard to approach the subject with one whom he loved infinitely more dearly than he had ever loved his cousin. But love brings tact and the knowledge of fitness, besides having the effect of partially hiding the past and exaggerating the future into an eternity of rose-colored happiness; wherefore Ronald supposed that everything would come right in time, and that the time for everything to come right could not possibly be very far off.

On the day after he had seen Joe in Boston he rode over to Sherwood in the morning, as usual, upon one of Vancouver's horses. He was lighter at heart than ever, for he had somewhat dreaded the revelation of his intentions to Joe; but she had so led him on and helped him that it had all seemed very easy. He was not long in reaching his destination, and having put his horse in the hands of the single man who did duty as gardener, groom, and dairyman for old Mr. Sherwood, he entered the garden, where he hoped to meet Sybil alone. He was not disappointed, for as he walked down the path through the wilderness of shrubbery he caught sight of her near the summer-house, stooping down in the act of plucking certain flowers that grew there.

She, too, was dressed all in white, as he had seen his cousin on the previous day; but the difference struck him forcibly as he came up and took her outstretched hand. They had changed places and character, one could almost have thought. Joe had looked so tired and weary, so "wilted," as they say in Boston, that it had shocked Ronald to see her. Sybil, who had formerly been so pale and cold, now was the very incarnation of life; delicate and exquisitely fine in every movement and expression, but most thoroughly alive. The fresh soft color seemed to float beneath the transparent skin, and her deep eyes were full of light and laughter and sunshine. Ronald's heart leaped in his breast for love and pride as she greeted him, and his brow turned hot and his hands cold in the confusion of his happiness.

"You have been away again?" she asked presently, looking down at the wild white lilies which she had been gathering.

"Yes, I was in Boston yesterday," answered Ronald, who had immediately begun to help in plucking the flowers. "I went to see Joe. She looks dreadfully knocked up with the heat, poor child."

And so they talked about Joe and Boston for a little while, and Sybil sat upon the steps of the summer-house on the side where there was shade from the hot morning sun, while Ronald brought her handfuls of the white lilies. At last there were enough, and he came and stood before her. She was so radiantly lovely as she sat in the warm shade with the still slanting sunlight just falling over her white dress, he thought her so super-humanly beautiful that he stood watching her without thinking of speaking or caring that she should speak to him. She looked up and smiled, a quick bright smile, for she was woman enough to know his thoughts. But she busied herself with the lilies and looked down again.

"Let me help you," said Ronald suddenly, kneeling down before her on the path.

"I don't think you can—very much," said Sybil, demurely. "You are not very clever about flowers, you know. Oh, take care! You will crush it— give it back to me!"

Ronald had taken one of the lilies and was smelling it, but it looked to Sybil very much as though he were pressing it to his lips. He would not give it back, but held it away at arm's length as he knelt. Sybil made as though she were annoyed.

"Of course," said she, "I cannot take it, if you will not give it to me." Ronald gently laid the flower in her lap with the others. She pretended to take no notice of what he did, but went on composing her nosegay.

"Miss Brandon"—began Ronald, and stopped.

"Well?" said Sybil, without looking up.

"May I tell you something?" he asked.

"That depends," said Sybil. "Is it anything very interesting?"

"Yes," said Ronald. There seemed to be something the matter with his throat all at once, as though he were going to choke. Sybil looked up and saw that he was very pale. She had never seen him otherwise than ruddy before, and she was startled; she dropped the lilies on her knees and looked at him anxiously. Ronald suddenly laid his hands over hers and held them. Still she faced him.

"I am very unworthy of you—I know I am-but I love you very, very much." He spoke distinctly enough now, and slowly. He was as white as marble, and his fingers were cold, and trembled as they held hers.

For an instant after he had spoken, Sybil did not move. Then she quietly drew back her hands and hid her face in a sudden, convulsive movement. She, too, trembled, and her heart beat as though it would break; but she said nothing. Ronald sprang from the ground and kneeled again upon the step beside her; very gently his arm stole about her and drew her to him. She took one hand from her face and tried to disentangle his hold, but he held her strongly, and whispered in her ear,—

"Sybil, I love you—do you love me?"

Sybil made a struggle to rise, but it was not a very brave struggle, and in another moment she had fallen into his arms and was sobbing out her whole love passionately.

"Oh, Ronald, you mu—must not!" But Ronald did.

Half an hour later they were still sitting side by side on the steps, but the storm of uncertainty was passed, and they had plighted their faith for better and for worse, for this world and the next. Ronald had foreseen the event, and had hoped for it as he never had hoped for anything in his life; Sybil had perhaps guessed it; at all events, now that the supreme moment was over, they both felt that it was the natural climax to all that had happened during the spring.

"I think," said Sybil, quietly, "that we ought to tell my uncle at once. He is the only relation I have in the world."

"Oh yes, of course," said Ronald, holding her hand. "That is, you know, I think we might tell him after lunch. Because I suppose it would not be the right thing for me to stay all day after he knows. Would it?"

"Why not?" asked Sybil. "He must know it soon, and you will come to-morrow."

"To-morrow, and the next day, and the day after that, and always," said Ronald, lovingly. "But he will not like it, I suppose."

"Why not?" asked Sybil, again.

"Because I am poor," said Ronald, quietly. "You know I am not rich at all, Sybil dearest. We shall have to be very economical, and live on the place in Scotland. But it is a very pretty place," he added, reassuringly.

Sybil flushed a little. He did not know, then, that she had a fortune of her own. It was a new pleasure. She did not say anything for a moment.

"Do you mind very much, dearest?" asked Ronald, doubtfully. "Do you think it would bore you dreadfully to live in the country?"

Sybil hesitated before she answered. She hardly knew whether to tell him or not, but at last she decided it would be better.

"No, Ronald," said she, smiling a little; "I like the country. But, you know, we can live anywhere we please. I am rich, Ronald—you did not know it?"

Ronald started slightly. It was indeed an unexpected revelation.

"Really?" he cried. "Oh, I am so glad for you. You will not miss anything, then. I was so afraid."

That evening Ronald telegraphed to Joe the news of his engagement, and the next day he wrote her a long letter, which was more remarkable for the redundant passion expressed than for the literary merit of the expression. It seemed far easier to write it since he had seen her and talked with her about Sybil, not because he felt in the least ashamed of having fallen in love within six months of the dissolution of his former engagement with Joe, but because it seemed a terribly difficult thing to speak to any one about Sybil. Ronald was very far from being poetical, or in any way given to lofty and medieval reflections of the chivalric sort, but he was a very honest fellow, loving for the first time, and he understood that his love was something more to be guarded and respected than anything that had yet come into his life; wherefore it seemed almost ungentlemanly to speak about it.

When Joe received the intelligence her satisfaction knew no bounds, for although she had guessed that the climax of the affair was not far off, she had not expected it so very soon. Had she searched through the whole of her acquaintance at home and in America she could have found no one whom she considered more fit to be Ronald's wife, and that alone was enough to make her very happy; but the sensation of freedom from all further responsibility to Ronald, and the consciousness that every possible good result had followed upon her action, added so much to her pleasure in the matter, that for a time she utterly forgot herself and her own troubles. She instantly wrote a long and sympathetic letter to Ronald, and another to Sybil.

Sybil replied at once, begging Joe to come and spend a month at Sherwood, or as much time as she was able to give.

"I expect you had best go," remarked Miss Schenectady. "It is getting pretty hot here, and you look quite sick."

"Oh no, I am very well," said Joe; "but I think I will go for a week or ten days."

"Well, if you find you are going to have a good time, you can always stay, any way," replied the old lady. "I think if I were you I would take some books and a Bible and a pair of old boots."

Miss Schenectady did not smile, but Joe laughed outright.

"A Bible and a pair of old boots!" she cried.

"Yes, I would," said her aunt. "Old Tom Sherwood cannot have seen a Bible for fifty years, I expect, and it might sort of freshen him up." The old lady's eye twinkled slightly and the corners of her mouth twitched a little. "As for the old boots, if you conclude to go, you will want them, for you will be right out in the country there."

Joe laughed again, but she took her aunt's advice; and on the following day she reached Newport, and was met by Sybil and Ronald, who conveyed her to Sherwood in a thing which Joe learned was called a "carryall."

Late in the afternoon, when Ronald was gone, the two girls sat in an angle of the old walls, looking over the sea to eastward. The glow of the setting sun behind them touched them softly, and threw a rosy color upon Joe's pale face, and gilded Sybil's bright hair, hovering about her brows in a halo of radiant glory. Joe looked at her and wondered at the change love had wrought in so short a time. Sybil had once seemed so cold and white that only a nun's veil could be a fit thing to bind upon her saintly head; but now the orange blossoms would look better there, Joe thought, twined in a bride's wreath of white and green, of purity and hope.

"My Snow Angel," she exclaimed, "the sun has melted you at last!"

"Tell me the story of the Snow Angel," said Sybil, smiling. "You once said that you would."

"I will tell you," said Joe, "as well I can remember it. Mamma used to tell it to me years and years ago, when I was quite a small thing. It is a pretty story. Listen."

"Once on a time, far away in the north, there lived an angel. She was very, very beautiful, and all of the purest snow, quite white, her face and her hands and her dress and her wings. She lived alone, ever so far away, all through the long winter, in a valley of beautiful snow, where the sun never shone even in the summer. She was the most lovely angel that ever was, but she was so cold that she could not fly at all, and so she waited in the valley, always looking southward and wishing with all her heart that the sun would rise above the hill.

"Sometimes people passed, far down below, in sledges, and she almost would have asked some one of them to take her out of the valley. But once, when she came near the track, a man came by and saw her, and he was so dreadfully frightened that he almost fell out of the sled.

"Sometimes, too, the little angels, who were young and curious, would fly down into the cold valley and look at her and speak to her.

"'Pretty angel,' they would say, 'why do you stay all alone in this dreary place?'

"'They forgot me here,' she used to answer, 'and now I cannot fly until the sun is over the hill. But I am very happy. It will soon come.'

"It was too cold for the little angels, and so they soon flew away and left her; and they began to call her the Snow Angel among themselves, and some of them said she was not real, but the other ones said she must be, because she was so beautiful. She was not unhappy, because angels never can be, you know; only it seemed a long time to wait for the sun to come.

"But at last the sun heard of her, and the little angels who had seen her told him it was a shame that he should not rise high enough to warm her and help her to fly. So, as he is big and good-natured and strong, he said he would try, and would do his best; and on midsummer's day he determined to make a great effort. He shook himself, and pushed and struggled very hard, and got hotter than he had ever been in his whole life with his exertions, but at last, with a great brave leap, he found himself so high that he could see right down into the valley, and he saw the Snow Angel standing there, and she was so beautiful that he almost cried with joy. And then, as he looked, he saw a very wonderful sight.

"The Snow Angel, all white and glistening, looked up into the sun's face and stretched her arms towards him and trembled all over; and as she felt that he was come at last and had begun to warm her, she thrust out her delicate long wings, and they gleamed and shone and struck the cold clear air. Then the least possible tinge of exquisite color came into her face, and she opened her lips and sang for joy; and presently, as she was singing, she rose straight upward with a rushing sound, like a lark in the sunlight, the whitest and purest and most beautiful angel that ever flew in the sky. And her voice was so grand and clear and ringing, that all the other angels stopped in their songs to listen, and then sang with her in joy because the Snow Angel was free at last.

"That is the story mamma used to tell me, long ago, and when I first saw you I thought of it, because you were so cold and beautiful that you seemed all made of snow. But now the sun is over the hill, Sybil dear, is it not?"

"Dear Joe," said Sybil, winding her arm round her friend's neck and laying her face close to hers, "you are so nice."

The sun sank suddenly behind them, and all the eastern water caught the purple glow. It was dark when the two girls walked slowly back to the old house.

Joe stayed many days with Sybil at Sherwood, and the days ran into weeks and the weeks to months as the summer sped by. Ronald came and went daily, spending long hours with Sybil in the garden, and growing more manly and quiet in his happiness, while Sybil grew ever fairer in the gradual perfecting of her beauty. It was comforting to Joe to see them together, knowing what honest hearts they were. She occupied herself as she could with books and a few letters, but she would often sit for hours in a deep chair under the overhanging porch, where the untrimmed honeysuckle waved in the summer breeze like a living curtain, and the birds would come and swing themselves upon its tendrils. But Joe's cheek was always pale, and her heart weary with longing and with fighting against the poor imprisoned love that no one must ever guess.

Chapter XXI

The wedding-day was fixed for the middle of August, and the ceremony was to take place in Newport. It is not an easy matter to arrange the marriage of two young people neither of whom has father or mother,.though their subsequent happiness is not likely to suffer much by the bereavement. It was agreed, however, that Mrs. Wyndham, who was Sybil's oldest friend, should come and stay at Sherwood until everything was finished; and she answered the invitation by saying she was "perfectly wild to come,"—and she came at once. Uncle Tom Sherwood was a little confused at the notion of having his house full of people; but Sybil had been amusing herself by reorganizing the place for some time back, and there is nothing easier than to render a great old-fashioned country mansion habitable for a few days in the summer, when carpets are useless and smoking chimneys are not a necessity.

Mrs. Wyndham said that Sam would come down for the wedding and stay over the day, but that she expected he was pretty busy just now.

"By the way," she remarked, "you know John Harrington has come home. We must send him an invitation."

The three ladies were walking in the garden after breakfast, hatless and armed with parasols. Joe started slightly, but no one noticed it.

"When did he come—where has he been all this time?" asked Sybil.

"Oh, I do not know. He came down to see Sam the other day at our place. He seems to have taken to business. They talked about the Monroe doctrine and the Panama canal, and all kinds of things. Sam says somebody has died and left him money. Anyway, he seems a good deal interested in the canal."

Mrs. Wyndham chatted on, planning with Sybil the details of the wedding. The breakfast was to be at Sherwood, and there were not to be many people. Indeed, the distance would keep many away, a fact for which no one of those principally concerned was at all sorry. John Harrington, sweltering in the heat of New York, and busier than he had ever been in his life, received an engraved card to the effect that Mr. Thomas Sherwood requested the pleasure of Mr. Harrington's company at the marriage of his grandniece, Miss Sybil Brandon, to Mr. Ronald Surbiton, at Sherwood, on the 15th of August. There was also a note from Mrs. Wyndham, saying that she was staying at Sherwood, and that she hoped John would be able to come.

John had, of course, heard of the engagement, but he had not suspected that the wedding would take place so soon. In spite of his business, however, he determined to be present. A great change had come over his life since he had bid Joe good-by six months earlier. He had been called to London as he had expected, and had arrived there to find that Z was dead, and that he was to take his place in the council. The fiery old man had died very suddenly, having worked almost to his last hour, in spite of desperate illness; but when it was suspected that his case was hopeless, John Harrington was warned that he must be ready to join the survivors at once.

In the great excitement, and amidst the constant labor of his new position, the past seemed to sink away to utter insignificance. His previous exertions, the short sharp struggle for the senatorship ending in defeat, the hopes and fears of ten years of a most active life, were forgotten and despised in the realization of what he had so long and so ardently desired, and now at last he saw that his dreams were no impossibility, and that his theories were not myths. But he knew also that, with all his strength and devotion and energy, he was as yet no match for the two men with whom he had to do. Their vast experience of men and things threw his own knowledge into the shade, and cool as he was in emergencies, he recognized that the magnitude of the matters they handled astonished and even startled him more than he could have believed possible. Years must elapse before he understood what seemed as plain as the day to them, and he must fight many desperate battles before he was their equal. But the determination to devote his life wholly and honestly to the one object for which a man should live had grown stronger than ever. In his exalted view the ideal republic assumed grand and noble proportions, and already overshadowed the whole earth with the glory of honor and peace and perfect justice. Before the advancing tide of a spotless civilization, all poverty, all corruption and filthiness, all crime, all war and corroding seeds of discord were swept utterly away and washed from the world, to leave only forever and ever the magnificent harmony of nations and peoples, wherein none of those vile, base, and wicked things should even be dreamed of, or so much as remembered.

He thought of Joe sometimes, wondering rather vaguely why she had acted as she had, and whether any other motive than pure sympathy with his work had made her resent so violently Vancouver's position towards him. It was odd, he thought, that an English girl should find such extreme interest in American political doings, and then the scene in the dim sitting-room during the ball came vividly back to his memory. It was not in his nature to fancy that every woman who was taken with a fit of coughing was in love with him, but the conviction formed itself in his mind that he might possibly have fallen in love with Joe if things had been different. As it was, he had put away such childish things, and meant to live out his years of work, with their failure or success, without love and without a wife. He would always be grateful to Joe, but that would be all, and he would be glad to see her whenever an opportunity offered, just as he would be glad to see any other friend. In this frame of mind he arrived in Newport on the morning of the wedding, and reached the little church among the trees just in time to witness the ceremony.

It was not different from other weddings, excepting perhaps that the place where the High Church portion of Newport elects to worship is probably smaller than any other consecrated building in the world. Every seat was crowded, and it was with difficulty that John could find standing room just within the door. The heat was intense, and the horses that stood waiting in the avenue, sweated in the sun as they fought the flies, and pawed the hard road in an agony of impatience.

Sybil was exquisitely lovely as she went by on old Mr. Sherwood's arm. The old gentleman had consented to assume a civilized garb for once in his life, and looked pleased with his aged self, as well he might be, seeing that the engagement had been made under his roof. Then Ronald passed, paler than usual, but certainly the handsomest man present, carrying himself with a new dignity, as though he knew himself a better man than ever in being found worthy of his beautiful bride. It was soon over, and the crowd streamed out after the bride and bridegroom.

"Hallo, Harrington, how are you?" said Vancouver, overtaking John as he turned into the road. "You had better get in with me and drive out. I have not seen you for an age."

John stood still and surveyed Vancouver with a curiously calm air of absolute superiority.

"Thank you very much," he answered civilly. "I have hired a carriage to take me there. I dare say we shall meet. Good-morning."

John had been to Sherwood some years before, but he was surprised at the change that had been wrought in honor of the marriage. The place looked inhabited, the windows were all open, and the paths had been weeded, though Sybil had not allowed the wild shrubbery to be pruned nor the box hedges to be trimmed. She loved the pathless confusion of the old grounds, and most of all she loved the dilapidated summer-house.

John shook hands with many people that he knew. Mrs. Wyndham led him aside a little way.

"Is it not just perfectly splendid?" she exclaimed. "They are so exactly suited to each other. I feel as if I had done it all. You are not at all enthusiastic."

"On the contrary," said John, "I am very enthusiastic. It is the best thing that could possibly have happened."

"Then go and do likewise," returned Mrs. Sam, laughing. Then she changed her tone. "There is a young lady here who will be very glad to see you. Go and try and cheer her up a little, can't you?"

"Who is that?"

"A young lady over there—close to Sybil-dressed in white with roses. Don't you see? How stupid you are! There—the second on the left."

"Do you mean to say that is Miss Thorn?" exclaimed John in much surprise, and looking where Mrs. Sam directed him. "Good Heavens! How she has changed!"

"Yes, she has changed a good deal," said Mrs. Wyndham, looking at John's face.

"I hardly think I should have known her," said John. "She must have been very ill; what has been the matter?"

"The matter? Well, perhaps if you will go and speak to her, you will see what the matter is," answered Mrs. Sam, enigmatically.

"What do you mean?" John looked at his companion in astonishment.

"I mean just exactly what I say. Go and talk to her, and cheer her up a little." She dropped her voice, and spoke close to Harrington's ear—"No one else in the world can," she added.

John's impulse was to answer Mrs. Wyndham sharply. What possible right could she have to say such things? It was extremely bad taste, if it was nothing worse, even with an old friend like John. But he checked the words on his lips and spoke coldly.

"It is not fair to say things like that about any girl," he answered. "I will certainly go and speak to her at once, and if you will be good enough to watch, you will see that I am the most indifferent of persons in her eyes."

"Very well, I will watch," said Mrs. Wyndham, not in the least disconcerted. "Only take care."

John smiled quietly, and made his way through the crowd of gaily-dressed, laughing people to here Joe was standing. She had not yet caught sight of him, but she knew he was in the room, and she felt very nervous. She intended to treat him with friendly coolness, as a protest against her conduct in former days.

Poor Joe! she was very miserable, but she had made a brave effort. Her pale cheeks and darkened eyes contrasted painfully with the roses she wore, and her short nervous remarks to those who spoke to her sounded very unlike her former self.

"How do you do, Miss Thorn?" John said, very quietly. "It is a long time since we met."

Joe put her small cold hand in his, and it trembled so much that John noticed it. She turned her head a little away from him, frightened now that he was at last come.

"Yes," she said in a low voice, "it is a long time." She felt herself turn red and then pale, and as she looked away from John she met Mrs. Wyndham's black eyes turned full upon her in an inquiring way. She started as though she had been caught in some wrong thing; but she was naturally brave, and after the first shock she spoke to John more naturally.

"We seem destined for festivities, Mr. Harrington," she said, trying to laugh. "We parted at a ball, and we meet again at a wedding."

"It is always more gay to meet than to part," answered John. "I think this is altogether one of the gayest things I ever saw. What a splendid fellow your cousin is. It does one good to see men like that."

"Yes, Ronald is very good-looking," said Joe. "I am so very glad, you do not know; and he is so happy."

"Any man ought to be who marries such a woman," said John. "By the bye," he added with a smile, "Vancouver takes it all very comfortably, does he not? I would like to know what he really feels."

"I am sure that whatever it is, it is something bad," said Joe.

"How you hate him!" exclaimed John with a laugh.

"I—I do not hate him. But you ought to, Mr. Harrington. I simply despise him, that is all."

"No, I do not hate him either," answered John. "I would not disturb my peace of mind for the sake of hating any one. It is not worth while."

Some one came and spoke to Joe, and John moved away in the crowd, more disturbed in mind than he cared to acknowledge. He had gone to Joe's side in the firm conviction that Mrs. Wyndham was only making an untimely jest, and that Joe would greet him indifferently. Instead she had blushed, turned paler, hesitated in her speech, and had shown every sign of confusion and embarrassment. He knew that Mrs. Wyndham was right, after all, and he avoided her, not wishing to give a fresh opportunity for making remarks upon Joe's manner.

The breakfast progressed, and the people wandered out into the garden from the hot rooms, seeking some coolness in the shady walks. By some chain of circumstances which John could not explain, he found himself left alone with Joe an hour after he had first met her in the house. A little knot of acquaintances had gone out to the end of one of the walks, where there was a shady old bower, and presently they had paired off and moved away in various directions, leaving John and Joe together. The excitement had brought the faint color to the girl's face at last, and she was more than usually inclined to talk, partly from nervous embarrassment, and partly from the enlivening effect of so many faces she had not seen for so long.

"Tell me," she said, pulling a leaf from the creepers and twisting it in her fingers—"tell me, how long was it before you forgot your disappointment about the election? Or did you think it was not worth while to disturb your peace of mind for anything so trivial?"

"I suppose I could not help it," said John. "I was dreadfully depressed at first. I told you so, do you remember?"

"Of course you were, and I was very sorry for you. I told you you would lose it, long before, but you do not seem to care in the least now. I do not understand you at all."

"I soon got over it," said John. "I left Boston on the day after I saw you, and went straight to London. And then I found that a friend of mine was dead, and I had so much to do that I forgot everything that had gone before."

Joe gave a little sigh, short and sharp, and quickly checked.

"You have a great many friends, have you not?" she said.

"Yes, very many. A man cannot have too many of the right sort."

"I do not think you and I mean the same thing by friendship," said Joe. "I should say one cannot have too few."

"I mean friends who will help you at the right moment, that is, when you ask help. Surely it must be good to have many."

"Everything that you do and say always turns to one and the same end," said Joe, a little impatiently. "The one thing you live for is power and the hope of power. Is there nothing in the world worth while save that?"

"Power itself is worth nothing. It is the thing one means to get with it that is the real test."

"Of course. But tell me, is anything you can obtain by all the power the world holds better than the simple happiness of natural people, who are born and live good lives, and—fall in love, and marry, and that sort of thing, and are happy, and die?" Joe looked down and turned the leaf she held in her fingers, as she stated her proposition.

John Harrington paused before he answered. A moment earlier he had been as calm and cold as he was wont to be; now, he suddenly hesitated. The strong blood rushed to his brain and beat furiously in his temples, and then sank heavily back to his heart, leaving his face very pale. His fingers wrung each other fiercely for a moment. He looked away at the trees; he turned to Josephine Thorn; and then once more he gazed at the dark foliage, motionless in the hot air of the summer's afternoon.

"Yes," he said, "I think there are things much better than those in the world." But his voice shook strangely, and there was no true ring in it.

Joe sighed again.

In the distance she could see Ronald and Sybil, as they stood under the porch shaking hands with the departing guests. She looked at them, so radiant and beautiful with the fulfilled joy of a perfect love, and she looked at the stern, strong man by her side, whose commanding face bore already the lines of care and trouble, and who, he said, had found something better than the happiness of yonder bride and bridegroom.

She sighed, and she said in her woman's heart that they were right, and that John Harrington was wrong.

"Come," she said, rising, and her words had a bitter tone, "let us go in; it is late." John did not move. He sat like a stone, paler than death, and said no word in answer. Joe turned and looked at him, as though wondering why he did not follow her. She was terrified at the expression in his face.

"Are you not coming?" she asked, suddenly going close to him and looking into his eyes.

Chapter XXII

Joe was frightened; she stood and looked into Harrington's eyes, doubting what she should do, not understanding what was occurring. He looked so pale and strange as he sat there, that she was terrified. She came a step nearer to him, and tried to speak.

"What is the matter, Mr. Harrington?" she stammered. "Speak—you frighten me!"

Harrington looked at her for one moment more, and then, without speaking, buried his face in his hands. Joe clasped her hands to her side in a sudden pain; her heart beat as though it would break, and the scene swam round before her in the hot air. She tried to move another step towards the bench, and her strength almost failed her; she caught at the lattice of the old summer-house, still pressing one hand to her breast. The rotten slabs of the wood-work cracked under her light weight. She breathed hard, and her face was as pale as the shadows on driven snow; in another moment she sank down upon the bench beside John, and sat there, staring vacantly out at the sunlight. Harrington felt her gentle presence close to him and at last looked up; every feature of his strong face seemed changed in the convulsive fight that rent his heart and soul to their very depths; the enormous strength of his cold and dominant nature rose with tremendous force to meet and quell the tempest of his passion, and could not; dark circles made heavy shadows under his deep-set eyes, and his even lips, left colorless and white, were strained upon his clenched teeth.

"God help me—I love you."

That was all he said, but in his words the deep agony of a mortal struggle rang strangely—the knell of the old life and the birth-chime of the new. One by one, the words he had never thought to speak fell from his lips, distinctly; the oracle of the heart answered the great question of fate in its own way.

Josephine Thorn sat by his side, her hands lying idly in her lap, her thin white face pressing against the old brown lattice, while a spray of the sweet honeysuckle that climbed over the wood-work just touched her bright brown hair. As John spoke she tried to lift her head and struggled to put out her hand, but could not.

As the shadows steal at evening over the earth, softly closing the flowers and touching them to sleep, silently and lovingly, in the promise of a bright waking—so, as she sat there, her eyelids drooped and the light faded gently from her face, her lips parted a very little, and with a soft-breathed sigh she sank into unconsciousness.

John Harrington was in no state to be surprised or startled by anything that happened. He saw, indeed, that she had fainted, but with the unerring instinct of a great love he understood. With the tenderness of his strength he put one arm about her, and drew her to him till her fair head rested upon his shoulder, and he looked into her face.

In a few moments he had passed completely from the old life to a life which he had never believed possible, but which had nevertheless been long present with him. He knew it and felt it, quickly realizing that for the first time since he could remember he was wholly and perfectly happy. He was a man who had dreamed of all that is noble and great for man to do, who had consecrated his every hour and minute to the attainment of his end; and though his aim was in itself a good one, the undivided concentration which the pursuit of it required had driven him into a state outwardly resembling extreme egotism. He had loved his own purposes as he had loved nothing else, and as he had been persuaded that he could love nothing else, in the whole world. Now, suddenly, he knew his own heart.

There is something beyond mere greatness, beyond the pursuit of even the highest worldly aims; there is something which is not a means to the attainment of happiness, which is happiness itself. It is an inner sympathy of hearts and souls and minds, a perfect union of all that is most worthy in the natures of man and woman; it is a plant so sensitive that a breath of unkindness will hurt it and blight its beauty, and yet it is a tree so strong that neither time nor tempest can overthrow it when it has taken root; and if you would tear it out and destroy it, the place where it grew is as deep and as wide as a grave. It is a bond that is as soft as silk and as strong as death, binding hearts, not hands; so long as it is not strained a man will hardly know that he is bound, but if he would break it he will spend his strength in vain and suffer the pains of hell, for it is the very essence and nature of a true love that it cannot be broken.

With such men as John Harrington love at first sight is an utter impossibility. The strong dominant aspirations that lead them are a light too brilliant to be outshone by any sudden flash of hot passion. Love, when it comes to them, is of slow growth, but enduring in the same proportion as it is slow; identifying itself, by degrees so small that a man himself is unconscious of it, with the deepest feelings of the heart and the highest workings of the intellect. It steals silently into the soul in the guise of friendship, asking nothing but loyal friendship in return; in the appearance of kindness which asks but a little gratitude; in the semblance of a calm and passionless trustfulness, demanding only a like trust as its equivalent pledge, a like faith as a gauge for its own, an equal measure of charity for an equal; and so love builds himself a temple of faith and charity, and trust and kindness, and honest friendship, and rejoices exceedingly in the whole goodness and strength and beauty of the place where he will presently worship. When that day comes he stands in the midst and kindles a strong clear flame upon the altar, and the fire burns and leaps and illuminates the whole temple of love, which is indeed the holy of holies of the temple of life.

John Harrington, through five and thirty years of his life, had believed that the patient labor of a powerful intellect could suffice to a man, in its results, for the attainment of all that humanity most honors, even for the wise and unerring government of humanity itself. To that end and in that belief he had honestly given every energy he possessed, and had sternly choked down every tendency he felt in his inner nature toward a life less intellectual and more full of sympathy for the affairs of individual mankind. With him to be strong was to be cold—to be warm was to be weak and subject to error; a supreme devotion to his career and a supreme disdain of all personal affections were the conditions of success which he deemed foremostly necessary, and he had come to an almost superstitious belief in the idea that the love of woman is the destruction of the intellectual man. Himself ready to sacrifice all he possessed, and to spend his last strength in the struggle for an ideal, he had nevertheless so identified his own person with the object he strove to attain that he regarded all the means he could possibly control with as much jealousy as though he had been the most selfish of men. Friends he looked upon as tools for his trade, and he valued them not only in proportion to their honesty and loyalty of heart, but also in the degree of their power and intelligence. He sought no friendships which could not help him, and relinquished none that could be of service in the future.

But the world is not ruled by intellect, though it is sometimes governed by brute force and yet more brutal passions. The dominant power in the affairs of men is the heart. Humanity is moved far more by what it feels than by what it knows, and those who would be rulers of men must before all things be men themselves, and not merely highly finished intellectual machines.

The guests were gone, no one had missed Harrington and Joe, and Ronald and Sybil had gone into the house. They sat side by side in the little bower at the end of the long walk—Joe's fair head resting in her unconsciousness upon John's shoulder. Presently she stirred, and opening her eyes, looked up into his face. She drew gently away from him, and a warm blush spread quickly over her pale cheek; she glanced down at her small white hands and they clasped each other convulsively.

John looked at her; suddenly his gray eyes grew dark and deep, and the mighty passion took all his strength into its own, so that he trembled and turned pale again. But the words failed him no longer now. He knew in a moment all that he had to say, and he said it.

"You must not be angry with me, Miss Thorn," he began, "you must not think I am losing my head. Let me tell you now—perhaps you will listen to me. God knows, I am not worthy to say such things to you, but I will try to be. It is soon said. I love you; I can no more help loving you than I can help breathing. You have utterly changed me, and saved me, and made a life for me out of what was not life at all. Do not think it is sudden—what is really to last forever must take some time in growing. I never knew till to-day-I honored you and would have done everything in the world for you, and I was more grateful to you than I ever was to any human being. But I thought when we met we should be friends just as we always were, and instead of that I know that this is the great day of my life, and that my life with all that it holds is yours now, for always, to do with as you will. Pray hear me out, do not be afraid; no man ever honored you as I honor you."

Joe glanced quickly at him and then again looked down; but the surging blood came and went in her face, coursing madly in her pulses, every beat of her heart crying gladness.

"It is little enough I have to offer you," said John, his voice growing unsteady in the great effort to speak calmly. There was something almost terrible in the strength of his rising passion. "It is little enough—my poor life, with its wretched struggles after what is perhaps far too great for me. But such as it is I offer it to you. Take it if you will. Be my wife, and give me the right to do all I do for your sake, and for your sake only." He stretched out his hand and took hers, very gently, but the strained sinews of his wrist trembled violently. Josephine made no resistance, but she still looked down and said nothing.

"Use me as you will," he continued almost in a whisper. "I will be all to you that man ever was to a living woman. Do not say I have no right to ask you for as much. I have this right, that I love you beyond the love of other men, so truly and wholly I love you; I will serve you so faithfully, I will honor you so loyally that you will love me too. Say the word, my beloved, say that it is not impossible! I will wait—I will work—I will strive to be worthy of you." He pressed his white lips to her white hand, and tried to look into her eyes, but she turned away from him. "Will you not speak to me? Will you not give to me some word—some hope? I can never love you less, whatever you may answer me—yes or no—but oh, if you knew the difference to me!"

Pale as death, John looked at Joe. She turned to him, very white, and gazed into the dark gray depths of his eyes, where the raging force of a transcendent passion played so wildly; but she felt no fear, only a mad longing to speak.

"Tell me—for God's sake tell me," John said in low, trembling tones, "have I hurt you? Is it too much that I ask?"

For one moment there was silence as they gazed at each other. Then with a passionate impulse Josephine buried her face in her hands upon John's shoulder.

"No, it is not that!" she sobbed. "I love you so much—I have loved you so long!"

Chapter XXIII

John Harrington and Josephine Thorn were married in the autumn of that year, and six months later John was elected to the Senate. With characteristic patience he determined to await a favorable opportunity before speaking at any length in the Capitol. He loved his new life, and the instinct to take a leading part was strong in him, but he knew too well the importance of the first impression made by a long speech to thrust himself forward until the right moment came.

It chanced that the presidential election took place in that year, just a twelvemonth after John's marriage, and the unusual occurrences that attended the struggle gave him the chance he desired. Three candidates were supported nearly equally by the East, the West, and the South, and on opening the sealed documents in the presence of the two houses, it was found that no one of the three had obtained the majority necessary to elect him. The country was in a state of unparalleled agitation. The imminent danger was that the non-election of the candidate from the West would produce a secession of the Western States from the Union, in the same way that a revolution was nearly brought about in 1876, during the contest between Mr. Hayes and Mr. Tilden.

In this position of affairs, the electors being unable to agree upon any one of the three candidates, the election was thrown into the hands of Congress, in accordance with the clause of the Constitution which provides that in such cases the House of Representatives shall elect a president, each State having but one vote.

Harrington had made many speeches in different parts of the country during the election campaign, and had attracted much attention by his calm good sense in such excited times. There was consequently a manifest desire among senators and representatives to hear him speak in the Capitol, and upon the day when the final election of the President took place he judged that his opportunity had come. Josephine was in the ladies' gallery, and as John rose to his feet he looked long and fixedly up to her, gathering more strength to do well what he so much loved to do, from gazing at her whom he loved better than power, or fame, or any earthly thing. His eyes shone and his cheek paled; his old life with all its energy and active work was associated in his mind with failure, with discontent, and with solitude; his new life, with her by his side, was brilliant, happy, and successful. He felt within him the strength to move thousands, the faith in his cause and in his power to help it which culminates in great deeds. His strong voice rang out, clear and far-heard, as he spoke.

"MR. PRESIDENT,—We are here to decide, on behalf of our country, a great matter. Many of us, many more who are scattered over the land, will look back upon this day as one of the most important in our times, and for their sakes as well as our own we are bound to summon all our strength of intelligence and all our calmness of judgment to aid us in our decision.

"The question in which a certain number of ourselves are to become arbitrators is briefly this: Are we to act on this occasion like partisans, straining every nerve for the advantage of our several parties? or are we to act like free men, exerting our united forces in one harmonious body for the immediate good of the whole country? The struggle may seem at first sight to be a battle between the East, the West, and the South. In sober earnest, it is a contest between the changing principles of party politics on the one hand and the undying principle of freedom on the other.

"I need not make any long statement of the case to you. We are here assembled to elect a President. Our position is almost unprecedented in the history of the country. Instead of acquiescing in the declared will of the people, our fellow-citizens, we are told that the people's wish is divided, and we are called upon to act spontaneously for the people, in accordance with the constitution of our country. By our individual and unhampered votes the life of the country is to be determined for the next four years. Let us not forget the vast responsibility that is upon us. Let us join our hands and say to each other, 'We are no longer Republicans, nor Democrats, nor Independents—we are one party, the party of the Union, and there are none against us.'

"A partisan is not necessarily a man who asserts a truth and defends it with his whole strength. A partisan means one who takes up his position with a party. There is a limit where a partisan becomes an asserter of falsehood, and that limit is reached when a man resigns his own principles into the judgment of another, his conscience into another's keeping; when a man gives up free thought, free judgment, and free will in absolute and blind adherence to a set of thoughts, judgments, and decisions over which he exercises no control, and in the formation of which he has but one voice in many millions. Every one remembers the fable of the old man who, when dying, made his sons break their staves one by one, and then bade them bind a bundle of others together, and to try and break them by one effort. In the uniting of individuals in a party there is strength, but there must also be complete unity. If the old man had bidden his sons bind their staves in several bundles instead of in one, the result would have been doubtful. That is what party spirit makes men do. Party spirit is a universal solvent; it is the great acid, the aqua fortis of political alchemy, which eats through bands of steel and corrodes pillars of iron in its acrid virulence, till the whole engine of a nation's government is crumbled and dissolved into a shapeless and a worse than useless mass of broken metal.

"Man is free, his will is free, his choice, his judgments, his capacity for thought, and his power to profit by it are all as free as air, just so long as he remembers that they are his own—no longer. When he forgets that he is his own master, absolutely and entirely, he becomes another man's slave.

"The contest here is between political passion roused to its fiercest pitch by the antagonism of parties, and the universal liberty of opinion, which we all say we possess, while so few of us dare honestly exercise it. This passion, this political frenzy that seizes men and whirls them in its eddies, is a most singular compound of patriotism, of enthusiasm for an individual, and of the personal hopes, fears, generosity, and avarice of the individual who is enthusiastic. It is a passion which, existing in others, can be turned to account by the cool leader who does not possess it, but which may too easily bring ruin upon the man who is led.

"The danger ahead is this same party spirit, this wild and thoughtless frenzy in matters where unbiased judgment is most of all necessary. It is a rock upon which we have split before; it has taken us many years to recover from the shock, and now we are in danger of altogether losing our political life upon the same reef. Unless we mend our course we inevitably shall. Men forego every consideration of public honor and private conscience for the sake of electing a party candidate. The man at the helm of the party ship has declared that he will sail due north, or south, or east, or west, whatever happens, and his crew laugh together and keep no lookout; they even feel a certain pride in their leader, who thus defies the accidents of nature for the sake of sailing in a fixed direction.

"What is the result of all this? It is here before us. The country is splitting into parties. Three candidates are set up for the office of President. Three distinct parties stand in the field, each one vowing vengeance, secession, revolution, utter dismemberment of the Union, unless its chosen champion is elected to be chief of the Executive Department. Is this to be the life of our Republic in future? Is this all that so many millions of free citizens can do for the public good and for public harmony? What shall we gain by electing the candidate from the North, if the defeated candidate from the South is determined to produce a revolution; and if the disappointed candidate from the West threatens to touch off the dry powder and spring the mine of a great western secession? Have we not seen all this before? Has not the bitter cry of a nation's broken heart gone up to heaven already in mortal agony for these very things to which our uncontrollable political passions are hourly leading us?

"The contest is between political passion on the one hand and universal liberty on the other.

"Liberty in some countries is a kind of charade word, an anagram, a symbol representing an imaginary quantity, a password invented by unhappy men to express all that they do not possess; a term meaning in the minds of slaves a conglomerate of conditions so absurd, of aspirations so futile, of imaginary delights so fantastically unreasonable, that if the ideal state of which the chained dreamers rave were realized but for one moment, humanity would start in amazement at the first glimpse of so much monstrosity, and by and by would hold its sides with laughter at the folly of its deluded fellows. In most countries where liberty is talked of it is but a dream, and such a dream as could only occur to the sickened fancy of a generation of bondsmen. But it means something else with us. It is here, in this country, in this capital, in this hall, it is in the air we breathe, in the light we see, in the strong, free pulses of our blood; it is the heritage of men whose sires died for it, whose fathers laid down all they had for it, of men whose own veins have bled for it—and not in vain. In these United States, liberty is a fact.

"We must decide quickly, then, between the conditions of our liberty and the requirements of frantic political passion. We must decide between peace and war, for that is where the issue will come in the end. Between freedom, prosperity, and peace on the one side, and a civil war on the other; an alternative so horrible and inhuman and hideous, that the very mention of it makes brave men shiver in disgust at the memories the word recalls. Do you think we are much further from it now than we were in 1860? Do you think we were far from it in 1876? It is a short step from the threat to the deed when political passion is already turning to bitter personal hate.

"In our times there is much talk of civilization and culture. Two words define all that is necessary to be known about them. Civilization is peace. The uncivilized state of man is incessant war. Culture is conscience, because conscience means the exercise of honest judgment, and an ignorant people can form no honest judgment of their own which can be exercised.

"In a state of peace, educated and truthful men judge fairly, and act sensibly on their decisions. In other words, the majority is right and free. In times of war and in times of great ignorance majorities have rarely been either free or right.

"It is a bad sign of the times when education increases and truth disappears. They ought to grow together, for education means absolutely nothing but the teaching and learning of what is true. If it does not mean that, it means nothing. In some countries the idea of truth is coexistent with the idea of destroying all existing forms of belief. Some silly person recently went so far as to raise the cry in this country, 'Separate Church and State!' If there is a country where they are absolutely separated, it is ours; but let the beliefs of mankind take care of themselves. I dare say there will be Christians left in the world even when Professor Huxley has written his last book, and when Colonel Ingersoll has delivered his last lecture. I am reminded of the Chinese philosopher and political economist, who answered when he was asked about religious matters: 'Do you understand this world so well that you need occupy yourselves with another?'

"The issue turns upon no such absurdities, neither does it rest with any consideration of so-called platforms—free trade, civil service, free navigation, tariff reform, and all the rest of those things. The real issue is between civilization and barbarism, between peace and war.

"Be warned in this great strait. I believe we need few principles, but universal ones. I believe in the republic because it was founded in simplicity, and has been built up in strength by the strongest of strong men; because its existence proves the greatest truth with which we ever have to do, namely, that men are born equal and free, although they may grow up slaves to their evil passions, and become greater or less according as they manfully put their hands to the plough, or ignobly lie down and let themselves be trampled upon. The battle of life is to the stronger, but no man is so weak that he cannot raise himself a little if he will, according to the abilities that are born in him; and nowhere can he raise himself so speedily and securely as on this free soil of ours. Nowhere can he go so far without being molested; for nowhere can man put himself so closely and trustfully in the keeping of nature, certain that she will not fail him, certain that she will yield him a thousand fold for his labor.

"There are indeed times in the history of a great institution when it is just as well as necessary to reconsider the principles upon which it is founded. There are times in the life of a great nation when it behooves her chief men to examine and see whether the basis of her constitution is a sound one, and whether she can continue to grow great without any change in the fundamental conditions of her development. It is a bad and a dangerous time for a growing nation, but it is an almost inevitable stage in her life. Thank God, that time is past with us! Let us not think of the possibility of exposing ourselves again to civil war as an alternative against retrogression into barbarism.

"Civilization is peace, and to extend civilization is to increase the security of property in the world—of property and life and conscience. The natural and barbarous state of man is that where the human animal satisfies its cravings without any thought of consequences. The cultivated state is that where humanity has ceased to be merely animal, and considers the consequences first and the cravings afterwards. Civilization unites men so that they dwell together in harmony; to separate them into parties that strive to annihilate each other is to undo the work of civilization, to plunge the state into civil war; to hew it in pieces, and split it and tear it to shreds, till the magnificent body of thinking beings, acting as one man for the public good, is reduced to the miserable condition of a handful of hostile tribes, whose very existence depends upon successful robbery and well-timed violence.

"Party spirit, so long as it is only a force which binds together a number of men of honest purposes and opinions, is a good thing, and it is by its means that just and powerful majorities are formed and guided. But where party spirit loses sight of the characters of men, and judges them according as they are Republicans or Democrats, instead of considering whether they are good or bad citizens; when party spirit becomes a machine for obtaining power by fair or foul means, instead of a fixed principle for upholding the fair against the foul—then there is great danger that the majority itself is losing its liberty, and upon the liberty of majorities depends ultimately the stability and prosperity of the republic.

"Consider what is the history of the average politician to-day, of the man whose personal character is as good as that of his neighbor, who has always belonged to the same party, and who looks forward to the hope of political distinction. Consider how he has struggled through all manner of difficulties to his present position, striving always to maintain good relations with the chiefs of his party, while often acknowledging in his heart that he would act differently were his connection with those chiefs a matter of less vital importance to himself. He probably will tell you that his profession is politics. He has sacrificed much to obtain his seat in Congress, or his position in office, and he knows that henceforth he must live by it or else begin life over again in another sphere. At all events, for a term of years, his personal prosperity depends upon the use he can make of his hold upon the public goods. He is not individually to be blamed, perhaps, for he follows a precedent as widely recognized as it is universally pernicious. It is the system that is to be blamed, the general belief that a man can, and justly may, support himself by clinging to a set of principles of which he does not honestly approve; that he may earn his daily meal, since it comes to that in the end, by doing jobs which in the free state he would despise as unworthy, and by speaking boldly in support of measures which he knows to be injurious to the welfare of the country. That is the history, the epitome of the ends and aims and manner of being of the average politician in our day. He has ventured into the waters of political life, and they have risen around him till he must use all his strength in keeping his head above them, though the torrent carry him whither it will and whither he would not. There are no compromises when a man is drowning.

"There are many who are not in any such position. There are men great and honest, and disinterested in the highest sense of the word—men whose whole lives prove it, whose whole record is one of honor and truth, whose following consists of men they have themselves chosen as their friends. We are not obliged to select a drowning man for our President; we can choose a man who stands on his own feet upon dry ground.

"There is an old proverb which contains much wisdom: 'Tell me who are your friends, and I will tell you what you are.' Is a man fit to stand at the head of a community of men when he has associated with a set of parasites, who live upon his leavings, and will starve him if they can, in order to enjoy his portion? Consider what is the position of the President of the United States. Think what vast power is placed in the hands of one man; what vast interests of public and private good are at stake; what an endless sequence of events and results of events must follow upon the individual action of the chief of the Executive Department; and remember how free and untrammeled that individual action is. A people who elect an officer to such a position need surely to be cautious in their choice and circumspect in their judgment of the man elected. They must satisfy themselves about what he is likely to do by judging honestly what he has done; they must know who are his friends, his supporters, his advisers, in order to judge of the friends he will make. They must take into their consideration also the character of his colleague, the vice-president, and the effect upon the country and the country's relation with, the world, should any disaster suddenly throw the vice-president into office. We cannot afford to elect a vice-president who would destroy the national credit in a week, should the President himself be overtaken by death. We must remember to count the cost of what we are doing, not passing over one item because another item seems just. We cannot overlook the future, nor disregard the influence which our election has upon the next; the steps which men, once in office, may take in order to secure to themselves another term, or to strengthen the position of the men whom they desire to succeed them.

"In a word, we must put forth all our strength. We must be cool, far-sighted, and impartial in such times as these. And yet, how has this campaign been hitherto conducted? Practically, by raising a party cry; by exciting every species of evil passion of which man is capable; by tickling the cupidity of one man and flattering the ambitions of another; by intimidating the weak, and groveling before the strong; by every species of fawning sycophancy on the one hand, and brutal overbearing bullying on the other.

"Party, party, party! A man would rather commit a crime than vote against his party. The evil runs through the country from East to West, from North to South, eating at the nation's heartstrings, gnawing at her sinews, and undermining her strength. The time is coming, is even now come, when two or three parties no longer suffice to express the disunion of the Union. There are three to-day: to-morrow there will be five, the next day ten, twenty, a hundred, till every man's hand is against his fellow, and his fellow's against him. The divisions have grown so wide that the majority and the minority are but the extremities of a countless set of internecine majorities and minorities.

"Members of parties are bound no longer by the honest determination to do the right, to choose the right, and to uphold the right—they are bound by fearful penalties to support their own man, were he the very chiefest outcast of the earth, lest the man of another party be elected in his place. The adverse candidate is perhaps avowedly better fitted for the office, a hundred times more honest, more experienced, more worthy of respect. But he belongs to the enemy. Down with him! let him perish in his honesty and righteousness! There is no good in him, for he is a Democrat! There is no good in him, for he is a Republican! He is a scoundrel, for he is a Southerner! He is a thief, for he is a Northerner! He is the prince of liars, for he comes from the West! He is the scum of mankind, for he is from the East! The people rage and rend each other, and the frenzy grows apace with the hour, till honor and justice, truth and manliness, are lost together in the furious chaos of human elements. The tortured airs of heaven howl out curses in a horrid unison, this fair free soil of ours, dishonored and befouled, moans beneath our feet in a dismal drone of hopeless woe; there is no rock or cavern or ghostly den of our mighty land but hisses back the echo of some hideous curse, and hell itself is upon earth, split and rent into multiplied hells.

"And the ultimate expression of the senses of these things is money. There is the chiefest disgrace. We are not worse than the old nations, but we have a right to be very much better; we have the obligation to be better, the unchanging moral obligation which lies upon every man to use the advantage he has. We alone among nations are free, we alone among nations inhabit a quarter of the world by ourselves, and live and grow great in our own way with no thought of the rest. Let us think more of living greatly than of prosecuting greatness for the sake of its pecuniary emoluments. Let us elect presidents who will give their efforts to making us all great together, and not to making some citizens rich at the expense of others who are also citizens. A President can do much toward either of these results, bad or good. He has the future of the republic in his hands, as well as the present. Let us be the richest among nations, since the course of events makes us so, but let us not be the most sordid. Let it never be said, in the land which has given birth to the only true liberty the world has ever seen, that liberty can be sold for a few dollars in the market-place, and bartered against the promise of four years of civil employment at a small salary!

"This party spirit, this miserable craving for the good things that may be extracted from the service of a party, has produced the crying evil of our times. A certain class—a very large class—call our politics dirty, and our politicians dishonest. Young men whose education and position in the commonwealth entitle them to a voice in public matters withdraw entirely from all contact with the real life of the country. Liberty has become a leper, a blind outcast in the eyes of the gilded youth of to-day. She sits apart in ashes and in rags, and asks a little charity of the richest of her children—a miserable mother despised and cast out by her sons. They will not own her for their mother, nor spare one crust to feed her from their plenty. They pass by on the other side, staring in admiration at the image they have set up for themselves—the image of what they consider social excellence, an idol compounded of decayed customs, and breathing the poisonous emanations of a dead world, a monument raised to the prejudices of former times, to the petty thirst for aristocratic distinctions which they cherish in their hearts, to their love of money, show, superficial culture, and armorial bearings.

"Truly let them perish in the fruition of their contemptible desires! Let them set up a thing called society and worship it; let them lose themselves in the contemplation of objects whose beauty they can never appreciate save by counting the cost; let them disgrace the names their honest fathers bore, by striving to establish their descent from houses stained with crime and denied with blood; let them disown their fathers and spit in their mothers' faces,—but let them not call themselves free, nor give themselves the airs of men. They toss their foolish heads in scorn of all that a man holds truest and best. We can afford to let them speak, if they please, even words of contempt and dishonor; we can afford to let them say that in laboring for our country we are groveling in mud and defiling our hands with impurity; but we cannot afford to let them steal our children from us, nor to submit to the pestilent influence of their corruption in our ranks. Those who would be of the republic must labor for the public good, instead of insolently asserting that there is no good in the public on which they have fattened and thriven so well.

"All honor to those who have set their faces against the growing evil, to check it if they can, and to lay the foundation of a barrier against which the tidal wave of corruption and dishonesty shall break in vain. All praise to the brave men who might live in the indolent lotus-eating atmosphere of wasteful idleness, but who have put their hand to the wheel of state, determined to bear all their might upon the whirling spokes rather than see the good ship go to pieces on the rock ahead. They have begun a good work, and they have sown a good seed; they ask for no reward, nor look for the reaping of the harvest. They mean to do right, and they do it, because right is right, not because they expect to be rewarded with the spoils or fed with fat tit-bits from the feast of party. Upon such men as these, be they rich or poor, we must rely. The poor man can make sacrifices as great as the rich, for he can forego for his country's sake, the promise of ease and the hope of wealth as well as any million-maker in the land.

"In the tremendous issue now before us we are called to decide upon the life of the country during the next four years. We are chosen to direct the course of a stream from its very source, and to turn it into a channel where it will run smoothly to the end. For the four years of an administration are like a river. The water rises suddenly from the spring and flows swiftly, ever increasing in volume as it is swollen by tributaries and absorbs into itself other rivers by the way. It may run smoothly in a fair stream, moistening barren lands and softening the parched desert into fertility; moving great engines of industry with a ceaseless, even strength; bearing the burden of a mighty and prosperous commerce on its broad bosom; spreading plenty and refreshment through the wide pastures by its banks, fed on its way by waters so clear that at the last it merges untainted and unsullied into the ocean, whence its limpid drops may again be taken up and poured in soft, life-giving rain upon the earth.

"But in digging for a spring men may find suddenly a torrent that they cannot control. It suddenly bursts its bounds and banks, and rushes headlong down, carrying everything before it in a resistless whirl of devastation, tearing great trees up by the roots, crashing through villages and towns and factories, girding the world with a liquid tempest that sends the works of man spinning down upon its dreadful course, till it plunges into the abyss, a frantic chaos of indiscriminate destruction, storm, and death.

"Can any of us here present say that he will, that he dare, take upon himself the responsibility of electing a President from motives of party prejudice? Having it in our power to agree upon the very best man, would any of us remember this day without shame if we disgraced those who trust us, by giving our votes to a mere party candidate? The danger is great, imminent, universal. We can save the country from it, I would almost say from, death itself, by acting in accordance with our honest convictions. Is any man so despicable, so lost to honor, that in such a case he will put aside the welfare of a nation for the miserable sake of party popularity? Are we to stand here in the guise and manner of free men, knowing that we are driven together like a flock of sheep into the fold by the howling of the wolves outside? Are we to strut and plume ourselves upon our unhampered freedom, while we act like slaves? Worse than slaves we should be if we allowed one breath of party spirit, one thought of party aggrandizement, to enter into the choice we are about to make. Slaves are driven to their work; shall we willingly let ourselves be beaten into doing the dirty work of others by sacrificing the nobility of our manhood? Do we meet here, like paid gladiators of old, to cut each other's throats in earnest while attacking and defending a sham fortress, raised in the arena for the diversion of those who set us on to the butchery and promise to pay the survivors? Are we to provide a feast of carrion for a flock of vultures and unclean beasts of prey, when we need only stand together, and be true to ourselves and to each other, to accomplish one of the greatest acts in history? The vultures will leave us alone unless we destroy each other; we need not fear them. We are not slaves to be terrified into compliance with evil, neither are we sheep that we need huddle trembling together at the snarling of a wolf."

"No, no, indeed!" were the words heard on all sides in the audience, now thoroughly roused.

"I do not say, elect this candidate, or that one. I am not canvassing for any candidate. It is too late for that, even if it were seemly for me to do so. I am canvassing for the cause of liberty against slavery, as better men have done before me in this very house. I am defending the reputation of unity against the slanderous attack of disunion, against the fearful peril of secession. I appeal to you, as you are men, to act as men in this great crisis, to put out your strong hands together and avert the overwhelming disaster that threatens us; to stand side by side as brothers,—for we are indeed brothers, children of one father and one mother, heirs of such magnificent heritage as has not fallen to the lot of mortality before, co-heirs of freedom, and inheritors of the free estate, five and fifty millions of free children, born to our mother, the great republic, who bow the knee to no man, and call no man master."

Loud applause greeted this part of the speech.

"I appeal from license to law, from division to harmony, from the raging turmoil of angry and devouring passion without to the calm serenity that reigns within these walls. As we turn in horror and loathing from the unbridled fury of human beings, changed almost to beasts, so let us turn in hope and security to those things we can honor and respect, to the dignity of truth and the unbending strength of unquestioned right.

"I appeal to you to make this day the greatest in your lives, the most memorable in our history as a nation. Lay aside this day the memories of the past, and look forward to the brightness of the future. Throw down the weapons of petty and murderous strife, and join together in perfect harmony of mutual trust. Be neither Republicans, nor Democrats, nor Independents. Be what it is your greatest privilege to be—American citizens. Cast parties to the winds, and uphold the state. Trample under your free-born feet the badges of party bondage, the ignoble chains of party slavery, the wretched hopes of party preferment."

"Yes. Hear, hear! He is right!" cried many voices.

"Yes," answered John Harrington, in tones that rose to the very roof of the vast building.

"'Yes, by that blood our fathers shed,
    O Union, in thy sacred cause,
 Whilst, streaming from the gallant dead,
    It sealed and sanctified thy laws.'

"Yes, and strong hearts and strong hands will hold their own; the promise of brave men will prevail, and echoing down the avenues of time will strike grand chords of harmony in the lives of our children and children's children. So, in the far-off ages, when hundreds of millions of our flesh and blood shall fill this land, dwelling together in the glory of such peace as no turmoil can trouble and no discontent disturb, those men of the dim future will remember what we swore to do, and what we did; and looking back, they will say one to another: 'On that day our fathers struck a mighty blow, and shattered and crushed and trampled out all dissensions and all party strife forever and ever.'

"Choose, then, of your own heart and will a man to be our President and our leader. Elect him with one accord, and as you give your voices in the choice, stand here together, knee to knee, shoulder to shoulder, hand to hand; and let the mighty oath go thundering up to heaven,

"'This Union shall not be broken!'"

Francis Marion Crawford was born in Bagni di Lucca, Italy on 2nd August, 1854, the only son of the American sculptor Thomas Crawford and Louisa Cutler Ward. His aunt was Julia Ward Howe, the American poet, most famous for the words to 'The Battle Hymn of the Republic'.

After his father's death in 1857, his mother remarried to Luther Terry, with whom she had Crawford's half-sister, Margaret Ward Terry.

Crawford's education began at St Paul's School, Concord, New Hampshire and then went on to Cambridge University, the University of Heidelberg and finally the University of Rome.

In 1879, Crawford went to India to study the ancient language of Sanskrit and to edit Allahabad, The Indian Herald.

Returning to America in February 1881, he enrolled at Harvard University for a year to continue his studies in Sanskrit. Crawford had no real career path at this time although for two years he contributed to various periodicals, mainly The Critic.

Early in 1882, Crawford established a close, lifelong friendship with Isabella Stewart Gardner, a noted and eccentric heiress from Boston who over the years built up a large and eclectic collection of art.

Crawford lived most of his time in Boston with his Aunt Julia and Uncle Sam. The family were concerned by his lack of ambition, prospects in general, and his financial ones in particular.

His mother had hoped he might train in Boston for a career as an operatic baritone based on his private renditions of Schubert lieder. With that in mind it was, in January 1882, that George Henschel, the conductor of the Boston Symphony Orchestra, was called in to assess young Crawford's talents. Henschel was direct and to the point. Crawford would 'never be able to sing in perfect tune'. His Uncle Sam, knowing that Crawford was keen on literary pursuits, proposed that his years in India might be good source material to write about. Crawford agreed. He set to work. Uncle Sam also set about developing contacts with a number of New York publishers.

Events moved very quickly. By December of that year Crawford had completed his first novel, 'Mr Isaacs', based on modern Anglo-Indian life flavoured with a touch of Oriental mystery. It was an immediate success. Crawford set about writing a second novel and the result was 'Dr Claudius' in 1883.

In October 1884 he married Elizabeth Berdan, the daughter of the Civil War Union General Hiram Berdan. The marriage would produce two sons; Harold and Bertram, and two daughters; Eleanor and Clara.

Crawford, buoyed by his excellent start, now decided to return to Italy and to live there permanently. The couple initially went to Sorrento and lived at the historic Hotel Cocumella during 1885 before moving permanently to Sant' Agnello, where the purchase of the Villa Renzi would now be rededicated as Villa Crawford.

As a writer Crawford had more than his fair share of detractors but, perhaps due to the physical distance between author and these detractors, they did not distract from his prolific output.

Each year seemed to bring a new F. Marion Crawford novel. His popularity was evident although some works, such as 1896's offering 'Adam Johnstone's Son', was described by his left-wing English contemporary, George Gissing, as "rubbish". Over half of his novels are set in Italy. He also wrote three long historical studies of Italy and was nearing completion on a history of Rome in the Middle Ages when he died.

His 'Saracinesca' series are considered his best works. The third in the series, 'Don Orsino' (1892) was told against the background of a real estate bubble and is especially effective. The volume immediately after was 'Corleone' (1897), and the first major treatment of the Mafia in literature.

Crawford himself was fondest of 'Khaled: A Tale of Arabia' (1891), a story of a genie who becomes human. 'A Cigarette-Maker's Romance' (1890) was dramatized, and had considerable popularity on the stage as well as in its novel form.

Towards the end of the 1890's Crawford ventured down another path with his writing. He began his historical works. 'Ave Roma Immortalis' was published in 1898, followed by 'Rulers of the South' (1900), and 'Gleanings from Venetian History' (1905). Most were re-titled with longer more explanatory titles for the American market. Within them all his careful and precise knowledge of the local Italian history together with his literary talents combined to great effect.

Whilst on an American Lecture tour in the winter of 1897-1898 Crawford was researching and gathering technical information for his historical work 'Marietta' (published 1901), that describes glass-making in late medieval Venice. Whilst visiting a glass-smelting plant in Colorado he suffered a severe lung injury when he inhaled toxic gasses. This would eventually contribute to his death a decade or so later.

Crawford's commercial popularity and appeal at the time was such that in 1901, the American Macmillan firm began a deluxe uniform edition of his novels as his works came up for re-printing. In 1904 the P. F. Collier Company in New York was authorized to publish a 25-volume edition (which was later expanded to 32 volumes).

In 1902 he wrote a stage play 'Francesca da Rimini', that was produced in Paris by his friend and legendary actress Sarah Bernhardt.

Towards the end of his life Hollywood had begun to realise that his works were a valuable source of stories and ideas and several were turned into movies and continued to be so for decades after his death.

Crawford also had a gift for pulling off excellent short stories. Several, such as 'The Upper Berth' (1886), 'For the Blood Is the Life' (1905, a vampiress tale), 'The Dead Smile' (1899), and 'The Screaming Skull' (1908), are among the most anthologized classics of the horror genre. After his death several collected volumes were published from various sources.

After most of his fictional works had been published, most had the view that he was a gifted narrator; and his books of fiction, were full of historic vitality and energy as well as dramatic characterization. He was widely popular among readers to whom literature was more for escapism than a confrontation with reality or pages of subjective analysis. In 'The Novel: What It Is' (1893), Crawford was both resolute and disarming in defending his literary approach, self-conceived as a combination of romanticism and realism, defining the art form in terms of its marketplace and audience. The novel, he wrote, is "a marketable commodity" and "intellectual artistic luxury" that "must amuse, indeed, but should amuse reasonably, from an intellectual point of view .... Its intention is to amuse and please, and certainly not to teach and preach; but in order to amuse well it must be a finely-balanced creation ...."

Francis Marion Crawford died at Sorrento on Good Friday 1909 at Villa Crawford of a heart attack.

F. Marion Crawford – A Concise Bibliography

Novels

Mr. Isaacs: A Tale of Modern India (1882)
Dr. Claudius (1883)
To Leeward (1884)
A Roman Singer (1884)
An American Politician (1884)
Zoroaster (1885)
A Tale of a Lonely Parish (1886)
Saracinesca (1887)
Marzio's Crucifix (1887)
Paul Patoff (1887)
With the Immortals (1888)
Greifenstein (1889)
Sant' Ilario (1889); sequel to Saracinesca
A Cigarette-Maker's Romance (1890)
Khaled: A Tale of Arabia (1891)
The Witch of Prague (1891)
The Three Fates (1892)
Don Orsino (1892); sequel to Sant' Ilario
The Children of the King (1893)
Pietro Ghisleri (1893)
Marion Darche (1893)
Katharine Lauderdale (1894)
The Upper Berth (1894); with "By the Waters of Paradise"
Love in Idleness (1894)
The Ralstons (1894); sequel to Katharine Lauderdale
Casa Braccio (1895); related to Katharine Lauderdale and The Ralstons.
Adam Johnstone's Son (1896)
Taquisara (1896)
A Rose of Yesterday (1897)
Corleone (1897)
Via Crucis (1899)
In the Palace of the King (1900)
Marietta (1901)
Cecilia (1902)
Man Overboard! (1903)

The Heart of Rome (1903)
Whosoever Shall Offend (1904)
Soprano (1905); U.S. title: Fair Margaret.
A Lady of Rome (1906)
Arethusa (1907)
The Little City of Hope (1907)
The Primadonna (1908); sequel to Soprano/Fair Margaret
The Diva's Ruby (1908); sequel to The Primadonna
The White Sister (1909)
Stradella (1909)
The Undesirable Governess (1910)
Wandering Ghosts; British title: Uncanny Tales.

Non-fiction

Our Silver (1881)
The Novel: What It Is (1893)
Constantinople (1895)
Bar Harbor (1896)
Ave Roma Immortalis (1898)
Rulers of the South (1900; 1905 in the U.S. as Southern Italy and Sicily and The Rulers of the South)
Gleanings from Venetian History (1905; in the U.S. as Salvae Venetia and in 1909 as Venice; the People and the Place)

Drama

In the Palace of the King (1900) with Lorrimer Stoddard.
Francesca da Rimini (1902) The piece was adapted into an opera by Franco Leoni in 1904.
Evelyn Hastings (1902) Unpublished typescript discovered in 2008.
The White Sister (1909) with Walter C. Hackett.

Filmography

A Cigarette-Maker's Romance, directed by Frank Wilson (UK, 1913, based on the novella)
The White Sister, directed by Fred E. Wright [it] (1915, based on the novel)
In the Palace of the King [it], directed by Fred E. Wright [it] (1915, based on the novel)
Whosoever Shall Offend, directed by Arrigo Bocchi (UK, 1919, based on the novel)
Il cuore di Roma, directed by Edoardo Bencivenga (Italy, 1919, based on the novel)
A Cigarette-Maker's Romance, directed by Tom Watts (UK, 1920, based on the novella)
Saracinesca [it], directed by Gaston Ravel (Italy, 1921, based on the novel)
Sant' Ilario [it], directed by Henry Kolker (Italy, 1923, based on the novel)
The White Sister, directed by Henry King (1923, based on the novel)
In the Palace of the King, directed by Emmett J. Flynn (1923, based on the novel)
Son of India, directed by Jacques Feyder (1931, based on the novel Mr. Isaacs)
The White Sister, directed by Victor Fleming (1933, based on the novel)

The Screaming Skull, directed by Alex Nicol (1958, named after the short story)
The White Sister, directed by Tito Davison (Mexico, 1960, based on the novel)